NONE OF THIS WOULD HAVE HAPPENED IF PRINCE WERE ALIVE

NONE OF THIS WOULD HAVE HAPPENED IF PRINCE WERE ALIVE

A NOVEL

CAROLYN PRUSA

ATRIA BOOKS

NEW YORK   LONDON   TORONTO   SYDNEY   NEW DELHI

ATRIA
BOOKS

An Imprint of Simon & Schuster, Inc.
1230 Avenue of the Americas
New York, NY 10020

First Atria Books hardcover edition November 2022

ATRIA BOOKS and colophon are trademarks of Simon & Schuster, Inc.

For information about special discounts for bulk purchases, please contact Simon & Schuster Special Sales at 1-866-506-1949 or business@simonandschuster.com.

The Simon & Schuster Speakers Bureau can bring authors to your live event. For more information or to book an event, contact the Simon & Schuster Speakers Bureau at 1-866-248-3049 or visit our website at www.simonspeakers.com.

Interior design by Jill Putorti

Manufactured in China

1 3 5 7 9 10 8 6 4 2

Library of Congress Cataloging-in-Publication Data has been applied for.

ISBN 978-1-9821-8886-3
ISBN 978-1-9821-8888-7 (ebook)

For Kevin.

TABLE OF CONTENTS

1

THE CONE OF UNCERTAINTY

OCTOBER 5, 2016

11:12 A.M.

"I'm not worried," my mother says. "Ramona. There's no need to panic."

When I pull down the slats of the blinds in the break room, I see a pale blue sky over the roofs of the Victorian District. *Worried* isn't the word I'd pick, and I wouldn't use *panic*, either. It's more like, *one more thing*.

"I just saw they're evacuating in South Carolina," I tell her.

"Well," she says. "That seems premature."

"Maybe. But they're usually in the path, so."

"What does Desmond think?"

"He's nervous. He says Savannah has been lucky so far but this one could be major."

"Des is nervous. Really?"

Neither my mother nor I come from Savannah. We depend on my husband's insider knowledge for situations like these:

hurricanes, salamanders clinging to the flue in the fireplace, the best place to find parking for the Saint Patrick's Day Parade.

"Kinda," I tell her, nodding to one of the developers shuffling by me with a shiny periwinkle bike under his left arm. The frame is skinny, maybe the width of a paper clip. "We'll talk about it tonight. Mom, I need to get some work done."

I hear the ice rustle in her 20 oz. Parker's cup. She's probably on her second Diet Coke of the day. She likes them with chewy ice and a splash of Dr Pepper, uses the same cup, tells us she's saving the earth.

"All right, honey. You know, don't worry, it's fine. Savannah has made it through plenty of these things."

"You think?"

My mother, Adelaide Burkhalter, terror of the senior tennis scene and the last woman on earth who describes pants as slacks. Even though I disagree with ninety percent of the stuff she says, my mother did teach me basic things like, accent your eyes or your lips, if you do both, you look like a hussy; check both ways before you cross the street. I can't completely disregard her opinion.

"Ramona, really," she says. "We don't need to evacuate."

In my office everything is open.

No cubicles for this bunch. The idea is, like, openness, togetherness, amid the exposed pipes and industrial lighting.

It also means no privacy.

I'd take a pat of privacy when one of the people who rely on me—my mother, my husband, my seven-year-old son, my daughter just shy of three—would like to chat. Or when I need to drop everything because someone's puking or worse, there's a birthday party, which means I need to sneak out of the office to purchase a remote control truck to plunge in an oversize gift bag with polka dot tissue paper recycled from past celebrations.

I'm not complaining about my family or my office. Having a job is great. It pays all right. Steady, which is key, especially when my husband's roofing business is up and down, and I earn health insurance for our family, which is a big deal. You could buy a boat for what we used to pay each year trying to cobble a family health plan together through Des's work, and the reason I know this is because people who live in Savannah care about boats.

I got this job because my friend Lindsay knows Alden, the guy who owns the company, a tech firm specializing in developing e-commerce sites for small businesses. Alden fled Silicon Valley so he could run a business between surfing on Tybee and playing the bass in a Christian band. He needed a project manager, and Lindsay told him, my friend Ramona's a graphic artist or something, when they bumped into each other in the olive section of Whole Foods. Then, to me, at Taco Tuesday at Foxy Loxy, Lindsay said, are you ready to go back to work?

I applied for the job. Online they asked me to include a recent photo and tell them my favorite song and movie. I lied about these, providing cooler answers I've now forgotten instead of my actual favorites: "Little Red Corvette" and *The Wedding Singer*. I had three interviews, all conducted online via Google Hangouts, even though I live less than a mile from the office, but convenient, because I could wear a blouse with a chunky necklace and nobody had to know I couldn't fit into my old work pants. I plunked my children in front of the TV with a bag of Pirate's Booty, closed the door to our office/guest room, and emphasized my passion for design while trying to avoid the smaller me in the corner of the screen emphasizing my passion for design.

Now, it's been a year and a half. They call me a project manager, but I technically never had project management experience except for packing up the family for a day at the beach.

It turns out I'm good at this. I like interacting with clients and I feel tiny jolts of joy when they are pleased, like the one time a restaurant owner described a website banner we created as "resplendent."

Just one thing.

The people are nice enough. Most of them are dudes, they call each other "bro," and say things like, "fan-bloody-tastic swipe gesture." At lunch they conduct entire conversations about people I assume are alive but they're not—they are characters in a video game. Sometimes I'll walk up to a coworker's desk without realizing they're on headphones because they are wireless. I'll be yakking away for five minutes until they sense my presence and jump.

I'm thirty-eight, it's not like I'm seventy. I don't want them to think I lost touch with the present day during the wormhole of creating humans and keeping them alive. I don't want them to think I don't belong here.

They're nice enough.

We have an office manager, Cailyn, who looks like Frodo. Her job is to keep the fridge stocked with brain snacks and caffeine to keep us calm, healthy, and productive. When I first started, Cailyn said, it's nice to have another woman in the office, it looks like your earring is about to fall off, what are your favorite snacks? I told her bananas and honey roasted almonds, and she wrote it down on a lavender notepad with an ultrafine Sharpie. She keeps buying wasabi almonds. I eat them because she seems so fragile and I don't want to hurt her feelings. But they are too spicy and leave green powder on my fingers.

11:37 A.M.

"Ramona," says Kenneth.

I jump, and then relax, because my monitor displays a spreadsheet for one of our clients, a nut butter company, instead of the quiz I was taking on Which *Friends* Character Are You. I'm Chandler, apparently, which hurts my feelings because I consider myself more of a Gunther at Central Perk.

"You worried about Matthew?" Kenneth is the creative director of our company. He leans against my desk and folds his skinny arms across his chest.

"Is he new?"

"The hurricane," he says. Kenneth looks like he's a buck twenty soaking wet, wears pants so tight there's no mystery as to the shape of his stuff or what it's doing at any moment, and has dark lamb chops like ski slopes tracing a line from his ears to his jaw.

Now I remember. "Oh, *that* Matthew. No, not yet. Should I be?"

"Maybe," Kenneth says. "They'll have a better idea tomorrow."

"The meteorologists, you mean."

"Yeah."

"The people on TV," I say.

Silence. I wonder if Kenneth smells the rotting Granny Smith apple in the top drawer of my desk I brought last Friday.

"So," he says. "Laser Life loved the new shopping cart."

I perk up like someone announced there's a puppy in the office. "Yeah?"

"Really great," he says.

"But."

"They want something bolder."

"Like, all caps."

It's a laser hair removal company. I didn't eat that apple because I wanted a Panera scone instead, one with tiny pockets of cinnamon hiding in canyons distributed across the rough bready terrain. Kenneth's pants are so tight and they don't reach very far down. I can see the entirety of his twiggy ankles and nubbly gray socks.

He snorts, "Right."

My phone buzzes. We both look at it. I am aware I have more personal obligations than all these bearded designers combined. I am the only working mom in the office. I'm not the only parent—we all have grinning school photos and artwork of stick people with disproportionately long fingers Scotch taped to our shelves. But I am the solo mother in the office, which HR may claim is no different but come on, ladies, we know.

"Or the bold font," I continue.

"You're hilarious, Ramona," he says. "Like, more in your face, they want people to access services and the shopping cart on every page."

"Gotcha," I tell him, sneaking a peek at my phone. "Just to let you know. We're billing them ten hours over budget and Xavier already started on the butter people."

"I know," Kenneth says. "Both parties are going to freak the fuck out."

"That's kind of what I thought."

"Thing is, they're desperate to go live by next week. That's why I'm lucky to have you to smooth things out."

"I'll talk to Xavier," I tell him.

I was actually thinking the font on their homepage was too small, unless they are marketing to lady elves who want to spruce up their bikini line.

In the pause my phone buzzes that I've got a message. I wait. Sometimes after these check-ins Kenneth asks about my children or if I've tried a new restaurant. I think this is to bookend the client's feedback with a personal connection. Maybe it's something he learned from a leadership course or a management app.

Not today.

"Cool," he says, pronouncing it, "kewl." This is how I visualize the spelling in my head because sometimes he signs off on emails in that fashion. He glides across the office like he's on a mini Segway.

The message is from my husband. It says, "Matthew, wtf?" I will work for seven minutes to show Kenneth that whatever is on my phone doesn't interfere with productivity and then I will call Des back.

12:04 P.M.

I'm eating Skittles in the break room.

"It looks bad," says Desmond.

"That's just hype," I tell him.

"Babe. Have you looked online?"

"Of course, I have! I'm on my computer. Or was. Now I'm in the break room."

"The Weather Channel predicts Level 4 winds," he says. "They're already evacuating South Carolina. It's supposed to make landfall here on Friday."

My husband's voice is soft with a Georgia accent that borders on tinny when he's telling a story he finds hilarious. He has an impish cleft in his chin and can lift one eyebrow at a time, which you might miss because they are the color of cantaloupe flesh. He knows two Cat Stevens songs on a guitar he can't tune and he suffers from psoriasis, mainly on his elbows.

"I know that," I tell him.

Outside the break room window a woman on her balcony shaves her legs with an electric razor on a white and lime-green plastic lawn chair.

Desmond: "Just sayin'." I sense he's shrugging, then cocking his head to the side, and I'm annoyed.

"I hate that phrase, *just saying*," I tell him. "People use it as a preemptive move before they say something snarky. It's like, *bless your heart*. That's it—that's what bugs me. It's the modern day equivalent of *bless your heart*."

"No, bless *your* heart."

I sigh. "Desmond. How are you watching the Weather Channel?"

"On my phone. I'm on-site."

"You're on someone's roof?" I secure the phone between my ear and shoulder so I can use both hands to tip over the bag of Skittles and a rush of candy slides to the table and then I quickly herd the rainbow balls rolling in every direction with my cupped hand.

"I'm in my truck, Ramona."

"You've called me from roofs before," I point out.

"True," he says. "But I haven't been on one in three months. I have people now."

The fact that Desmond now has people is a big deal. He has a general contractor named Jeremiah who manages a team of workers who help Des with the roofs and his Spanish. It occurs to me that a hurricane might be good for business. Which also means less Desmond to help with the kids.

The sky in Savannah is still pure blue with faint vapor trails. It's hard to imagine any major weather patterns moving in. A slight breeze sways the twinkly lights on the balcony where the woman, now finished shaving, is lying on her lawn chair with a magazine over her face. I can't read the headlines but I know them. *Trump Says Mexico Should Build a Wall. You Don't Get the Kids, Angie Tells Brad.*

"We could probably go to Augusta. To Christopher's?"

Christopher is my oldest friend from college who I met on day one of studio art class. Then he was a tiny seventeen-year-old from Valdosta in a wife-beater tank, a welder helmet, and elbow-length gloves. Over a shared Parliament on the steps of the Lamar Dodd School of Art we pinky swore not to let cute boys distract us from our art.

"I guess. Does he have room for us? He still with the physical therapist? The dude with the Airstream?"

See how that pinky swear worked out.

"No, that's way over," I tell Desmond. "He has a new boyfriend. A lawyer. Fred or Frank or something. I don't want to evacuate," I admit. "I'm tired. And I don't want to take Nanette's potty in the van."

"Huh?"

"She is not even close to the clear in potty-training, babe."

"Right."

"I'm actually starting to think she doesn't give a rat's ass about peeing in the potty or in her unders."

"I'm getting that, too," he says. "Yesterday she wouldn't try because she didn't want to stop working on her rainbow loom. So she half-assed it to the bathroom and then pissed in the living room. Also, she's so stubborn, she doesn't want us to be right. Like, us telling her to go potty is another way the man is keeping her down."

"If we left and got stuck in traffic? I can see us trapped in the middle of miles of cars. The kids losing their minds and Nanette has to go."

"Do other parents take the plastic potty in the car?"

"Maybe. Kinda gross."

"Yeah," he says.

"Pee sloshing around back there."

The melted candy coat of Skittles decorates the inside of my palm in a camo design of red, purple, and green. I'm in charge of so many things every day and I still don't feel like a grown-up.

Desmond is listening but he's not. "Wouldn't we pull over and dump it out?"

"I guess? Let's just stay," I say, like I'm deciding for all four of us. I feel a wave of relief. I don't have to think about the potty. Maybe the office will close—we'll have a staycation! A day or two without alarm clocks, dress codes, apologizing for auto correct in a work text during carpool. It could be just what we need.

Desmond, focused again: "You wanna stay?"

"Maybe." I hear the waning confidence in my voice. "I gotta go. Let's talk about it later."

"Category Four, just sayin'."

1:13 P.M.

Nicole's photo pops up on my caller ID. It's a selfie where her face is barely visible behind her towheaded twins. In the picture one of them is sucking on a Tootsie Roll Pop and the other one sticks out her tongue. Looks like the flavor was cherry.

I brace myself. "Hey, girl, hey."

Nicole watches Nanette in the afternoons for a babysitting fee under market rates. If I get a call from school or a babysitter at work my body initiates the flight-or-fight response and I immediately imagine Alex or Nanette in King Kong's fist, dangling from a jump rope off the Talmadge Bridge, or more likely leaving a lunch box in the driveway after abandoning it for a rock that looked like a shark tooth. Which would mean someone's cubby is now sans sandwich so basically the earth has stopped spinning.

Nicole hesitates. "I don't want to stress you out, but."

"But."

"Can you pick up Nanette earlier today?"

Nanette. My curious, snot-encrusted, lisping three-year-old with burnt orange curls and a cleft in her chin, who accompanies Nicole and her twins home from preschool until I make the pickup rounds. Why do I need to scoop up my daughter early? It's only 1:15.

I'm a nail-biter. My ring finger on my right hand is my favorite. Upon hearing Nicole's request, my hand flies to my mouth.

"Of course," I tell Nicole. "How come?"

"Think we're busting loose," Nicole says. "We don't want to get stuck in traffic." Traffic with a nasally "a"—Nicole grew up in Michigan. She is also the friend I talk to most often due to our daily drive-by exchanges of Nanette. Suckily, I chat with college girlfriends and mom homies less and less as my days morphed from long stretches of hours to fill to tight rectangles of time with lists. Lucky Nicole.

"You're what?"

"Ramona," Nicole starts. "Are you keeping tabs on this storm? Once upon a time there was a hurricane named Matthew."

"It's Wednesday. The hurricane is supposed to come Friday."

"We're in the Cone of Uncertainty."

I find that phrase delightful. "Like my career."

"Or my marriage," she says.

"Isn't this a little alarmist?"

"Not if you don't want to be stuck in nine hours of traffic on the way to Macon with twin toddlers."

Nanette's mobile fire engine potty flashes to my mind. Also the R.E.M. video for "Everybody Hurts." Nope, nope, nope, no.

"Well," I say, pulling up the Weather Channel site on my monitor. There's an apostrophe shape swirling over the Atlantic with an angry red-purple center. Next to it is a model of rainbow-colored spaghetti noodles hugging the East Coast. "Holy guacamole."

"If we wait too long, the traffic will be awful."

"Right," I murmur.

"Maybe I should buy adult diapers," she says.

"Do you remember the lady astronaut who bought adult diapers to drive from Texas to Florida to get revenge on her husband's mistress? Or maybe she was the mistress. She didn't want bathroom breaks to slow her down."

"I don't," Nicole says. "But never underestimate a woman on a mission."

"I don't know how much time she really saved with the diapers. Because you've got to stop for gas."

"Unless you can get there with just one tank. So, I'm packing. Jonathan wants to leave right now." Of course he does—I roll my eyes. Nicole can't see me, only Cailyn witnesses my flippant expression as she plods past me with a brown box from Back in the Day Bakery. In this office it's someone's birthday every half hour. "We can bring Nanette to your office. If that's easier."

It's an idea. Then again, Nanette at my office. Skipping down the halls. Eating rubber cement. Practicing somersaults between the partitions. The polite smiles of my hipster coworkers, the frantic typing as they instant message each other, complaining. Me, asking her if she needs to use the potty every five minutes, Nanette screaming no, and crumpling into a ball on the sisal carpet, flashing her soiled Elsa undies under her ruffled skirt.

Three desks away Kenneth hovers over Bearded Designer #3, who points to something on his screen. I watch my boss scratch his stubble, then his butt.

"Or," she continues, "want me to call Miss Sandy and ask if Nanette can go back to school with the full-day kids? I'm sorry to be a pain."

"Stop saying you're sorry! It's cool. She doesn't have Minneapolis. She doesn't nap much anymore, and she definitely won't without Minneapolis."

Minneapolis = Nanette's giraffe blanket.

"True," Nicole admits. "Sorry. I know it's not ideal. Better safe, though?"

"It's okay. That's the dark side of you turbo organized moms. You get paranoid about stuff. The good part is that I know my kid is safe."

Nicole's laugh sounds more fitting for a seasoned bartender slinging beers for stubbled football fans in Green Bay than a consultant turned stay-at-home mom—it's low, churning, and raspy.

"Or so you think," she says. In the background I hear Nanette and the twins banging on something—there's a crash, a pause, and three high pitched giggles.

"All right," I tell her. "Keep your Lululemons on. Someone will be there in thirty. Maybe me. Maybe Des or Adelaide."

"Excuse me."

"What."

"I'm wearing leggings from the Carrie Underwood collection for Dick's Sporting Goods."

"Oh. Good on you. Good on Carrie."

"You should probably get gas, too," she suggests. "And think about getting out of here."

I should also call Arrow Exterminators and tell them about the cockroach the size of my thumb that I found this morning on our kitchen floor, his legs bicycling the air in slow motion. And yet here we are.

1:42 P.M.

At first Mom is not picking up her phone. Then she calls me back, only to inform me too loudly she's in the waiting room at the dentist office, they are taking forever, and there's a new woman at reception who has no idea what she's doing. Des does not respond to my text so I reckon he's really on the roof this time.

Shit.

I am hyper aware of any kid-related absences that may be held against me. Even though I try to play down my momminess, it rises to the surface. Like when I'm trying to speed thaw frozen chicken by plunging it into hot water in a Ziploc bag. It keeps floating up so that parts of the breast get a squishy texture while the edges remain solid with freezer crystals.

I need to scoop up Nanette from Nicole's house. I watch Kenneth making big hand gestures near the designer's desk—like, "Itsy Bitsy Spider" meets Bob Fosse—and I mentally write a letter to his back. It goes like this:

Dear Kenneth,

I feel nervous telling you I have to leave the office. At the heart of things I am a people-pleaser—believe you me, I am working on that. At the same time, I waffle back and forth between guilt and a feeling of outrage that I'm experiencing these emotions to begin with. I am responsible and I work hard. When I have kid emergencies, I never let one iota of work slip. By the way, it's 2016. We have a woman running for president. Also you may have heard of the internet, which means I can manage projects from anywhere. I should be home wearing my slippers and too small Purple Rain *T-shirt with the bleach stain on the right boob. Also when I said I was a multitasker in my interview, it was a lie. Yeah, I lied. The idea of keeping both my kids happy and safe in two different schools and making sure my house is not a toxic dump and trying to be a supportive partner for my husband instead of a cranky bitch and making sure the clients are happy is frankly, mind-blowing. I am smart, but that shit is hard. This is something you have never attempted to balance in your life, and maybe never will have to.*

Love,

Ramona

PS I suspect Intern MacKenzie slept here last Thursday night.

PPS Guesstimate is not a word. When you say it, I want to puncture my ear drums with the keys to my minivan.

Instead I call out, "Kenneth, I'm going to step out for a minute."

"Ramona, kewl."

2:07 P.M.

I sneak past Nicole's husband boarding up windows in his work khakis—that's a half hour conversation I don't have time for. Inhaling fresh plywood plucked from Home Depot, I wait on the front porch while Nicole flips over the dead bolt.

Nicole has a heart-shaped face with overplucked eyebrows. She got her boobs done last Christmas because she says nursing twins turned them into edamame husks. You can't see them today under the gray baggy University of Chicago sweatshirt she's wearing with cherry blossom printed leggings. Over her shoulder she exclaims, "Nan-nan Babycakes. Look who's here!"

Nanette is surprised to see me—it's earlier than usual—and she springs into my arms like we're long lost comrades. My daughter hugs with ferocity and smells like baby wipes and applesauce. Her joy at seeing me is temporary because next she remembers her snack and launches a tantrum at the idea she won't be able to finish it. Nicole says she can take it with her.

Dang, Nicole's house is clean. I bet you could run a white glove along any surface in Nicole's midcentury ranch and it would come up the color of fresh snow, printer paper, the mountain of cocaine on Tony Montana's desk. Women with far more responsibilities than me pull off everyday tasks with speed and efficiency and I don't understand how they do it. My mother-in-law gave us 23andMe kits for Christmas—it took me until August to spit on the thing—and I still haven't put it in the mail yet.

As Nicole pours goldfish into a Ziploc bag, we exchange the look of women who have been beaten down into Choosing Our Battles thanks to years of toddler dictatorships. I ease Nanette's small feet into faded silver glitter Mary Janes. We find her purple headband; I grab her bookbag from a basket and take her hand.

Nicole tells me she's getting a migraine from that "g-d hammering" and they haven't even packed a suitcase yet. At the door she gives me a hug—a real one with strong arms, not a cocktail party pat.

On the path to the car Nanette finds all kinds of cool sticks and leaves. I try to step into her universe and appreciate a child's innocent view of the world around her. It slows me down. Then the moment passes and I feel like a maniac again.

As we buckle up, Nanette emits a squeal of glee upon locating Minneapolis, who was scrunched in the cup holder of her crusty car seat. I sense Nicole's family's energy from inside the house. They're waiting for us to leave. As soon as my Sienna labors out of sight, they will stuff the kids inside the SUV and peel away like the Road Runner.

I remind myself Hurricane Matthew isn't here yet.

He's only just made it to Haiti.

"Where's Alex?" Nanette asks me. It's not "Aah-wex," anymore, it's "Alex." It's one of those bittersweet transitions, like the moment I realized Alex requested strawberries for breakfast instead of "tawbies."

I turn the ignition. "He's still at school."

"Why?"

"Well," I explain, backing out of Nicole's driveway. "I picked you up first today."

"Oh."

"Isn't that a fun surprise?"

As Nanette considers this idea, she lowers Minneapolis's gnarled horn from her lips.

"No," she says.

2

MOM DOWN, Y'ALL

2:34 P.M.

When I see Desmond's truck in the driveway, my first thought is, he must be more worried about the hurricane than I thought, *just saying*. Once I'm inside the house my second thought is: My husband is having an affair.

Turns out, both are true.

Nanette and I announce ourselves as we pour through the screen door—"Helloooooooo!"—only to be greeted by a flushed strawberry blonde in tight dark jeans tucked into cowboy boots holding a coconut La Croix in front of the fridge. I'm startled, a stranger is raiding our produce, then I recognize her—it's Sarah Ellen, one of the mothers from Alex's school. Her kid dressed up as Iron Man for Halloween last year. Caden or Jaden or something like that.

"Oh," she says.

"Hey," I say, and I'm confused as to why she's here, why she didn't greet me in a friendlier fashion, and why she's still loiter-

21

ing there—in front of our Maytag that I work hard to stock with mostly healthy foods but also reasonable ones you'd expect small children to eat, unlike Nicole, who makes her kids eat quinoa kale balls.

Desmond rounds the corner in a ratty Dave Matthews T-shirt, boxers, and a face that transforms from red to white.

And then I get it.

My husband, and this Sarah Ellen.

While I was at work or while they thought I was at work.

"Daddy!" Nanette leaves my side, and runs to Desmond, whose trance is broken by dimpled hands surrounding his thighs. "You're wearing your unders. Silly."

"Hey, Nanner!" Desmond says, his voice half-autopilot-cheerful and half-shaky.

I am still standing at the door holding Nanette's backpack. You know when people flatline on the operating table and float over their bodies? I see how that happens now. There I am in the kitchen—five foot six and a half, slightly squishy around the middle, a brunette bob with frizzy gray baby hairs, sassy bohemian blouse and work pants, practical but professional shoes, the strap of an Elsa backpack in my right hand, two rings on my left.

"This is bad," Sarah Ellen says.

Her voice: quavering. The refrigerator beeps because the door has been open too long, she presses it shut.

"Yes," I hear my voice say. "It is."

"Ramona," Desmond says. "Monie."

That was probably the last coconut La Croix. The ones left

are peach-pear, I don't even like those. I only buy them because Desmond does. These are the things I consider while my heart is breaking. I also have the emotional capacity to feel irritated my son left his soccer cleats in the front hall after I nagged him about it, twice. The soles are encrusted with dirt from the field which when dry, molts from the shoe in the shape of rabbit pellets.

Desmond repeats my name: "Ramona."

Nanette has released his leg and wandered off. My body starts to thaw. It's passed lukewarm and gone straight to fire. Now I feel hot molten magma running through my veins. I want to set the kitchen on fire.

"No," I tell him. "Get out of this house. Both of you."

"Get out?" he repeats.

"I should go," Sarah Ellen says. Thin gold bangles circling her wrist jingle as she lifts both hands to cover her mouth. I only see her eyes—hazel and red-rimmed. To me: "I'm so sorry. This is a mess."

"You're right. You should go," I say. "I have to get Alex."

"What?" Desmond says. "I don't think you should drive."

Now he walks toward me.

Like he's going to touch me.

I put up my hand: Stop.

"You will back the fuck away from me. You will leave me alone. You will leave my children alone. I will go. I'm going to go. When I come back you will not be here. Either of you. You will be gone."

Sarah Ellen clears her throat. I brush past both of them to find Nanette in her brother's room, busy dumping out all the Hot

Wheels cars in the bin. She's capitalizing on this rare brotherless window to raid his toys.

Mom voice: "Come on, sweetie, it's time to get Alex."

"No," she says.

I'm desperate, cajoling. "You can bring the cars."

"No, I'm playing," she says. She reaches into the red plastic bin and plucks out a faded aquamarine sedan. "I want to stay with Daddy."

Goddamn, goddamn.

"I'm sorry, honey, we have to go."

"No, Mommy."

I pick her up and she starts screaming, and there's no alternate route to the car except the one past my husband and that woman again so I march through the kitchen and I don't care how much of a fool I look like. Turns out I'm the biggest asshole, anyway, some kind of cuckoldette, so why not haul a shrieking toddler wearing one sock and currently slapping me, and there it is—OUCH—the bite in my upper right arm, *goddamn goddamn,* as I scramble to find the keys in my purse and try to shove Nanette in the car seat. She's still screaming.

Desmond, now in navy track pants, hovers next to my door.

"Ramona, I know this is rough—I'm sorry, okay? This is bad, this is bad."

Is he crying? He is.

I slam the door and clutch the steering wheel, hands at ten o'clock and two. Nanette throws a sippy cup at my head, she misses. I retrieve it from the valley on the passenger's side and place it in a cup holder. I reverse out of the driveway, narrowly

avoiding a woman walking a senior golden retriever—sorry!—
and a beat-up red Taurus. Underneath the basketball hoop in our
driveway Desmond stands with his hands on his hips. I see his
mouth moving, *come on.*

No.

Nanette continues to wail until we get to Skidaway Drive.
Everything feels dry: my mouth, my eyes, my hands.

The sky is clear blue, not a cloud in sight.

APRIL 2016

The moment I learned Prince died I was at the post office mail-
ing a birthday present to Desmond's mother—a splashy floral
scarf she would probably never wear and a card we'd all signed.

When it was my turn in line, I hustled to the far station where
I was helped by an employee with dark brown skin and false
eyelashes thick with mascara. She had a silver cross necklace
grazing the first button of her uniform and a picture of a chubby-
cheeked baby in a striped onesie Scotch taped to the inside of
the partition.

First class, two-day, or next day, she asked me.

I rested my elbow on the counter, which was high, so it came
up to my chest. I handed over the package, a lightweight yellow
envelope with my hurried writing, the 4 in my mother-in-law's
address kind of looking like a 9.

Regular mail is fine, I said.

The postal service clerk didn't really look at me. That was also
fine. This exchange was between two women with shit to get

done. She was looking at her monitor and typing in my mother-in-law's zip code.

Her eyes moved from the screen to her phone, then back to her phone, which was buzzing. She picked it up, sparkling hot pink nails curling around the case like tulip petals, and gasped.

Prince, she said.

I reached inside my purse for my wallet: What?

Prince died.

I thought she said, *the* prince.

Prince William?

No, she said, Prince. She turned her phone to show me a news alert from CNN. I leaned closer.

Prince Dead at 57. Musician Found Unresponsive at Paisley Park.

No, I said.

Next in line, said the attendant two stations down from us.

Above the article was a photo of him—one from a recent concert. His hair was slicked back. He was holding the guitar in one hand and the other was held to his ear, as if he was waiting to hear an answer from the audience.

The woman placed her palm over her heart.

I can't believe this, she said.

Me, neither, I said.

He was so young, she said.

The rest of the post office bustled along like nothing awful just happened.

I idled at the counter. I didn't know then you can feel heartbreak over losing someone you don't really know. Someone you've never seen. Not even from the nosebleed seats.

I guess you can. I wasn't the only one. Though we'd been passing ships just two minutes ago, now the woman across from me and I locked eyes across the counter.

It seems too early for Jesus to be calling him home, but he must have.

Way too early, I heard my voice say, and break, just a little.

She issued a long sigh, twisted in her chair, and slapped a sticker on my package.

Four dollars, twenty-two cents. It'll get there by Monday.

I slid my credit card into the machine on autopilot and signed the electronic receipt. I put my wallet back into my purse, next to wipes, a package of ToastChee crackers, and a pair of promotional earbuds I'd got from a client.

Outside it was drizzling on and off. It occurred to me the rain should have turned purple. Because something had shifted in the universe. But it was regular colored rain. I pressed the remote to unlock the Toyota Sienna and drove out of the parking lot into a world without Prince.

2:56 P.M.

You're not supposed to be on the phone in carpool line. It's a strict rule at Oglethorpe Day School.

Come on, cut me some slack. They haven't even trotted out the kids yet. And the only reason I'm early today is because I just fled the scene of a tawdry discovery involving my spouse and a desperate housewife from the Landings.

At least I think Sarah Ellen lives in the Landings. Maybe she's in the Yacht Club neighborhood on Whitemarsh. Some HOA where you're not allowed to put signs in your front yard? With shaking hands I text Desmond: *Do not be there when I get back with Alex. No scene in front of kids. I hate you.* I try to add the red face angry emoji but I accidentally type the one that looks like it's sneezing so I delete it.

The Honda Odyssey in front of me inches along. Nanette has now distracted herself by crushing a water bottle she found against the window and singing about it. In my peripheral vision I see a bouncy figure in a tomato-colored visor and a white tennis skort and I slump down in the driver's seat. Right now I need this conversation like I need a yeast infection.

I roll down my window. "Hey, Trudy."

"Girl," she says. "How 'bout this storm?"

Hurricane Matthew. For real, I forgot about it.

"It's coming," I tell her. "Definitely I think it's coming."

"What are y'all going to do?"

"You know, Trudy. I'm just not sure yet."

I inch up a few feet and Trudy moves along with us, utilizing a side-to-side shuffle probably helpful when she's lunging for a volley. I say a brief prayer to the Goddess of the Private School Mom Scene. Please rain down mercy on me. *Por favor* divert this woman from my vehicle as she obviously cannot sense the shock I'm trying to hide under my CeraVe Moisturizer with SPF 30.

"We might go to Parker's parents' place in the Highlands," she says.

"Yeah?"

She reaches up to tighten her ponytail. "It's not around the corner. They'll have power, though."

"Right," I tell her. I know for a fact that Stay-At-Home-Moms don't sit around eating bonbons and watching their stories because I used to be one. Now that I'm back at a nine-to-five, I resent any woman who can make a hair appointment on a Tuesday at eleven and I don't like that about myself.

"And take pets."

"Pets," I repeat, and file that under Who Gives A Shit. "Well. Guess we'll figure it out tomorrow."

My phone buzzes. Out of habit I look down: *Please tell me when you're ready to talk, I am sorry. I love you. I will be at Scott's. Please check Weather Channel, they evacuated SC.*

You have no right. To text me, to check in on me, to tell me you love me, to worry about the hurricane. I already fucking know about South Carolina!

Trudy absentmindedly nibbles on her keychain—a monogrammed pink whale from Vineyard Vines whose lifted eyebrow suggests trouble to come.

"You know they called off school, right?" she tells me. "You gonna work from home?"

"What?"

"They just sent out an email blast," Trudy says. "Around two."

The email blast. Of course! The confounded email blast. I've got so much to finish at work and I can't remember if I brought my laptop home. How much do we pay to send these punks to private school? Can't they teach them on a day where the sky is perfectly blue and clear? There's nary a breeze rustling the tall grass. A white egret wades through the shallow water in the creek next to the carpool line. It looks like a painting you can buy at Bed Bath & Beyond to create a calming vibe in the waiting room at a doctor's office.

"Oh. I didn't check it. It's been kind of a day."

"And they already evacuated South Carolina."

"Mr. Banner is waving me up, Trudy." He's not, actually. Mr. Banner is examining a clipboard with another teacher wearing galoshes with penguins on them. Again: "I gotta move up, Trudy."

Trudy's eyes scan the distance between my windshield and bumper. "People swear by these. The automatic doors and everything. Do you love it?"

"Sure."

She smiles like she's about to tell Pat Sajak she'd like to solve the puzzle. "I just couldn't ever bring myself to drive a minivan."

"Yeah." Trudy, bless her heart, picked the wrong day to poke the bear in carpool line. "You're probably not cool enough."

I roll up the window, propel the car forward, and leave Trudy standing there. My hands, gripping the steering wheel, are white.

Once Mr. Banner moves forward to help a set of siblings board a massive silver truck, I spot Alex, my first grader, sitting on the step. He's holding a large picture book about volcanoes next to a girl in a leopard print dress and pink fuzzy boots. Only the top of his head is visible; his thick dark brown curls, while his light blue eyes are following the words on the page.

My vehicle hovers in front of my son for a good thirty seconds until his classmate nudges him. "Alex, your mom is here." He's jolted to action, reaching for the strap of his backpack, holding his still-open library book at the same time, stepping around the other kids, both shoelaces untied, a collection of slender limbs.

I press the button to open the sliding door of our ancient Toyota Sienna.

"Hi, sweetie!" I call out.

"What's Nanette doing here?" Alex asks, wriggling his backpack to the floor of the van and reaching across his shoulder for the seat belt.

"Change of plans."

"Okey-dokey, artichokey," Nanette says.

"Oh," says Alex. "Did you know there's going to be a hurricane?"

"Heard something about that," I tell him.

I can do this. On the inside, I feel like the spewing volcano on the cover of Alex's book. On the outside I will maintain a steadfast Mommy facade. I will be patient, I will use a calm voice, I will answer bizarre questions, I will negotiate power struggles, I will refresh sippy cups.

I slowly accelerate along the carpool line. Out of the corner of my eye I see Alex's teacher, Mrs. Wall, waving with a certain voracity—at me?—oh, at us, sure, so I stop the Sienna again and roll down the window. Mrs. Wall folds neatly trimmed nails over the passenger's side door. She's got a long, beakish nose, shiny at the tip, and a layer of gold hair lighter than the rest of her bob that curls under her chin like the hook of an umbrella.

"I caught you," she says.

"Hi, Mrs. Wall. Everything okay?"

"Well, we're a little crazy today, but I think we've got a handle on it. Just one thing—Alex is signed up to take Clarence Thomas home this weekend."

"Clarence Thomas?"

"The guinea pig? Our class pets are named after notable Savannahians."

"Huh."

"We were wondering if y'all wouldn't mind taking Clarence Thomas with you a couple days early? For the evacuation?"

My throat burns.

"Of course, we will. The more the merrier."

She smiles back at me. Apparently, Clarence Thomas is waiting for us inside the administrative office. I park and open all the windows so Alex and Nanette won't suffocate as I head inside to retrieve the rodent. There he is—a mini football with black fur and caramel patches and big inky eyes in a massive wire cage with wood-chip bedded plastic floor.

"Aren't you lucky," says the admissions director.

"All rodents remind me of my ex," says the receptionist.

"I can carry his food for you," offers Mrs. Wall, hoisting up a Whole Foods bag almost as large as the supersize cage. I lift up Clarence Thomas's cage and tread through the door another teacher holds open with Mrs. Wall trailing behind me, only on the second to last step, my right ankle wobbles, and I start to tumble. I clutch the cage, but the two of us end up on the ground, Clarence Thomas is tossed to the side of the habitat, and he squeals—a supernatural squawk—and the glass water bottle shatters into a thousand pieces.

"Oh my God," says Mrs. Wall.

I bet she doesn't say that in front of the students, she probably encourages them to say, *oh my gosh*. My knee is bleeding and I've scratched the palm of my right hand trying to catch myself—it stings.

Nanette and Alex, sticking their heads out the window, look alarmed, whether about me or the guinea pig, I'm not sure. The carpool line continues to inch around us: the sprawling woman, guinea pig, and broken glass. Mom down, y'all. Now the penguin galoshes appear at my side and the pre-K teacher has a broom and she's sweeping up the bits of glass. I turn the cage right side up, I'm staggering to my feet, brushing myself off, I've got to get out of here. The blood on my right knee seeps through my work pants in a splashy stain the shape of Texas.

"I'm so sorry," I tell Mrs. Wall.

Sarah Ellen rolls past us in a pristine gold SUV, Jaden or Caden or whatever his name is securely fastened in her backseat. She looks straight ahead. Her hair is in a ponytail now, she must have brushed it and bound it in an elastic band between fucking my husband and picking up her son at Oglethorpe Day School.

Just a typical Wednesday, huh, Sarah Ellen? Wonder what she's got lined up for later. Lacrosse practice? Piano lessons at Ms. Amy's School of Music? Maybe some light errands. What would I do if I were free, instead of locked up in my own cage of societal expectations like Clarence Thomas? Would I throw myself in front of her car? Utter a primal scream? Swing my jumper cables like a lasso until I crack her car windows?

We'll never know. Because I am a mother. We cannot lose control. We must push down all the feelings like pressing Nanette's felt Curious George back into his tin jack-in-the-box.

Once I secure Clarence Thomas and his accessories in the back-back of the minivan, I steer us out of the carpool line, offering brief waves here and there. *Hello, other parents, hi, semi-acquaintances, oh, hey, Piper's scary dad who drank too much at the oyster roast and said the n-word, what's up, people I don't know who watched me wipe out in front of the admin office.*

At the exit of the school I check traffic to the right and the left.

"Are you okay, Mommy?" asks Nanette.

Tenderness for my daughter surges in my chest. "I am, Nanner. Thank you for checking on me."

"You fell, Mommy," Alex says. "We saw you wipe out."

"At home," Nanette says. "We have SpongeBob Band-Aids. No more *Frozen* ones. Just SpongeBob."

"They evaporated South Carolina. Right now Hurricane Matthew is over the Pacific Ocean," Alex says.

"Pacific? Do you mean Atlantic?" I suggest. "Maybe near the Bahamas?"

"Bahama?" Nanette repeats, and chortles. "That's funny. Bahama."

Alex is defensive. "Maybe that's where it is."

"Thor makes hurricanes," Nanette announces.

"Not really," Alex says. "He uses Mjolnir to call the lightning in case he needs it for something."

"Sometimes he makes hurricanes," she says.

"No, he doesn't. Mommy. Tell her."

"Alex," I start, "technically I think you're right. However. I can see how your sister might be confused, since lightning is traditionally associated with storms. Also, she's three."

"In January I'm gonna be three and a quarter," she announces with pride.

Jan-ooh-ary.

"Yes," I press the brake at a red light. "You will."

"Noah's going to his grandma's house in Alabama," Alex says.

"He is?" I am turning right on DeRenne, crossing Skidaway, and reminding myself to breathe. "That sounds like a good time."

I don't like Noah. One time he came over and bragged about his father buying a boat from Paula Deen when I suspect the boat was actually purchased from some dude named Paul or Dean. We listen to a jingle about how it's not too early to do your winter checkup for your HVAC system and rumble down Paulsen to 53rd Street. I feel my stomach seize up as we approach our house. Will Desmond be there? There's no sign of his truck.

This is a relief.

It also makes me feel worse. We're pulling into the driveway, waving to the awkward high schooler—Bailey—two doors down who waters our plants when we're away. As I push the gear into park the check engine light comes on. We spill out of the car, a dust cloud of backpacks and Cheez-Its and BPA-free water bottles, and into our home. We deposit Clarence Thomas's cage in the corner of the TV room.

If you subtract the guest star rodent and my bloody work trousers, this all seems normal. It's just another day, us coming home from school, carrying things we'll toss everywhere, Alex darts to the bathroom, he's been holding it because he doesn't like to poop at school, Nanette pulls out her Octonaut toys for five minutes before asking me for another snack. I toss the contents of the Tupperware containers from their lunch boxes and wash them out one by one.

Except I spy the lukewarm can of La Croix on our kitchen counter. I consider hurling it against a wall and then decide that would be wasting my last coconut La Croix so I put it back in our fridge.

I plug the kids into a movie—a treat for after-school activity—which gives me one hour and twenty minutes, maybe two, depending on whether or not my kids fast forward the commercials, to process the information my husband is smack dab in an affair.

1997

One year Christopher dressed up as Apollonia and I was Prince for the eighties party at SAE. We approached the project with the same diligence as any assignment for our shared visual art major—so, a month planning costumes. That meant combing the Goodwill for our looks, losing our shit discovering key accessories, even taking a road trip to Atlanta for finishing touches, i.e., deece wigs. We pocketed beads and wire from the metal department to recreate Apollonia's dangly red earring from *Purple*

Rain and with a glue gun affixed studs atop the shoulders of a violet ladies' blazer for me.

Day of, we etched out an itinerary beginning at nine a.m. and ending at question mark in purple marker on the dry erase board in Christopher's tiny single. First: breakfast in downtown Athens—peanut butter banana pancakes and Diet Pepsi. Next, a nap to refuel our energy, which never happened because even though we had food comas, it's like when you can't fall asleep because Santa's coming. One hour in the dorm kitchen making deviled eggs with Nayonaise and purple sprinkles. Two to four p.m. for makeup and costumes accompanied by a Best of Prince mix I'd burned onto a CD and Korbel Extra Dry we turned purple (fuchsia, really) by adding raspberry Pixy Stix. We took the bus to the mall to take Glamour Shots in our flip-flops anticipating we couldn't last all night in the vinyl boots we'd bought and plus you can't see anyone's feet in the photo. What you can see in the glossy 8x10 flattened between art books in my attic: Christopher's bouncy feathered wig, magenta eyeliner, my voluminous lace collar and pout.

Before the party, we each popped a tablet of ecstasy Christopher had bought from Dimitri in my acrylics class, clomped two blocks south holding hands before bursting into the house with our container of deviled eggs. The music was loud. I found a pea green crushed velvet couch I decided was probably pretty close to how you would feel if your bed was a cloud and Christopher showed off his bustier to a bemused Ty Webb from *Caddyshack* at the keg. People were signing the cast of a girl who had broken her wrist playing lacrosse so I wrote my name, extending the R into long, swirling octopus tentacles, until she asked me to speed it up because she thought she might throw up.

The DJ was a dick. He said he'd played Prince before we got there. We decided we should bribe him, but deviled eggs didn't do the trick, so we walked around the house raising funds from partygoers. A girl from my astronomy class dressed as Madonna gave me a five and Christopher handed it to the DJ in a smooth handshake. As I was coming out of the bathroom with toilet paper stuck to my boot, I heard the opening organ of "Let's Go Crazy"—finally! I saw Christopher across the parquet floor, we screamed like it was the Rapture, nudged people to the side to dance wildly with flailing arms, sweating in fake leather.

We bailed on the party, thinking, if it was that hard to get the DJ to play Prince, we're not going to listen to him anymore. It was freakishly cold and it looked like the stars were one-upping each other to shine for us. We walked to campus, made plans to move to San Francisco together after graduation, make art, take lovers, and choose joy. We would bow to no one and create lives just as colorful as my canvases and Christopher's sculptures. We could survive by splitting half-price appetizers at Happy Hours and once a year we would put on these costumes again.

Our feet hurt. We took off our shoes, ran barefoot across campus, and Christopher said, now it's time for you to purify yourself in Lake Minnetonka. We plunged our feet in one of the fountains, which was ice cold. I said, I think it's Lake Michigan, and now I realize he was right. Soaked and coming down from the pills, we laid on the grass next to the fountain until a campus security guy came up and said, y'all go back to your dorms now.

We said, okay, stay funky, and walked back to Christopher's dorm swinging our boots. Halfway there we realized I left my Prince wig next to the fountain and we wondered if we should go back and get it and I decided it would make me so happy if a bird found it and made a nest out of it and what if all the bird's babies played guitar and wore high heels. Then we both passed out in the common room of Christopher's dorm and when I woke up my feet were filthy and the chest hair I'd drawn with eyeliner had darkened the torn up upholstery of the couch.

The eighties party sophomore year—that was before I met Desmond.

Sometimes I think about that night and I remember: how disgusting the deviled eggs were, how we danced like our bodies were possessed, how every corner I turned begged me to unearth its beauty, how I found crushed acorn caps ground in my heels. I wonder if Desmond was there, or at another party two houses down, and what would have happened if we never, ever met.

4:19 P.M.

I've got three texts from Kenneth and two from my husband, which I ignore. I kick off my shoes. I slide off my bloody work trousers, arrange them on a wooden hanger, and pull on my charcoal Old Navy yoga pants, pilled on the inside of the thighs. I feel simultaneously jacked up like I just drank a Monster Energy drink and sluggish like I'm moving through a vat of melted marshmallows.

I flop on my unmade bed before considering Des and Sarah Ellen might have been there. Maybe they picked someplace more exciting because you only have sex in bed with your wife. Still, if they were here, there could be fluids so I relocate to the foldout sofa in the office—it's olive with a light spot on the left arm where I tried to Resolve out the unicorns Nanette drew with a purple marker.

On the sofa I hug the decorative throw pillow I bought at HomeGoods for $24.99 and then I'm annoyed that the beading is scratchy so I flip it over to rest my head against the smooth side. Across the street I hear the creak as my neighbor opens and closes her mailbox and fusses at her beagle to stop chewing on the perennials. I anticipate a slow build from irritation into animalistic rage, followed by a shit-ton of tears. Big time tears. We're talking eighteen years down the drain kind of cry. Like a bullet to an aquarium.

Nothing.

Now I try to induce the crying. It's like when you've got a beast of a hangover and you know you'll feel better after you throw up so you think about disgusting things to prompt the puking reflex, like eating a hamburger with maggots inside. I visualize the two of them buck naked, in the throes of ecstasy, on the very pillowtop mattress I just abandoned. Sarah Ellen in front of the fridge. Desmond's blank look in his Dave Matthews T-shirt. Nanette finding it hilarious that her father isn't wearing pants.

Again, nada.

Outside the office the light fades behind Cream of Wheat–colored plantation shutters. I hear the kids cackling through our thin walls, next, the sound of them pushing the coffee table to the side. I assume they are now throwing all the pillows on the ground to play the Floor Is Lava. In the never-ending mom guilt that has used my body as a host ever since I gave birth, I chastise myself for not hanging out with Alex and Nanette. I should be enjoying this bonus time with them instead of wallowing in here.

No marriage is perfect. Each one is hard work and don't let anyone on Netflix or social media inspiring #couplegoals make you think differently.

But this.

I didn't know Desmond had it in him to do something like this. A move that hurts so badly that it seems my body doesn't even know how to respond. Why couldn't he tell me he was unhappy? If things sucked so much, why didn't he just bail, or we could take a break, or we could've done something, talked to someone about it. This Hallmark Channel plot pivot leads to the end of us? This is how we wrap up eighteen years together.

And Sarah Ellen. Why was she wearing cowboy boots? This is Savannah, not Dallas. I wonder if it was just a quick romp or multiple rolls in the hay, sweat and grunting and sticky stuff. If my husband put in the effort to make her come or if it happened easily. It would have been a whole new body to work with, different erogenous zones, sounds, style, and speed. For the love of Jesus did they use birth control and what kind? After they finished, did they change their clothes or brush their teeth to hide the evidence? Did they hop back in the car to go to work or swing by the Super Kroger to scoop up pizza with cauliflower crust for dinner?

I have many questions and no tears.

And I have to pee. In the bathroom the toilet paper is gone. There's just the cardboard tube, damn it all to tarnation. Cracking the door, I plead for my son to retrieve a fresh roll from the laundry room—*Alex, honey, c'mere*—he can't hear me over *The Lego Movie*. I open the trash can to see if there's any discarded tissues I can repurpose. There's a bunched-up piece I used yesterday when I smashed a spider against the wall so I un-wad the toilet paper and shake out the insect corpse.

Or is it love?

Of course that's worse, a million times worse, though both scenarios suck hard. Love hurts more than horniness. Maybe Desmond loves this stranger going through my fridge. Perhaps she's so different from me he found her refreshing. Her skin is softer than mine or she smells like sandalwood. Or she's really good at shaving so she never has spiky patches or cuts on her knees. Maybe she's easier to be with, she doesn't get cranky about things like not pushing the toothpaste cap down all the way— you need to hear a click.

I wasn't always like this. I used to wear vintage cocktail rings and eat two veggie samosas for lunch every day and I won second prize at the Sidewalk Chalk contest in Forsyth Park for my sketch of an underwater cellist.

I flush and tug up my yoga pants. Back on the couch I consider there may have been other women. In my mind I wade back to odd times Des visited sites or missed events with the kids because of work. Was it work or orgies all over Savannah? Richmond Hill, Port Wentworth, Pooler.

It's over. It's gotta be, right? We can't save this thing. I imagine what life would look like with just the three of us living in the house. Me, sleeping in the middle of the bed. Me, doing the crap that Des traditionally handles. Me, trimming the grass on our tiny lawn with the mower from 1985. The simple idea of breaking up our family feels like a tectonic shift that I can't even process.

No. It can't be over.

Is it?

I don't know.

This happened, Prince has been gone six months, and the world already feels less sparkly, specifically my world. He is never again going to don a shoulder-padded blazer with a billowing scarf and remind us that we are gathered here today to get through this thing called life. I don't even know how I'm going to get through *today,* Prince.

3

PRINCE DOESN'T ANSWER

5:49 P.M.

When my mother calls, a photo pops up: good old Adelaide sporting a green peacock hat at the Flannery O'Connor parade. In the fuzzy snapshot she's adjusting the hat, both hands pinching the brim, and her expression is all business, a straight mouth and a deep line between her eyebrows.

Before I press accept, the voice of emotionally healthy and strong communicator Ramona whispers, *Tell her. Tell your mother about Desmond and the Strumpet. You need to talk to someone. No woman is an island. It takes a village, or something. Not an island village.*

"Hey, cookie," she says.

"Hey, Mom."

In first grade an evil girl named Shoshanna kidnapped my favorite stuffed animal, Carmen, a ragged elephant with pastel pink tusks and ballerina shoes and a trunk hanging on by its last threads, and lied to the teacher and her mother, saying

I had given it to her as a gift. Then she disappeared with Carmen, bounding up the stairs of the bus. When my mother found me sobbing at carpool, we looked up Shoshanna's address in the phone book and drove to her house, and my mother demanded Carmen's return while I cowered in the backseat. At home we threw a welcome back party for Carmen, with Tab in plastic teacups and gummy worms.

Tell your mother what happened. She's not going to swoop in and comfort you, no, she's not that kind of mother. She will probably say, *that's what you get for marrying a Southern boy, they worship you at first then deep down they just want you to make dinner and raise the babies while they go shoot things on the weekend.* At this point, how could you feel worse?

"If you ask me," my mother starts, her favorite way to launch a topic, to which my brother and I have a shared knee-jerk reaction where we mouth, *I didn't*, "this is a whole lot of commotion about nothing."

"What?"

"Hurricane Matthew, Ramona," Mom says, semi-aghast. "Did you forget?"

Right, the hurricane.

"No, I didn't forget about it," I tell her. "It doesn't seem hurricane-y yet. I haven't been thinking about it." I reach my hand into the toaster oven while it's still on, something that infuriates Desmond—well, guess what, I'm going to do all the things that annoy him—and turn over the chicken tenders I'm heating up for the kids. I think they changed the recipe. They used to taste pretty close to Chick-fil-A and now they're slimy.

Mom goes on: "I can't believe South Carolina already evacuated. Figures those Charleston snoots don't want to get their loafers wet."

Recently my mother has embraced all sorts of Savannah attitudes despite the fact she spent most of her life in Mobile, Alabama, and then Delaware, and really only two and a half years here, when she and Dad bought a house on Wilmington Island to be closer to us.

I've noticed the way my mother has made modifications to adapt to her environment and it annoys me. Like the Savannah vs. Charleston rivalry, complaining about tourists, or the way she started wearing jewelry when she plays tennis like the other women in her league. Much of this identity flared up after we lost Dad from pancreatic cancer in 2014 and I resent her for this. Not that she doesn't deserve to reinvent herself or be happy after my father's death. More like I'm too tired to get to know this new version of my mother.

"Well. But, Mom," I say. "Savannah has been lucky so far."

"Or you just have to look at a map."

"Right," I say. I pull out a carton of blueberries from the fridge, toss them in a colander, and run them under the faucet.

"We're protected."

"I wish I felt protected," I say, spreading out the berries to dry on a paper towel. "If you look at that thing on the Weather Channel, it's no joke."

"We'll see. What are my grands up to?"

"No school tomorrow. They were watching *The Lego Movie*. Now they're in the backyard playing hockey with croquet mallets. Or just hitting each other with them. I need to feed them dinner."

"I'm having soup."

"What kind?"

"Southwestern Chicken. Progresso was BOGO at Publix on Sunday, you should get some."

"Oh. Maybe. That would be good with shredded cheese and sour cream."

"Whenever I buy sour cream I only use two spoonfuls, it seems like a waste. Where's Des? Does he think y'all should leave?"

"You can freeze it, I think. He's not home yet," I lie. "He's still at work."

"At work? I hope he's not banging on a roof on the eve of a hurricane. There's stupid and then there's stupid."

"He's probably on his way."

The timer on the toaster oven beeps.

"Well. Are y'all going to stay or go?"

"I don't know, Mom. If we have to scoot, I bet we can stay with Christopher in Augusta."

"All right, then. You okay? You sound frazzled."

Tell her. What are you trying to protect her from? You've never been able to hide stuff from your mother.

I sigh. "I'm fine. A little frazzled, but fine."

"I wish you could see this. Jerry's out there trying to pull his boat in like he's walking a dog. This is the funniest thing, I wish you were here. He's wading in the water, pulling it to the hitch like the thing's a damn Lhasa apso."

Through the back window I watch Alex and Nanette hurling big wheels at the fence we share with our neighbors.

"Mom, I gotta feed the kids."

"'Kay. Sure you're all right?"

She knows. She always knows.

"I'm fine. Just tired."

"All right then. Love you."

"I love you, too, Mom."

8:47 P.M.

I put Alex and Nanette to bed. Correction: My kids are in their bedrooms, they're not sleeping. While Nanette sings the months of the year to herself and Alex reads the *Star Wars Character Encyclopedia* by the light of the cracked door, I pour pinot grigio in my Prince mug and flip on the television. I can't remember what number the Weather Channel is so I scroll through the guide to find it.

It feels strange Desmond isn't here, and not strange—like there's a plausible explanation for his absence. He's ordering Dirty Bird Chicken Nachos and a Bud Heavy at Coach's for the Alabama game. He's fussing at his crew not to leave cigarette butts on the ground as they pack up the Southbridge property. He's stopping by Walmart—the nice new one on Abercorn, not the one that makes us sad—on his way home to grab a box of nighttime pull-ups for Nanette. I know those things aren't true but thinking about what is hurts like a motherfucker. And the wine tastes like fermented Mountain Dew.

I find the Weather Channel. All right, let's talk Hurricane Matthew. The programming bounces from the observations of a poncho-ed blonde in Miami—Daphne Glover—to Dan Munoz, an earnest-looking man with Dr. Spock–like eyebrows in Jacksonville. Then back to the storm tracker crew in the studio analyzing satellite imagery. I pull a *Highlights* magazine close for a coaster and unhook the sterling silver hoop on my right ear so I can rest my head on the couch without my earring stabbing me.

The news is daunting. Hurricane Matthew is the first Category 5 storm to hit the Southeast since Hurricane Mitch in 1998. Right now it's churning over the Bahamas. South Carolina already evacuated—I *know*, dammit. Daphne and Dan aren't panicking yet. They sure are worried, though. I like their rain slickers and kind of wish I had one. My body starts to morph into the couch—the wine is doing its job.

So, it's bad. It's a powerful and dangerous storm. Though isn't there still a chance the hurricane could veer east? Maybe it will mosey farther out in the Atlantic to stir up some marine habitats or get exhausted ripping up all those stucco houses in Florida. By the time it makes landfall here, Matthew could be too tired to do anything more than blow our trees around and dump a little rain.

Nobody on the Weather Channel mentions Savannah. I've only had a third of my pour and I feel a monster headache. That's what you get for drinking the cheap stuff. And forgetting to eat dinner. Wait. Did I eat lunch? I can't remember if I did. Or if I put a new roll of toilet paper in the bathroom. What is Des doing right now? Ordinarily he would be on the other side of the sofa holding one of my feet or dead asleep with his head thrown back, mouth open, softly snoring.

Now the Weather Channel is back to Dan in Jacksonville.

"Again, we're encouraging people along the coast," he says, "to head inland if possible. Better safe than sorry."

Dan is right. It's probably healthy to consider my marriage over and visualize the future. Only one parent living in this house—I'm thinking, me. Two parents showing up for events at school, coming and going in separate cars. Desmond will rent a generic carpeted apartment with a second bedroom that Alex and Nanette will share on his weekends. A nook decorated in a little kid design they're too big for. Or maybe their new bedroom will be awesome, with a PlayStation or Xbox so they'll think Dad is way cooler than me. He's never been as anal about limiting screen time. Somehow he'll have to master purchasing a card for his mom's birthday and Mother's Day, even manage to send it to her through the mail.

The kids will be okay. They'll be fine, right? I know plenty of products of divorce who grew up to be functional members of society, some of them even have healthy relationships. I wonder if I will date again. There are probably different trends in the bedroom and new strains of diseases I can catch.

I wonder where Desmond is and if he feels as confused as I do right now. Somewhere in Savannah my husband is brushing his teeth. Somewhere in Savannah my mother rinses off her soup bowl in the sink and places it on the top shelf of the dishwasher. Somewhere on I-16 Nicole hands squeezy packs to her twins in the backseat. Somewhere in Savannah my boss, Kenneth, wonders where I disappeared to after lunch and loads his wet clothes in the dryer.

On my mug Prince smolders at me, the volume of his hair competing with the frills on his lace shirt. In the midst of my heartbreak and cheap wine buzz, I still feel the pain of Prince's death.

"How could you leave us?" I ask him. "I need you."

Prince doesn't answer. He doesn't know what it feels like to be left in a world that used to have a tiny guitar-wielding deity shrouded in lush fabrics emanating freedom, sexuality, vulnerability, and funkiness and now it doesn't.

But we do. And things have gotten pretty shitty since Prince died. I mean, they really suck now. Not just in my own disastrous existence but also out there in the world. I'm starting to feel confident there is a connection between these two things.

"We are gearing up for what will very likely be Category 3 or 4 winds. If you are in the path of Hurricane Matthew, please consider evacuation."

I guess I should make a plan for Hurricane Matthew. He's coming and he's not concerned with anyone's crappy marriage. I'm exhausted and a little tipsy and every force in the universe prevents me from getting up from the couch. I pass out, things starting to spin a little, and then wake up at two. I stumble back to our bedroom, wonder where Desmond is, then I remember, and I can't go back to sleep again until four, when I toss and turn over dreams starring Sarah Ellen in front of my fridge.

MAY 2016

What I did for Alex's seventh birthday party at Adventure Zone, two weeks and two days after Prince died.

1. I negotiated the party date and price at Adventure Zone in person. The owner doesn't appear to like people, forget kids, so, odd career choice for him. However,

my visit ensured Alex's party was penciled in on the calendar.

2. I collected email addresses of parents for kids in Alex's class, fashioned an Evite, and responded to messages like, "Thanks for including us! Preston's MeMaw is driving here from Naples so our plans are up in the air."

3. I scoured the internet before choosing an Angry Birds Lego Set from Amazon and small ice cream maker from Bed Bath & Beyond for Alex's gift. I wrapped them in plaid paper from Christmas, hid the presents behind the boots in my closet, flattened the boxes, took them outside to the recycling bin while my children were sleeping, and almost had a heart attack when I saw a possum scuttling across my neighbor's lawn.

4. I ordered oversize plastic race car mugs for party favors, stuffed them with bags of Starburst jelly beans, tied them with fire engine red crimped ribbon, and used scissors to curl the ends.

5. I baked yellow cupcakes from a Duncan Hines mix, frosted them with chocolate icing, and misted them with red sprinkles.

6. I bought matching Hot Wheels plates and napkins at Party City, organic boxes of juice from Whole Foods, sparkling and bottled water for parents at Publix.

7. I packed a Ziploc bag with candles, lighter, and a dull knife in case Adventure Zone didn't have one. Extra napkins to wipe the knife off.

8. I loaded party supplies in the van, double-checked the backpack to make sure I had extra diapers and wipes for Nanette, responded to last minute texts about the time and location of the party, drove out to Adventure Zone with Alex to set up forty-five minutes before go time.

That's what I did. Desmond's job: Pick up ice and bring Nanette to the party. All he had to do was purchase one bag of ice at Chu's and chauffeur our daughter to Adventure Zone.

I was sweating and standing on a chair hanging Alex's favorite colored streamers—red and yellow—over a dated mural featuring kids wearing party hats when Des arrived. Alex, the birthday boy, was already bored, bugging me for quarters to play the video games in the lobby.

Me: I paid for this party so your friends can ride go-carts and jump on the bounce stuff, I'm not giving you bonus cash to stand in front of a screen and rot your brain more than you already have.

What is up, party people, Des said. Nanette popped out behind him, rocking an ensemble only the two of them could concoct: a purple princess dress, red leggings with a Christmas elf print, and too-small Crocs. Choose your battles.

Daddy! Alex threw himself into Des's arms, as if they were long lost father and son, instead of two people who just shared cinnamon toast waffles at breakfast. I noticed Des was wearing a hideous UGA football jersey and not carrying anything.

Hey, babe, I said. Ice?

Ice, Des repeated.

My heart started beating faster: Did you bring the ice?

Ice, ice, baby, Des said.

Stop, collaborate, and listen, Nanette recited, much to Des's delight, a routine that was cute six months ago, not today.

Ice is back with a brand-new invention, Des said.

You forgot it, I said. Scotch tape in one hand and half a roll of crinkled yellow streamers in the other, my arms fell by my side.

I did, Des said, avoiding eye contact. It's cool, I'll run and get some.

The blood rushed to my head.

Babe, I asked you to do one thing.

And I'm going to do it, he said, the beginning of an edge in his voice.

But I still have stuff to do, I said, gesturing to the party space and the box of supplies I hadn't put out, like in MTV *Cribs* when musicians point out their media rooms with couch floors. And you're going to bail now to get ice when you could be helping me.

Babe, Des said. You do this all the time.

Do what? Everything?

You totally freak out. It's a party.

It's a party, Nanette squealed.

Right, Des said. It's supposed to be fun. Mommy should probably chill out. Are y'all ready to have fun or what, he said, scooping up Alex and Nanette at the same time and swinging them around. They giggled. Mid-swing, Alex's sneaker knocked over a foldout chair, it made a metallic thud against the floor.

It's the worst to tell someone they're freaking out. Or stressed out. The end result is that the accused person feels backed into a corner. If I didn't feel stressed before, I sure as hell do now, and yet if I react in an emotional way, I prove Desmond was right.

It's lose-lose.

You don't get it, I hissed. This stuff doesn't happen by itself. It's a lot of work. I ask you to do one thing and you forget and instead of showing any remorse you make me the wet blanket while you're the fun party guy. Drives me fucking crazy.

Um, language?

I felt an urge to climb off my folding chair and bash him over the head with it, WWF-style. Yeah, it was a birthday party. I was aware it was supposed to be fun. Well, for the kids. Birthday parties are usually brutal for parents. More maddening was the way he pulled this shit all the time and acted like I was the wacko.

I made an effort to create a special moment for our family and he just rolled in and consumed everything—figuratively and literally. He'd take a piece of cauliflower and sweep it around the garlic hummus in a huge swath like a tsunami before the guests arrived. Then entertain everyone and take credit like he was host of the year. And me, the worker ant, the uptight one.

Prince would want you to enjoy yourself, Desmond said.

How dare he.

I wanted this day to be about Alex. I was trying to celebrate a milestone for my baby. Now I was filled with rage over my husband blowing me off. Wait, was I the one being the asshole? He was right—it was a party. It wasn't a big deal. So why was I shaking?

Nanette had pulled off her dress, balled it up, and stuffed it in a bucket of golf balls, and was licking the top of a juice box she'd stabbed with the cake knife.

I sighed. I wondered if raising my munchkins with Desmond meant more birthday parties like this. Does it get better when they're older? Or will it always be me, curling the ends of the ribbon on the party favors and seething.

Just go, I told him. Please go get ice. The kids will be here in ten minutes.

THURSDAY
6:39 A.M.

A small face appears by the side of my bed. I roll over and blink. The outline of her hair—wild curls with matted ends—is visible against the hall light.

"Where's Daddy?" Nanette asks me. "Hey. You're wearing the same thing from yesterday."

"Good morning, boo boo," I say. "Want a hug?"

Nanette considers this proposal—blank expression, scratching of head—before she responds.

"Yes." I pull her up, across my body. Dang, she's getting heavy. She wraps her arms around me and rests her head on my chest. The good stuff: the weight of a small child, her sniffing sounds, her morning breath, the curls itching my nose.

"Daddy stayed with a friend yesterday," I tell her.

"Oh," she says. Apparently my answer is satisfactory. "I'm hungry. Can you make breakfast?"

"I can do that."

She scampers off, Minneapolis in tow.

It's Thursday. No school today, South Carolina already evacuated. At least I don't have the morning routine—feed children, brush their teeth, make sure they are wearing clothes semi-appropriate for the weather, pack lunches, make myself presentable, botch my eyeliner, blot it with remover and start over, deliver my children to the correct schools—not today. My task, instead: Pretend to be emotionally stable and keep my children alive.

Can I do that?

Prince, if you're listening, shine your purple light down on me from whatever cool version of heaven you've found. Give me strength.

Yes, I can.

But work, freaking work—Kenneth! I feel a spur in my stomach. I scooted early yesterday and forgot to follow up. And I can't go in today—I'm going to have to work from home. Kenneth won't close the office because of a hurricane. He won't give two shits the schools are out. He probably reckons the natural disaster will fuel our creativity.

The comfort of holding my soft child to my chest is replaced by a pinot grigio headache like a bowling ball rolling around in my skull.

I pad down our dark hall, shifting a tipped picture frame back to level, bending over to pick up a mermaid doll lying facedown next to the air-conditioning vent. It feels odd, walking through my home, everything in the same place, nothing is the same.

I turn on Nick Jr. for Nanette. She's content, a tiny figure in a pile of throw pillows, sucking on Minneapolis's horn. I make a pot of coffee. Alex treads into the kitchen with a quilt wrapped around him like a toga and heaves himself onto a chair at the table.

"I had dreams about the hurricane," he says. "It brought lava, the hurricane did. It was covering everything. It was burning up the sidewalks."

"Hurricanes don't erupt," I tell him. "That's the one thing you don't have to worry about with those."

Alex, exasperated with me, it's not even eight a.m.: "I know, Mommy. It was just a dream."

"I don't want you to worry," I tell him.

"Okay," he says.

"You know what? We don't have school today. Let's have bacon and eggs. Let's live it up."

"Bacon?" Nanette echoes from the TV room.

"I don't like bacon," Alex says.

"Says no one, ever. All right, just eggs for you, then."

The doorbell rings.

Through the spyhole I see him on the step. Desmond. I am not prepared to talk to him at all, forget so early in the morning. I just poured half-and-half in my coffee and I haven't gotten the chance to stir it. In other news, my desire to stab him with a fireplace poker is mixed with a sense of pleasure he's come back to fight for me.

A flutter in my stomach. Could we refresh, could we move on from yesterday? He is my person and of course I still love him.

You can't click and drag that over to the recycling bin in one day. And yet the thing he did. I have never felt this gutted in the entirety of my thirty-eight years of sometimes lovely and occasionally rough existence.

Actually I'm not sure why Desmond is here. Maybe he stopped by to pick up his phone charger. I throw open the door lightning fast like a ninja, step out onto the front landing, and close the door behind me.

"Can I come in?" he asks me.

I hold a small spoon in my fist and every cell in my body is alert. "No."

"Ramona," he says. "Please." He looks awful and I'm delighted about that. His red hair is greasy, he's stubbly, he's rubbing his eyes.

"No."

"Listen," he says. "We have to go. They're recommending evacuating Chatham County now."

We.

"We," I tell him, "are not going anywhere with you."

"What?"

"If I have to evacuate, I'll do it," I hiss. "That does not include a road trip with you."

"You and me have a lot to talk about. But dude, they're my kids, too."

"Dude." My voice drips with mockery—who the hell calls his estranged wife, *dude*? "You should've thought about that before you fucked up everything."

He crams his hands in the pockets of the same track pants he was wearing yesterday. "Where are you going to go?"

"I don't know yet," I say.

"But you're going to, right? Evacuate? These branches. I mean, who knows."

"It's none of your business."

"Ramona. It *is* my business."

"Desmond, I am not prepared to talk to you. I'm hungover as hell. I haven't brushed my teeth yet. It may be a week until I am ready to talk to you. Or a year. You need to respect that. And get off my step."

"Ramona," he says, his tone half-pleading, half-irritated.

My body begins to transform into the Incredible Hulk. Must. Keep. Calm. I am a mother. We are not allowed to lose control. We must be unflappable.

"Please go," I say. "I don't know what I'm telling the kids and I don't want to flip out when they're here."

"Will you at least let me know what your plan is? That you're safe."

He looks pathetic.

I shake the small spoon in his face. "Just assume we are alive unless the news tells you otherwise."

"Ramona," he says. "You're acting like a child."

"Me?" I look behind me in case a small person has crept up—the coast is clear. "Me? I'm the child? I'm not the one who stepped outside the sacred bond of marriage with Botox Barbie just because I was going through a dry patch. I'm not that child."

"Babe. I am so sorry. I will say it a thousand times if you'll talk to me."

"I'm not ready. I will talk to you after the hurricane."

He rubs his eyebrows with his thumb and ring finger before grunting, "Okay."

"If we survive."

"Don't say that," he says.

"Turn around and walk back to your truck."

"I just want to tell you that I love you."

"If you don't move this instant, I'll be loving you under my shoe."

To prove my point, I launch a karate kick into the air.

"That was weird," Des says.

"Get gone."

He half turns, lowers his head, and I see extra flesh between his chin and his neck and skinny streaks of white interspersed with the red hair over his ear. "All right."

Inside, I turn the dead bolt and press my back against the front door. I listen for his footsteps moving down the path, I can't hear them, he's wearing sneakers. My breath comes quickly now.

As I walk by the kitchen I see him through the window. He's outside tying the legs of the grill to cinder blocks. I bang on the window and wave frantically for him to leave. He straightens up, gestures to the grill, and holds up his right hand like, *five minutes.* This makes me even more furious so I make bigger hand movements, pointing, and mouth, *fucking go, get out*! He shakes his head and trudges out of sight. I hear the truck door opening and slamming and the sound of his truck moving down the street.

Back in the kitchen, Alex asks, "Who was that?"

"FedEx," I lie. "They had the wrong house."

From his cage Clarence Thomas looks up at me with beady eyes. I pull out a carton of eggs from the fridge and a package of bacon. Somebody already opened the bacon, it's fastened with a chip clip, and a smog of grease covers the inside of the package.

Nanette informs the room she thinks the poopy is coming. We both sprint to the bathroom and I wait in the hall while she unsuccessfully attempts to land number two in the potty. As she sings the theme song of *Paw Patrol* to herself, I tap out an email to Xavier on my phone. *Laser Life wants bigger font. Shopping cart every page. In your face!* My hands smell like bacon. They shake as I search for the letters on my phone.

4

YOUR DISASTER SUPPLY KIT

7:54 A.M.

"I'm checking in on you," Nicole says.

"Thanks," I respond, and really, I'm grateful for someone to pull me out of the swirling darkness that is my brain. It's a horror film in there, with eighties hair and stabbings, Excel spreadsheets and flash drives, tubes of strawberry banana Go-Gurt and monster trucks.

"You betcha," Nicole says.

"Did you land in Macon?"

"We did," she says. "Only had to stop three times. Two wardrobe changes. For the same kid. Just a sweet start to what's probably going to be the best hurrication ever."

"Well, good."

"Nothing like extra time with the ol' mother-in-law. Or sleeping with your husband and twins in a guest suite the size of the dressing room at the Gap."

"I love the Gap," I say.

"Me too. Where are you guys headed today?"

I want to tell Nicole that I just can't right now. I know there's a hurricane on the way but I've got a lot on my plate—like, more than usual.

Instead I admit, "I'm not sure we're gonna."

"Ramona," Nicole says.

"What?" I scrape up my defense: "The most annoying thing would be losing power for a couple days. I'll round up some candles and buy peanut butter and jelly. The worst thing would be not having AC. If that happens, we open the windows. We'll be fine."

I visualize Nicole's diaper bag—a tasteful floral print with pink and blue containers inside for each twin: wipes, snacks, first aid, a change of clothes. Of course, she can't imagine anyone staying in Savannah. The majority of her day is spent predicting catastrophes that may befall the twins.

"Ramona," Nicole says. "I'm not sure that's the best idea. They're ordering a mandatory evacuation of Savannah now. All of Chatham County. Turn on your TV!"

This is what happens when super-educated women are plucked from being badasses in the corporate world and plunged into a daily routine consisting of watching *Wild Kratts* and cutting up avocado. My friend needs projects, and her next one is me.

"Mandatory?" I start to chew on the stump of nail on my middle finger. "New information. GD."

Nicole, incredulous: "Girl. How is this new information?"

"Mommy, are you talking to me?" Alex calls out.

I rest the phone against my left boob.

"No, sweetie. I'm on the phone with Miss Nicole."

"You're talking loud," he says.

"*Loudly*," I correct. Phone back to ear.

Nicole scolds, "Check the TV, hon."

"I will. I promise."

"Turn it on!"

"I will!"

"What have you been doing?" she asks me.

Trying to keep it together because my marriage is in deep doo doo. I'm simultaneously charmed by Nicole's concern and annoyed by her persistence. I have the right to get mauled by Hurricane Matthew if I want to. She doesn't need to impose her Black Hawk helicoptering on me.

"I just thought," I say. "It was probably a lot of hype."

"Nope, it doesn't appear to be. It's a Cat Four cruising toward you. Landfall tomorrow night."

"Okay, I'll go turn on the TV."

"Do it. And make a plan. Then text me when you have a plan."

"All right," I say.

"Ramona, my sweet. I'm going to keep bugging you until I know you're evacuating. It's me and my crazy kids trapped with my crazier mother-in-law. In freaking Macon. I've got plenty of time to stalk you."

8:14 A.M.

"I will now interrupt regularly scheduled programming to check on a natural disaster," I tell the kids, snatching the remote control from Alex's hand, and plopping on the couch.

"No, Mommy," says Nanette.

"We were watching Spider-Man," Alex says. On the screen Spider-Man perches on the roof of an abandoned warehouse, monologuing as usual. Something's poking me; I shift my weight so I can reach back and extricate a monster truck wedged between the couch cushions.

"You've seen this one," I say. "And to be honest, I don't know if Spider-Man is the best influence. He's whiny, and he thinks he's hilarious. That's the worst. People who think they're funnier than they really are."

"I'm funny," says Nanette.

"You are," I admit.

"Daddy's funny," Alex says.

"Sometimes," I mumble.

My son buries his head in my side and groans. He's too big for those pajama pants, now they barely reach his ankles.

"When is Daddy coming back?" he asks me.

"I don't know. He's helping somebody with their roof." I calculate how many lies I've told in the last twenty-four hours to my children, stacking them on top of each other like Lincoln Logs. "Okay, here we go."

On the Weather Channel Daphne is still on duty in Miami. I hope she gets overtime because that is one long shift. It looks gusty down there but not too bad. Dan must be on break—we're not getting updates from him. Instead we hear from a new guy—a shiny-faced man in a navy slicker—standing in front of a river in Jacksonville, where, again, the storm doesn't look major. What does look major, however, is that angry swirl on the digital map.

I announce, "Nobody is talking about Savannah."

"Why not?" Alex asks me.

"I'm not sure but it's odd, don't you think? If the hurricane was headed right toward us, wouldn't they say, people of Savannah, get out of Savannah."

"Get out of Savannah," Nanette repeats. "Get out of banana."

They cut to the local news. Pretty sure these folks are going to tell us South Carolina already evacuated.

"Checking in from WTOC serving Savannah, Hilton Head, and Bluffton, Mayor Eddie DeLoach has ordered a mandatory evacuation for Chatham County residents effective today."

"Aw, geez," I say.

"What does that mean, Mommy?" Alex asks me.

Mandatory.

We still don't have to go. Government officials are just covering their asses. We could stay. If things get dicey, we'll have a slumber party in the laundry room. Behind Mayor DeLoach the red swirl on the screen moves up to the border between Florida and Georgia. Next to him is a serene preacher from the African Methodist Episcopal Church whose presence encourages the community to trust the words emerging from the white man. A blazered blonde rapidly gestures, I don't know sign language, probably something to the effect of, *y'all, get the fuck out of here.*

Panic starts to spill over like water bubbling from a pot of Annie's noodles I left on the stove and forgot about. I need to get my babies out of Hurricane Matthew's path, and soon.

"It means," I tell him, "that we should probably skedaddle."

"Is the hurricane coming to our house?" he says.

"There's a good chance," I tell my son, reaching sideways and pulling him into a hug. "But we'll be okay." I kiss the top of his head.

"How do you know?" he asks, worried.

"Because we'll be together."

"But Daddy's not here," Nanette says. "And we have Clarence Thomas."

"Well, I'm here," I say. "And I will never ever let a hurricane get you guys. Or Clarence Thomas. If any wind tries to blow one single hair on your head I will stand up and fight it like Superman."

"Silly Mommy. You're not a super," says Nanette.

"Oh, aren't I? Okay, guys. I'll get your suitcases. Let's pack some stuff. Why don't you put your action figures and your ponies in a bookbag? I gotta call Grandma."

8:52 A.M.

I've got an email from Nicole: *"Please. Get. Out. Of. There."* All right. I will open your attachment, Nicole.

CEMA encourages citizens to make storm preparations now. Individuals, families, and businesses should:
—Secure any items that could be easily blown around by strong winds.

I can do that.

—Listen to local authorities for advice and protective actions.

Well?

—Check your disaster supply kit and make sure it has the necessary items to include food, water, a battery-operated radio, and medicines.

I don't have a radio. I've got Children's Advil, however, and let's not forget the last few drops of the pinot Mountain Dew.

—Don't forget to include pets in your preparations.

Thanks, Mrs. Wall, for bringing Clarence Thomas into my life.

—Create a family evacuation plan that details how and where you will evacuate and where you will meet if you are separated.

There are family members I'd like to avoid.

—Residents and tenants should inspect their homes to confirm that there is no damage that a hurricane could increase. Residents with yards should also make a list of anything lying on the ground outside that could get tossed into the air and become debris during high winds.

I've never classified myself as a list-maker.

—Back up your electronics: Aside from keeping extra batteries and chargers around during a hurricane, people are also encouraged to back up any electronic devices.

I need to charge the tablets.

9:27 A.M.

"Yup, I heard," Mom says. "Jerry came running over here with the news. He's got nine TVs in that crappy ranch and they're on all the time."

"Fox News?"

"Uh-huh. So, where you headed?"

"Probably Augusta," I tell her. "We can stay with Christopher."

"He still a gay?"

"I think so."

"What are you going to tell the kids about that?"

"That he's gay."

"Oh," she says, and I hear her tossing back Diet Coke from her Parker's Cup.

"Want to ride with us?"

"Nope," Mom says.

"Where are you going?"

"Nowhere."

Now I'm the ballbuster: "Mom. You live on the water. You can't stay."

"First of all, I'm sixty-eight. Second of all, I get to decide."

"Pack a bag and come with us," I tell her. "If we're too cozy at Christopher's we can find a Red Roof Inn somewhere. We'll figure it out."

"I appreciate the offer, Monie, but I'm staying put."

"Mom."

"Don't worry, I'll get supplies. I need to swing by Kroger anyway because I'm out of toothpaste."

"Mom!"

"Ramona. We've had hurricanes before. I'm going to be just fine."

This is a problem. While many people have tried (and failed) to outsmart Adelaide Burkhalter, my mother is no match for Hurricane Matthew, especially in her tiny house on the edge of the river.

I hear wails of frustration emerging from the bathroom—pretty sure Nanette shit her pants.

"Mom. Nanette just pooped. This isn't over. I'll call you later."

"No need," she says. "I'm fine. Love you."

To the phone, I whisper, "For fuck's sake."

"Mommy," Nanette calls out. "I went poopy."

"In the potty?"

I am old enough to know that there are grown-ups who will let me down but I will always cling to the hope my children are capable of achieving greatness.

"Nope," she replies, cheerfully. "It's in my unders."

10:02 A.M.

"Hey, Mrs. Arnold," calls Bailey, the high schooler from two doors down. "You need some help?"

I'm hauling the potted plants that aren't too heavy to the shed in the backyard. Also our Walmart Halloween decorations. I'm not going to board up windows but I'll feel like a putz if we have to replace them thanks to a plastic skeleton flying at my house at 90 miles per hour.

"Bailey, hey. Actually, that would be lovely."

He lopes over to me—a pale teenager with high cheekbones and bruised banana-colored bangs drooping over eyebrows, massive burgundy basketball sneakers looking cartoonish compared to his chicken calves and knobby knees. He's draped in a black piqué polo with a plastic name tag: Welcome to Party City Let Bailey Help You. He picks up a cracked pot of wilting geraniums.

"You moving all these?"

"Maybe just the lighter ones," I tell him.

"I can get this one," he says. "Hey, you're still in pajamas."

"I am. Kinda one of those mornings."

"I know what you mean," he says. We walk together down a gravel path to our small backyard, where I hoist open the shed door and shove to the side a gasoline can, a Cozy Coupe, a deflated basketball, a faded cornhole board, and a lime-green swimming noodle. "Y'all got a generator?"

"No," I tell him. "That would be helpful."

"We don't, either."

The sky is smoky light gray and the air feels still. I drop one pot—shit—and it rolls to the side, spilling soil inside my slipper. I stand on one foot, slide off one slipper, and shake the dirt out onto the grass.

"That sucks," Bailey says. "Think you'll put your lawn furniture in here?"

"I should."

He's surveying our backyard and deck.

"What about those lights?" he says.

"Yeah. Those should probably come down, too."

Since I don't hear any screaming from the house, I assume my children are still plugged in to Nick Jr. While it's disappointing Nanette pooped in her underwear—again—there's relief knowing I don't have to worry about poop for a few hours until the next time she needs to go.

I'm sweating now and my phone buzzes in the pocket of my robe. It's probably Desmond, ignoring my request for time to process, or Mom, maybe changing her mind about the evacuation, or Nicole, harassing me for my escape plan, or lack thereof, or maybe it's Kenneth, wondering where I am. Tell you what, Kenneth. I'm not in the office.

It's a Savannah area code, an unknown number. During a natural disaster I should probably answer calls. When I do, I hear a soft voice.

"Ramona?"

"This is she."

"Hey, Ramona, it's Sarah Ellen."

"Nope," I say.

"Wait," she says, louder. "Please. One minute."

"Nope, nope, no. How did you get my number?"

A pause. "School directory."

"Oh."

"Just," she says. "Can I ask you something?"

I roll my eyes even though she can't see it. "Like, about my-self?"

"No, a favor."

"You're," I say, reaching for the door handle of the shed like I need it to prop me up. "Asking *me* for a favor?"

"I know, I know. I have no right."

"You're darn tootin' you have no right, Sarah Ellen."

"Hey, Mrs. Arnold?" Bailey calls out across my backyard. When he realizes I'm on the phone he puts his hand over his mouth. In a quieter tone, "You got a ladder? These lights are hard to reach."

I point to the shed. Sweet kid. Why is Bailey helping me? Here I am gesturing to things like he works for me.

Sarah Ellen is still talking: "I'm sure you're angry."

"Kinda."

"It's just, I'd rather tell him," she says.

"Tell who?"

"My husband."

"Oh," I say, watching Bailey squint at our ancient aluminum ladder. "You think I'm going to call your husband?"

"Well," she says. "I'm sure you're mad."

"I sure am. But why do you think I give a rat's ass about your crappy relationship when mine is ending?"

"Yours is ending?" When she says this her voice changes, like she's finding out a pleasant piece of information: *oh, they're giving out free scoops at Leopold's if you recite the Pledge of Allegiance?* The new tone makes me want to heave the terracotta planter I'm holding against our storage shed.

"I don't know," I say. "Maybe. Maybe not. I can't think about that right now."

"Well."

"Yeah."

"It didn't mean anything," she says. "Desmond's a great guy, you two are good together, I'm sure you can work it out."

It didn't mean anything to them. It means everything to me.

"Oh," I sputter. "You're sure? *You're* sure?"

Of all the nerve in the whole wide world. I watch Bailey reaching up to pull down the twinkly lights, outdoor decor I practically killed myself hanging up for Desmond's thirty-fifth birthday party, that ingrate slimebucket. The bulbs are heavier than you'd think and one breaks. Tiny pieces of glass scatter on our yellow lawn. Worried, Bailey looks at me, and I wave and shake my head like no big deal and I realize what a jerk I am by being on the phone.

"Listen, Sarah Ellen? I gotta go. There's a hurricane coming, I need to prep my house, and get out of town."

"You're still in Savannah?"

"Yes," I respond through clenched teeth. "And before you tell me, I know South Carolina evacuated. Listen. I have no intention of calling your husband. Or shouting from the rooftops to anyone in Savannah who will listen. I haven't had any time to process this info or grieve or even drink myself into a stupor. So please let me be. One disaster at a time, lady."

I press end on the phone.

"Bailey," I call out. "That's so nice of you. You don't need to do that."

"I don't mind," he says.

I reach for the strands of lights he's holding, which he's expertly wrapped in a neat loop.

"Let me get those," I say, examining him. Bailey, who Des and I refer to as Awkward Teen Task Force, is taller than me now. I know his father is deployed. The last time I remember seeing the dad, he was power washing pollen off the siding of the house. Must have been last spring. The mom? I met her once when she delivered an Amazon package that ended up on her doorstep by accident—a skittish woman with thin platinum hair and a pantsuit too big for her. "You scoot. I'm sure your mom has stuff she needs help with. You going to hit the road?"

"Probably, ma'am," he says, smiling. "Looks like it's going to be a big storm."

"Okay. Be safe."

I watch him amble across the lawn and close the gate carefully behind him and I ache, like, what a lonely kid, then I remember the call I just got, and I feel another ache, like, what a lonely everyone.

2014

Desmond and I had plans to celebrate our eighth anniversary by riding our bikes in the Midnight Garden Ride. He has a fancy mountain bike he takes on trails—the kind where you hook your shoes into the pedals—and I have a rusty seafoam Huffy I pedal to the pool.

We're not talking Tour de France. It was something different for a night out. We booked my mother to babysit, an ask we reserve for special occasions because you never know when things can backfire on you with Adelaide.

In October it's still humid in Savannah, so I slid on a scoop-neck T-shirt that could get sweaty and skinny jeans. I traced eyeliner above my lashes and coated them with waterproof mascara. After I finished applying makeup, I was startled by my face in the mirror. It was like bumping into an old friend at a place you rarely go to, like the office where you pick up a new cable box.

Our date was kind of a big deal. We needed a change of scenery that didn't involve wiggly children or stressing about a new expense we didn't see coming. We were so tired. I was in the trenches of newborn-induced sleep deprivation, Des was working all the time, and cancer was decimating my father.

My mother arrived at the front door with the James Patterson novel she'd reserved from the Islands library branch, her reading glasses secure in an embroidered burrito-shaped case, and her Parker's cup filled to the rim. She waved off my instructions with one or two comments like, *this isn't my first rodeo*, and *I'm pretty sure you and your brother grew up just fine without me buzzing around you like horseflies over a carcass.*

The Midnight Ride started at nine, not midnight. Appropriate because nine feels like midnight when you can't remember the last time you cobbled together five hours of sleep.

Of course Des knew half the folks lined up outside Daffin Park for the ride. He always recognizes more people than me, partly because he grew up here, partly because I'm an introvert. He rolled down the window and heckled some guy standing next to the Porta Potty about the Alabama game. We parked, extracted our bikes from the back of Des's truck, and strapped on our helmets. We giggled and gave each other high fives.

Some bikers had cool glow wheels and flashing accessories. Some participants were dressed in legit cycling clothes—tight jerseys, cleats, and spandex stopping at the knee. One guy had an oversize fanny pack boasting three cans of beer. We hadn't really prepped like that—it didn't matter. I felt like I'd already won for putting on makeup and leaving my house after dark.

Eight years, I heard Des tell a man gripping the handlebars of a cherry-red cruiser. So what better way to celebrate than bike around town with a bunch of drunk people?

Can't think of one, the man said.

That's my beautiful bride, Des said. Not only can she pedal like no one's business but she makes amazing babies.

I was crouched down, double knotting the laces of my sneakers. I nodded and waved. Desmond introduces me with over-the-top descriptions, which make me cringe yet nudge me to see myself the way he does. The Most Talented Artist in Athens. Maker of the Most Amazing Chili in Midtown. The Smartest Broad in the Advertising Biz. My Lady Most Fair from Delaware.

I don't have titles for Desmond. But I always felt special being included in the wide net he cast. I'm the fish you wouldn't expect at the party but is having a great time. I was proud to be with him and I liked that when the party was over, I got to go home with him.

We started pedaling in a cluster of people. We were in the middle of the pack, between a trio of dudes and a family with tweens wearing glittery unicorn helmets. As we crossed over the quiet streets of Ardsley Park, chatter and giggles emerged from our group. The streetlights shined a soft orange glow, muted flashlights against the live oak trees. Passing a gas station, two officers interrogated a disheveled woman next to the car wash, their hands on their hips.

I'm going to ride behind you, Des said, as we cruised down Victory past a large house with an iron gate, so I can look at your butt.

Cool, I told him.

Or do you want to look at mine?

We can alternate. I like your ass.

Language! Unicorns on the starboard side.

Oops, I said.

Eight years, Ramona the Best. Eight years.

The temperature started to drop. My thighs burned a little from pedaling and I was awake. As we picked up the pace, the air brushed my cheeks and forearms and Des rode at a steady pace on my left side.

We were headed to a tent near Chippewa Square, where we were promised snacks. But when we crossed over East Taylor Street, my bike started wobbling side to side. Something was up with the back wheel. I steered to the outer band of the pack, found the ground with tippy toes, and slowed to a stop. Des didn't notice at first, he was talking to another couple on the ride.

Babe, I said. Hold up a sec.

He didn't hear me.

Des, I called out, louder.

He heard me that time. He circled back around, along with another guy, some buddy from a project downtown.

I think something's wrong with my bike, I said.

With your bike? Des said.

Yes, with my bike.

To his friend: We'll catch up with y'all.

We used the flashlight on my phone to check the back wheel. It looked like the chain had fallen off the part that connected the rear wheel with the frame because something had come loose. Maybe a bolt or a screw? We looked around for the part by shining the flashlight on the last stretch I'd ridden but it was gone. I felt around on the cobblestones—dusty, smooth—in case my eyes were failing me.

The last cyclists in the group sailed by us. A woman slowed down to ask if everything was okay.

Sure, I said. We'll figure it out.

We retraced my route to the place where I first started feeling wobbly. Even though we could still hear the crowd of cyclists, they were now out of sight. We were whales who beached themselves during migration and our other whale friends didn't give a shit about us. I couldn't find any hardware and I actually wasn't sure what I was looking for.

I'm sorry, babe, I said.

Don't worry, Des said, his voice too cheerful.

I mean. We're still out. And we have a babysitter. Let's get a beer.

Okay, he said.

I could tell he was bummed. We pushed our bikes another block to Pinkie Masters. A cranky bartender in Harry Potter glasses informed us we couldn't wheel our bikes in the bar, we didn't bring locks, and Des wouldn't leave his outside because he was nervous someone would steal it. All was not lost! We could find a joint somewhere with a patio so we could keep an eye on our bikes.

Desmond and I faced each other on the sidewalk, both of us holding the handlebars. A group of bachelorettes stumbled down Liberty, linked arms and matching Tervis cups.

I'll just ride back and get the truck, Des said.

No! My tone sounded like my toddler son.

Babe.

You don't have to do that, I insisted. We could call an Uber.

An Uber that can fit two bikes? And we already paid for the tickets for the Midnight thing. We don't need to spend more money on Uber and drinks when we have Miller Lite at home.

Now I was sweating in my skinny jeans with a sinking feeling. I could save the night, I could.

Des, I said. This sucks but let's figure something else out.

It's cool, babe, I'll get the truck.

He had already started to click his shoes into his fancy pedals. My throat burned and my shoulders slumped.

Seriously?

Yeah, he said.

I wasn't going to try to convince him to stay when for him the night was already over. This wasn't how the evening was sup-posed to go—Desmond and me, parting ways like we're both bailing from an awkward date. Sure, it's tough to stay connected in a marriage when you have little kids. And we'd have more, better date nights, right?

Off he went, a hunched figure retreating in and out of the shadows between the streetlights. When I couldn't see him anymore I leaned my bike against the brick—I didn't care if it got stolen. I went inside Pinkie's, bought myself a PBR in a to-go cup, and pounded it too quickly. I made a second trip for a vodka and soda. I leaned against the wall, slid down to the sidewalk to a squat, and sipped my drink while I waited for Desmond, who pulled up to the curb forty-five minutes later. We loaded my bike into his trunk. On the ride home, I don't think we said a word to each other.

5

JESUS AND THE FISH OR WHATEVER

10:43 A.M.

The house is ready for a Category 4 storm.

Ready-ish. I'm sure there's more I should do, however, I feel confident that if anything destroys our house it will either be from nature (beyond my control) or jackasses on our street who didn't put away their stuff (also, beyond my control). I'm sweating in my bathrobe, and I head back inside where the kids are playing ghosts, chasing each other with chenille throw blankets over their heads, bumping into walls.

I should pack.

I stuff two pairs of jeans and three T-shirts in a duffel bag. In my plastic overnight case I toss my hairbrush, facial cleanser, makeup, and deodorant. I don't have much deodorant left because I dropped the solid powder stick on Monday morning. It broke into three white chalky chunks, which I then tried to squish back into the applicator with mediocre results.

"Guys," I call out. "Did you two put some of your toys in the Spider-Man suitcase?"

My query is greeted with squealing and a loud crash. Our bedroom looks like marriage, interrupted. My husband's jeans thrown over a chair. On his dresser: receipts, loose change, a worn brown leather belt. When my phone buzzes, I peek at caller ID.

Of course.

"Kenneth," I say, tugging at the zipper on my duffel bag. "Hey."

"Hey, Ramona!"

"I meant to text you, I'm so sorry."

Now I'm rummaging through the closet for our small navy suitcase, the one with the missing wheel that stores a stack of shoeboxes holding shoes my feet don't fit into anymore because they went up a size after I had Nanette.

Kenneth: "It's cool, it's cool. So, I'm at the office."

"You are?"

"Yeah," he says, and I picture him pulling at his ear, an unconscious habit. "There's a few of us here, so."

One of Kenneth's trademark moves is ending sentences with the word, "so." It's been a while since I studied grammar but I seem to recall that "so" is an adverb or conjunction depending on context. However Kenneth prefers to use it as a passive-aggressive weapon implying that whoever he is speaking to has made a dubious or confusing choice.

"Oh." In the closet I press the icon for speaker and prop the phone against a plastic container of handbags while I pick up shoeboxes.

"Well," he says. "Most people are taking off, I mean, we're not really sure how long this whole . . . evacuation . . . thing . . . will last. Maybe you can pop in and grab the feedback on Laser Life? I dropped it by your desk yesterday, it looked like you had already left, so."

My heart starts beating quickly.

"Kenneth, I'm evacuating with my kids to Augusta today. I may be able to work on it. Want to email it to me, or send me a shared doc?"

"It's just that it's handwritten. Lots of notes."

"Oh."

"Yeah," he says. "I guess MacKenzie could scan it for you? She's not in yet because she took her rabbit to get its teeth filed. If you don't do it they grow into, like, hooks. Probably would've been easier to go over it in person but you weren't here, so."

"Yup. I can do that. I'll stop by the office."

My voice sounds clipped and sharp. I sit down in the closet. The hem of a linen bridesmaid dress from J.Crew grazes my forehead.

Right. I will stop by the office on my way to Augusta because I am committed to my company. Also, I will bring my kids inside and let them snatch up every aesthetically pleasing knickknack and reach their grubby hands into the jars of trail mix in the staff room.

Of course I'm going to get the job done and I'm going to do it well. It's this passive-aggressive nonsense and nitpicking about tiny tasks that makes me want to burn down the office. But there's no time to dwell. I need to finish packing and get the heck out of Dodge.

I pack toothbrushes for the kids, Children's Advil, Band-Aids. Seven pairs of underwear for Nanette. I'd bring more but that's all

I got. Socks. Two hoodies, just in case. Minneapolis for Nanette and Beary for Alex. Alex's Doc Hudson pillow. Nan's *Frozen* night-light. A sound machine.

My stomach growls, a deep gurgle in a low octave.

That's what I forgot to do.

Eat.

11:04 A.M.

When I think about Desmond and Sarah Ellen together, a kind of seizure, which feels like a flash, one with colors—purple, orange, red—takes over my body.

I scan my memory for incriminating information. Sarah Ellen was enrolled in the infant swim class at the Chatham County Aquatic Center with her son—a teeny guy, who was colicky if I remember—with baby Alex and me.

Alex adored that class. He took to the water, splashing and heaving his body forward like he was joining a mosh pit. Funny, considering he's more of a cautious guy now. I was squeezed into an ill-fitting one-piece from Kohl's I bought last minute because I didn't know what kind of suit was appropriate for a baby swim class or my postpartum body with boobs overzealous with milk.

The smell of chlorine was powerful. Our instructor, Miss Melissa, wore a fleece leopard print robe, which she placed over a bench before lowering herself into the pool. She encouraged our babies to grab floating yellow ducks, blow bubbles, and the scariest thing—submerge their heads underwater. I hated that part.

The babies squealed like dolphins and the sound reverberated from the lofted ceiling. Miss Melissa was a soft talker. She was giving us instructions I couldn't hear.

I asked Sarah Ellen, "What did she say? I can't hear the teacher."

Sarah Ellen's baby was clinging to her in fear, tiny fists grasping at her neck, a wail that seemed disproportionate to the size of the kid. I remember Sarah Ellen's face had the polite expression you put on when someone is making an effort to talk to you—she bent her head to listen and raised her eyebrows. Then her face fell.

"I only hear screaming," she said. "All the time. I just hear screams."

I can't believe my husband cheated on me. And yet. Once the purple-orange-red flash fades, the thought occurs to me—what if this is a gift? Suppose I recover from the immediate pain from Desmond's affair. Assume I trek through the logistics of dissolving a marriage with enough blood to survive. Could this be a path to assume control of a life where I'm not taking care of someone else all the time or resenting the partner who isn't? And really, is that so bad? Sure, it's the end of a dream. Could it also be, let's quit while we're ahead?

It's hard to think of it that way right now.

11:44 A.M.

It's almost lunchtime. By this hour on a regular Thursday I've delivered both children to school and I'm on my third cup of coffee and knee deep in shared Google Docs.

Cool, I have my shit packed in the duffel, supplies for the kids in the navy rolling suitcase, and their toys/lovies zipped up in the miniature Spider-Man carry-on. In the pool cooler I loaded snacks for the road trip and ice water in Avengers cups with lids. I charged the technology, including my laptop, double birds to Kenneth. I folded the power cords into a free mesh makeup bag from Clinique and stuffed it in the glove compartment of the Sienna on top of a stack of napkins from Chick-fil-A.

I dive into the fridge, tossing perishables in a trash bag, taking thirty seconds to mourn half a tub of pimento cheese, and throwing salvageable stuff in our Coleman cooler that looks like it's from the Reagan administration. My phone buzzes in my pocket. It's Nicole: *Are you still there? Q: What does a shepherd say to his sheep? A: Let's get the flock out of here.*

I know there's something else to do in here. I'm grinding my teeth and gnawing on my nails at the same time. If Des were here I'd make a joke about fighting tooth and nail, or maybe he would. At some point our weirdo senses of humor morphed into one shared cloud like our family data plan.

Alex races into the kitchen, sliding in green-and-white striped socks with a hole near his right pinkie toe.

"When are we leaving?" he asks me.

I'm kneeling next to the cooler with the freezer door open.

"When Mommy has us packed," I tell him.

"When is that going to be?"

"In seventeen minutes."

Satisfied, he skates off across the hardwood floor in his socks and I hear Nanette say, "Oh, you're back."

The fridge is mostly empty. I leave a box of baking soda and a bottle of Tito's in the fridge—a reward in case I make it back alive. As

I toss our suitcases and the cooler in the back of the van, I consider how disgusted Desmond would be by my anarchic loading style, which makes me smile. He packs our luggage in a perfect order like he's playing Tetris, sliding shapes side to side to make a row.

Outside it's calm, eerily so. Overcast skies stretch over the bungalows on the opposite side of our street. The air is cooler than usual but still stuffy. A hint of wind ruffles the leaves on the trees and nudges the Spanish moss. I'm distracted by the sound of a ball bouncing against plexiglass—Bailey practicing free throws in his driveway.

My phone buzzes again: Mom.

"Thanks for calling me back," I tell her.

"I had to do my Zumba video."

"Oh." I pull down the door of the van.

"You can't answer your phone during Zumba," Mom says. "That defeats the whole purpose."

"You're right. It's a meditation. Listen, we're off. What's your plan?"

"What do you mean?"

"Mom." I stop dead in my tracks on our front stoop. "You're not staying."

"All right," she says. "I'm not staying. I'm driving to Guyton with Susan in her awful Volvo to stay with her awful daughter."

My shoulders relax. "You could always stay with *your* awful daughter."

"And her two kids and husband and the gays?"

"Sure," I tell her.

Minus the husband.

"It's all right," she says. "Susan's good fun except she turns down the radio when she needs to tell me something. Why doesn't she just keep it at a low volume? Maybe I'd rather hear the radio instead of whatever she's saying."

"When are you leaving?"

"Who knows," she says. "I packed a bag, the little bumblebee one, and now I'm watching Kathie Lee and Hoda waiting for Susan to roll over here and fetch me."

"Mom, will you let me know when you're on the road?"

"Of course, I will, honey. And you let me know when you get to Gayville."

"I will," I say.

"222 Gay Road."

"That's not their address," I say.

"Sure, it isn't."

My mother cackles and takes a swig from her Parker's cup.

I guess I didn't imagine us going different ways in the hurricane. It will be fine. Susan is solid and she'll drive slower than a wounded armadillo. She'll be super cautious and Mom will probably be trapped in Guyton for a week, even if Hurricane Matthew ends up being a sprinkle. All right, I can cross that item off the list in my head of shit I need figured out.

"Okay," I say. "Love you."

"Don't get all sappy now. I'll see you next week at Fresh Market for Little Big Meals on Tuesday. And for the record, this evacuation is silly business."

"All right."

"Be safe, Ramona," Mom says.

I slide my phone into the back pocket of my jeans. Across the street our neighbor trudges down a stone path to retrieve his newspaper. When he bends over, his glasses slide down his nose, so he pushes them back up. I wave at him, and he shakes the newspaper in a reciprocal gesture. When I head back inside, I realize the front door has been wide open this whole time—there's probably a block party of mosquitoes in my house.

I scan the kitchen with my hands on my hips. What am I forgetting? From the corner of the room emerges a small grunt and crunching of cedar chips. Clarence Thomas. I can't forget the damn guinea pig.

"I believe Anita Hill," I tell him. "For your file."

12:22 P.M.

"Does anyone need to use the bathroom?"

"No!" Alex says.

"No!" Nanette echoes.

We're clustered at the side door of the kitchen. By some miracle everyone's got on both shoes and socks, at the same time, even me. Alex holds his volcano book up to his face and the plastic wrapping from the library crinkles under his grip. Nanette, clutching Minneapolis between her teeth, repeatedly knocks her head against the pantry door.

"Can you guys, just, try?" I say. "We're going to be in the car for a while."

"I don't have to go," Alex says.

"What's the worst thing that could happen if you try?"

"I could waste my time trying to pee instead of reading." Alex has gray-blue eyes like me, the pupil outlined with a fuzzy rim the color of slate. Desmond says it's freaky to see my eyes looking out from a child. It's not freaky for me because I don't have to look at my face as often.

"Will you tie your shoes, then?" I ask him.

Alex releases the sigh of all sighs, the exhale heard around the world, places his book on the floor, and kneels down to loop the laces of his orange New Balance sneakers. Another reminder of how I'm just the worst. What kind of evil troll wants to make sure her kid emptied his bladder and doesn't break his neck tripping over shoelaces?

I wipe the sweat from my brow with the sleeve of Alex's camo hoodie. Nanette informs me, "I'm hungry, Mommy," and Minneapolis falls to the floor.

"Are we going to eat lunch?" Alex says. "I'm hungry, too."

"Of course we are. Listen, munchkins. I need you to be patient with me. We're going to have to go with the flow over the next couple days. Know what I mean?"

"Roll with it," Alex says.

"Yes. Exactly. Nanette, I'm bringing your mobile potty in case you have to go right away while we're in the car."

Nanette, horrified: "Mommy, no."

"You're doing great with it, honey, it's still new, though."

"I don't use that potty," she says. On the verge of tears. "No, Mommy."

"Well, all right. It's in the car if you change your mind."

"Take it out," she says. "You should take it out!"

"Let's just—let's just go."

"Is Daddy going to meet us?" Alex asks me.

I am reminded of a deodorant commercial from the eighties that told women to never let them see you sweat. Even though I am so angry with Desmond that I can't see, the idea of separating him from our children, today or down the line, opens up a painful fissure. He might be an unfaithful douchebag but he's always been a present father. If I decide we can't work things out, am I the one who breaks up the family?

"Maybe," I tell him. "We have to stop by Mommy's office and then we're going to take an awesome road trip to Mr. Christopher's and find all the fun things to do in Augusta."

I lock the side door and double-check the dead bolt in the front. This paranoia about looters circulating on Facebook is dorky. Even if there are looters after Hurricane Matthew, what are they going to take? They can help themselves to our splashy floral prints from Bed Bath & Beyond or my HP printer from 2008 with the broken scanner.

The wind has started to pick up. I slide into the driver's seat and slam the door. We're ready.

"Goodbye, house," I call out. "Good luck in the hurricane."

"Goodbye," Nanette says.

"Take it sleazy," Alex says.

"Take it sleazy!" Nanette repeats, giggling. I back out of our driveway and turn down 53rd Street. I wave goodbye to Bailey and then pull up to the stop sign on Reynolds.

Hold up. I linger at the intersection for an extra beat. Then instead of taking a right on Reynolds I circle back to our house.

In front of Bailey's small brick bungalow I roll down the window and lean across the large gulf between my seat and the passenger's side.

"Bailey?"

"Hey, Mrs. Arnold," he calls out.

I'm gesturing for him to come closer to my car—he can't hear me over the yelps of my children. He dribbles over to us, balances the basketball between his right palm and hip.

"Are you going to evacuate?" I ask him.

"Oh, yes, ma'am."

"Where are you going?"

"They are taking people on buses. You gotta get to the Convention Center."

"Bailey, where's your mom?"

He leans down so his face is visible in the opposite window. "She's out of town."

"Your mom's not here?" My voice rises to a squawky pitch. "You're taking a bus—to where? Where do the buses go?"

Bailey shrugs, tosses the basketball from one hand to another.

"The last one leaves tomorrow at noon," he says. "I gotta get there before that."

There are so many questions. Where the hell is this child's mother on the eve of a hurricane? Or doesn't he have friends or cousins he could catch a ride with? People from Savannah seem to have an average of 16,000 cousins.

I start to nibble on my nails and then drop my hand. If Desmond were driving the car, he wouldn't have turned around. If Desmond were driving the car, he would have nodded to Bailey and said, what a nice kid. If Desmond were driving the car, I'd wonder out loud about Bailey's situation, and Desmond would say, *he's not your responsibility, Monie, we got enough on our plate.*

I shift the gear from drive to park.

"No," I say. "Bailey, you should come with us. Why don't you grab some things? Pack an overnight bag. Call your mother and tell her you're going to Augusta with your neighbor, Mrs. Arnold."

Bailey's face lights up. "Really?"

"It's not like a prize vacation. But if you can put up with this lot, you're welcome to join us."

"Okay, cool," he says.

His name tag tilts toward the buttons on his collar. "Are you . . . working today?"

Bailey looks down.

"Oh, no. I was wearing this yesterday."

He drops the basketball on the grass, where it keeps rolling until it stops at the base of a bush, and sprints into his house. I turn off the car entirely.

"Why you brake, Mommy?" Nanette says.

"We're picking up another passenger," I tell her.

"You said we don't have room for Daniel Tiger."

"I did?"

"Or my mermaid."

"We don't," I tell her. "But we have room for neighbor kids. It's like Jesus and the fish or whatever. You keep cutting the fish into smaller pieces so everyone gets some."

She fixes me with a suspicious stare and bites on Minneapolis's horn.

6

YOUR HEART WALKING AROUND

How to Lose Yourself in Eight Short Years

1. Grow a massive hemorrhoid during your first pregnancy which forces you to sit on a round pillow during work to minimize pressure on the anus. (After you give birth, this will transform into a permanent skin tag.)

2. Talk to another woman at the playground for two hours without learning her profession yet leave with an in-depth understanding of the way she transitioned her son from the family bed into a big boy one.

3. Hear yourself saying out loud, "No, thank you. We do not touch our privates during story time. On top or underneath the pants."

4. Find yourself opening clickbait on how Jessica Biel whipped her body back into shape after having a baby and theorize that Justin Timberlake needs to be the star in the relationship.

5. Scream at your husband that he's wasting liquid gold after he leaves a half-consumed bottle of pumped breast milk on a bookshelf instead of replacing it in the fridge.

6. Feel confused that My Little Pony has a new sexy image and worry about the message this is sending your daughter.

7. Forget that you worked really hard on becoming pretty good at something, like painting, because you will never have time for it again.

8. Insert KY Liquibeads up your vagina before you have sex with your husband so it's more comfortable for you and he thinks you're turned on.

9. Find yourself humming the theme of Thomas the Tank Engine when extracting rocks, wrappers, feathers, and Lego minifigures from the pockets of various articles of clothing before loading them into the washer.

10. Listen to someone on a podcast describing children as your heart walking around outside your body. Burst into tears and tell your children, it's so true, only to have them look confused and ask for (another) snack.

1:31 P.M.

It is a piece of cake to find parking downtown. Glass half full.

"This is great!" I tell my vanload of kids. For now I am a mother of three.

The doors of the Sienna slide open and I usher them out into the salty air. We hear the repeated low horn blast of a container ship on the river while we shuffle along the sidewalk toward my building at a pace too pokey for my liking.

"Come on, sweeties," I say. "This way! We're walking, we're walking."

"Nanner, keep up!" Alex urges.

Nanette waves at herself in the windows of Banana Republic. In her reflection she can't see her tongue sticking out so she turns sideways to spot it in her silhouette.

"Nanette, we're walking," I repeat. So far Bailey, now in a fresh white T-shirt celebrating Pi Day and tapered track pants, is the only one of my children who follows directions. He's head and shoulders over Alex, who ambles along with both shoelaces untied.

"This is where you work, Mrs. Arnold?" Bailey asks me.

I flash my ID card at the keypad on the ground floor.

"Yup," I say. "Glamorous, isn't it?"

Even though my children have visited my office before, when my miniature team assembles on the second floor they do find it glamorous and for a moment I'm happy to impress them. The high ceilings, exposed brick, the faux grass carpet, the Ping-Pong table, the bikes hanging on the walls.

"That bike looks like it's flying!" Alex says.

"Kind of," I tell him. "Okay, team. I need to grab something from my desk, then we're out of here. Alex, *por favor*, your shoelaces."

From the entrance I see only two people in the office. One developer doesn't look up from his headphones and the other one, I think her name is Ainsley, gives us a small nod. *Hey, what's up.* This is a relief because in my head I'd created a movie where the office is crowded with dedicated employees who wouldn't dream of letting weather interfere with their productivity.

Cool. Let's do this—in and out. I'll catch up on my emails once we get to Christopher's house.

It's not hard to find the documents on my desk because they are right in the center with a fluorescent green Post-it: "Notes for Ramona." Resentment flares up in my belly and I squash it like I'm pounding moles with a foam sledgehammer at Chuck E. Cheese. Nanette starts squeezing my stapler—*crunch, click*—and Alex squats to tie his shoe before losing his balance and rolling under my desk. Bailey hovers near the station opposite mine, examining a coworker's framed photos.

"I want to work somewhere like this," he says. "I went to my mom's office once. It didn't look anything like this. They had free mints, though."

"That's something," I tell him, stuffing the stack of papers into my purse.

"Ramona!" I spin around to see Kenneth taking large strides toward us in another set of ridiculously tight pants.

I exhale. "Hey."

"You found the notes—great," he says. "I see you brought some new interns today. Hey, gang."

Bailey nods at Kenneth. My children ignore him.

"Yes. Parenting doesn't stop for natural disasters."

"I bet," he says. "Well, I'm glad you made it in."

"Mommy," Alex says. "Can we go look at the bikes?"

"Those bikes cost more than our mortgage this month, honey," I tell him. Ainsley looks up, alarmed, either from the threat to her bike or the concept of home ownership. I point to a room near the windows with an eggplant-colored door. "Yesterday there were Skittles in there if you want to check."

"Ooooh!" Nanette says. They scuffle down the corridor past clusters of desks, Bailey leading and my kids trailing him like Pigpen's dust cloud in *Peanuts*.

"It would be great if you could have those back to me by tomorrow. We're way behind on the launch and the client is antsy."

I repeat, "Antsy?"

In my head I say, *tomorrow?*

"That's sort of," he says, "putting it mildly."

"Kenneth. Tomorrow there's a Cat 4 hurricane touching ground in our fair city."

"Right. But the client is in Columbus." I stare at him. He stares back at me. If only this contest were about blinking instead of a bizarre power standoff. "Columbus, Ohio."

No, you didn't, Kenneth. Did he just pull some Big City patronizing shit on me? Like, since I live in Savannah, I would instinctively assume he's talking about Columbus, Georgia?

"I'll see what I can do, Kenneth."

"Great, Ramona," he says. "You're the best."

"I know I am."

"And you always crack me up."

"I crack myself up, too," I say. Hyena shrieks emerge from the break room. "I need to grab them, Kenneth. Be safe, okay?"

"You, too, Ramona." He spins and I watch his twiggy figure take long strides down the path between the desks.

Columbus, Ohio. If Kenneth would just get out of my way. If he allowed me the space to blossom into the project management badass that's lurking below the surface, I could devote my energy to maintaining strong relationships with clients instead of fantasizing about microwaving his Apple Watch.

In the break room, Nanette spoons someone's almond butter into her mouth with a plastic fork. It's a sample from our client but there's a name written in Sharpie on the label: Kenneth.

"Nanette!" I scold.

Alex and Bailey are giggling.

"We told her it was poop butter," Alex says.

"She still tried it," Bailey says.

"Well," I hiss, in a low voice. "It's not *my* poop butter! We gotta put it back!"

I yank the jar from Nanette, who cries out like a wounded animal, replace it—a little bit stickier—in the fridge, and then I drag her to the sink, where I wipe down her hands and face with eco paper towels. I rub too hard, and she whines, but it's really on there. It's drying on her skin like papier mâché around a balloon.

The corners of Nanette's mouth droop down. My body tenses in anticipation of her tantrum. No, no, not now. I wish for anything to stop her unfurling—distract from it, even—but she starts to cry, big droplets rolling down pink cheeks changing to fuchsia. Next a wail which reverberates through the break room.

Bailey's eyes grow bigger. Alex makes a smiley face with thumbtacks on a cork board next to the fridge.

I reach for her: "Honey."

"No!" She swats my arm away.

The wail escalates into a scream. It alternates between two octaves like the siren of an ambulance. My teeth clench. Blood rushes to my head, and my instinct is to squeeze her pipe cleaner arms and shake her and scream at her to stop. I can't do that. Parents can't do that or discuss the sensation of wanting to do that.

Nanette's eyes are desperate. I step closer again, trying to make physical contact. This time she allows me to take her hands.

"Nanner, I know you are upset but that wasn't our snack, see, and there's people here trying to work and it's time for us to get moving."

My daughter looks at me as if I've said something cruel. Her mouth shifts from the shape of an O to a squiggly line. When I pull her body into mine, her heart beats double time, hiccups rock her frame, and she deposits a layer of snot on my shoulder.

"You hurt my face with that napkin."

"I'm sorry, love. I didn't mean to." At the same time I'm trying to recover from my tantrum, the one nobody sees. "Anyone need to go to the bathroom?"

"No," Alex says, still giggling.

"Poop butter," Nanette says, having rebounded from the injustice of the face scrubbing and everything that followed. I calculate how much time has passed since she achieved number one or number two, either in the toilet or in her underpants.

"Nanette, want to try potty here? Otherwise you have to hold it or use the one in the car."

"I'm *not* using the potty in the car."

I shift the strap of my purse over my shoulder and start herding my party toward the exit. Kenneth has disappeared and the programmers stare into their monitors. Bailey reaches a long thin arm up to tap the petal of a shamrock decoration nobody bothered to take down clinging to the doorframe next to the elevator.

Nanette presses the button for the main floor and we descend together in silence.

2015

On the elevator ride to my office floor, I realized I was wearing my boatneck shirt backward. So when the man delivering Jimmy Johns got off on the second floor, I dropped my laptop, rapid-fire suctioned my arms inside my top, spun it around, and then pushed my arms back through the sleeves. When the door opened, I was face-to-face with the account team from PicnicATL.

The trio consisted of a jowly white guy, an Indian man in a purple bow tie, and a bobbed blond woman towering over them. I knew them by their email addresses. They were leaving the meeting I just missed with folders I'd stickered tucked under their arms.

Hi, I said, straightening up.

I considered introducing myself as the person who set up the meeting and created that resplendent PowerPoint but that seemed silly now. They were probably spitballing on where to grab dinner, so I muttered, excuse me, and pushed open the doors to reception.

Everyone was looking at me as I speed-walked to my desk. Xavier lifted his eyes from his monitor to me and then dropped them. Cailyn, clasping a box of printer toner, froze when she saw me and then issued a sympathetic smile. Through the windows of the conference room Kenneth beckoned to me.

How'd it go, I asked him.

My heart was thumping hard. Kenneth was wearing a shiny gray tie tucked into a cotton candy–pink V-neck sweater. For a weaselly guy he radiates a commanding presence.

It went fine, he said. Except for a couple technical difficulties.

With the PowerPoint?

That and other things.

I put it on a flash drive for Xavier, I said. Everything was set up.

Well, the battery in the remote was dead, Kenneth said. So then Xavier and MacKenzie spent five minutes looking for a replacement while I tried to kill time making conversation, and then MacKenzie ran downstairs to Walgreens to buy new batteries.

I frowned. But you could have just manually forwarded the slides using the laptop.

I could have, Kenneth said. And that's what we ended up doing. But not before Xavier hit the wrong button while MacKenzie was gone and launched an update that took ten more minutes.

Then what happened?

I carried the laptop over to the table and showed them the presentation on that.

Okay, then, I said.

Not okay, Ramona, Kenneth said, shaking his head. Not okay. We looked like wankers. We probably won't get the account.

You don't know that.

I have a pretty strong hunch.

That sucks.

You should've been here.

Kenneth, I'm sorry. Something came up.

You should have been here. You should consider every worst possible scenario and prepare accordingly.

I'm sorry, Kenneth. I made the PowerPoint. I set up the projector. I ran the flash drive to Xavier. Everything was ready.

Where were you?

My son, Alex, collapsed and the school nurse called and I had to race to the ER.

I said, my son. He wasn't feeling great. I had to step out.

I consider telling Kenneth the whole story. That the school nurse called me at 10:47 and said my son, Alex, passed out on the playground. The nurse called an ambulance and the kindergarten teacher rode in the back with him. I sped over to Memorial Hospital absolutely sure that my son had some obscure and deadly virus and I was so nervous I ran a red light on Abercorn. I couldn't get in the entrance at first because someone's shiny pink new baby balloon was stuck in the revolving door and people were trying to get it out. Alex had wood chips from the playground lodged in his curls. It turned out he didn't have a stroke. He was dehydrated because he didn't want to drink from his water bottle that week because a girl named Hazel had the same one and accidentally sipped from his. Alex didn't want to catch lactose intolerance from Hazel.

Ramona, Kenneth said.

Yes.

He drummed his fingers on the conference table. He said, you need to really think about whether or not you can balance your family commitments and excel at this position.

I can!

I could try to explain to Kenneth. I could describe how, for a window of forty-five minutes I couldn't breathe. Every muscle in my body tensed and my head was spiraling up into the sky in a swirl of absolute panic. That once I saw Alex's goofy smile with his front right tooth at an angle because it was loose but he was afraid to wiggle it free I could breathe again. Once I knew he was okay and home sipping Gatorade with Desmond on our sofa I felt euphoric. I actually considered myself a hero for coming back to work to see how the pitch meeting went.

I cannot lose another account because I can't trust you, Ramona, Kenneth said.

Noted. I tried to make my voice sound normal: all right.

I should have told him. I didn't because I've been conditioned to pretend that I can slide my children into file folders with different colored tabs in order to be taken seriously as a professional woman. Instead I stared at the tiny bald patch in his beard. When his Apple Watch buzzed, Kenneth spun his wrist inward to read the message.

Fuck me. I'm going to follow up with them and see if I can save it.

Dismissed, I skulked back to my desk. I was being reprimanded for a triple A battery? A dead battery and a subpar clicking experience. Ridiculous. If I had a baseball bat, I would swing it at each monitor on each desk. I would shatter the glass window separating the open concept office from the conference room. Did anyone have a Louisville Slugger handy? Or a crowbar—maybe even one of those long umbrellas.

The sucky thing was that I cared. I worked really hard on the PowerPoint and I think we could brand PicnicATL in a unique way. Even if they only jumped on one of our ideas for the YouTube channel, it would drive major traffic to their website.

I sat down at my desk and tried to steady my breath. I pressed a letter on my keyboard and my screen sprung to life, the wallpaper a photo of Desmond in the parking lot of Huc-A-Poo's with Alex and Nanette thrown over each shoulder in a fireman's carry. In the picture their faces look more babyish than they are now, Nanette wearing the rainbow leggings she refused to take off for a solid two months so that finally the fabric was as thin as a dryer sheet.

2:03 P.M.

Evacuation Take Two.

"Okay, guys. Now we're really ready to blast off!" We find our assigned seats again in the minivan. Seat belts, tablets, neighbor kid, check. A half a tank of gas, good enough. Laser Life notes now tucked into the side shelf on the passenger door, thanks for being you, Kenneth. Guinea pig, grunting in the way-back.

I take a left on Broughton and take MLK to Oglethorpe. Downtown is quiet—there's a few SCAD students walking around with large portfolios tucked under their arms like nothing unusual is going on. At a stoplight I tap Christopher's address into Google Maps. On my right a man with a tobacco-stained Santa Claus beard holds up a sign: *This is not the path I chose.*

"Mommy. You're not supposed to text and drive," Alex says.

"Correct," I tell him. "I am just typing Christopher's address into the map thingy so I don't drive us to Milwaukee by mistake."

I *did* remember to text my friend last night that we're coming and I feel proud of that. His response was: "Party! FYI we're doing Whole 30, so we don't have kid food." I vaguely remember the rules of Whole 30 based on the incessant Facebook posting of a mother from Alex's school who did it. Wait, is the Whole 30 the one where you can't have alcohol?

I did not mention to Christopher the guinea pig or the extra kid. That was on purpose—begging forgiveness versus permission. I feel warmth at the idea I will soon be in the scrawny embrace of my oldest friend from college. Christopher would never tell me there's not enough room in the inn.

The thoughtful voice on Google Maps informs me a trip from Savannah to Augusta in current traffic takes two and a half hours. That's not bad. The hard part—packing, cramming my children plus an extra in the car, and collecting notes at the office without muttering anything snarky—is behind me. Less stressful now that everybody is in one place moving a direction we want to go.

I should take 17-N to 321-N, then two more roads I won't remember until the Google lady reminds me. When I launch the minivan onto 17-N, it groans as I accelerate and on comes the check engine light, which I ignore. The Toyota Sienna is a faithful ally who would never let me down, unlike a certain person I know whose name starts and ends with a *d*.

We're moving along on roads hosting regular Thursday afternoon traffic. The way Nicole described it, I thought everybody had already left Savannah. I imagined empty roads stretching out in front of us, flat asphalt and flies buzzing around roadkill, like a scene from an apocalyptic movie where there's only four humans left alive. Is Savannah full of diehards, like Kenneth and my mother, who roll eyes at the evacuation order? Or maybe I'm not as behind at getting out as I thought.

My kids bow over their tablets with Stormtrooper headphones covering their ears, their fingers guiding the Subway Surfer or Minecraft Blocks or Monkey to his Lunchbox. The headphones squash some of Nanette's red curls and send the other ones every direction. Periodically she chuckles, a throaty thing gurgling up from her belly.

We rumble over the Savannah River. We pass Hutchinson Island into South Carolina. Bailey looks out the window, his long fingers fiddling with a patch of torn upholstery.

I'm surprised Alex has not attached himself to Bailey since

it's an established fact Big Kids Are The Coolest. Then again, Big Kids can't compete with technology. Bailey glances at a Galaxy phone and now he watches the scenery slide by the window.

"Bailey?" I call out.

"Uh-huh?"

"I'm not used to talking to someone in the back-back," I explain. "It feels like I need to yell. Did you tell your mom you're headed out of town with us?"

"Not yet, Mrs. Arnold."

"Better do that. Want to give her my number?"

"I can do that later," Bailey says. "For now I'll just say I'm going to Augusta."

"That sounds kinda," I tell him, "like you're making it up."

"What?"

"*For now, I'll just say I'm going to Augusta.* It sounds fake."

He frowns. "But we are, aren't we? Going to Augusta."

"We are. We should definitely call her later. If I were out of town with my kids in a separate place I'd be freaking out."

"Yeah," Bailey says.

He pushes his hair back. I study his face in the rearview mirror, unkempt eyebrows arching over deep-set eyes, sharp cheekbones, a chin he hasn't grown into. Scruffy hair that looks a little longer on one side, maybe that's how kids are wearing their hair these days. Giant headphones resting against his collarbones. He'll call her. Right? He doesn't seem like the kind of kid who goes out of his way to be a jerk to his mom.

In the small window of silence, I'm ambushed by the memory

of the moment when Nanette and I walked in on them. Desmond's face, his T-shirt, boxers. I push the preset buttons on the car stereo to find a song I like.

"I'm hungry, Mommy," says Alex. We've driven six miles.

"Here's a snack," I tell him, fumbling in the cooler with my free hand for an apple cinnamon fruit and grain bar. "And we'll stop in a bit."

"But we never had lunch," he points out.

"We didn't?" He's right. We didn't. "Well, chow down on that and we'll have a late one or an early dinner. We'll stop somewhere."

"Then we'll still have regular dinner?"

My firstborn. This child needs order and routine or he feels like the carpet's been pulled out from under him.

"Yes," I tell him. "I'll figure it out, honey. You won't starve. Trust."

I listen to him fiddling with the wrapper. Alex has never knocked it out of the park with the fine motor skills and I hear him grunting with exasperation. Nanette, who missed the exchange thanks to her headphones, now notices Alex's snack and wants one, too.

She hurls, "*Mommy*" at me like I left her out of the will. Bailey doesn't request a fruit bar but I can't leave him out. I'm peeling the wrappers off fruit bars while holding the wheel and tossing them behind me like a trainer throwing fish to dolphins at SeaWorld.

"*You* get a fruit bar!" I tell them. "*You* get a fruit bar!"

My Oprah joke falls flat and for some reason I'm deflated. It's not Des's laugh I'm missing—it's my dad's, who went through an intense Oprah phase in the last year of his life. He would have laughed.

The kids make smacking noises. In my head I imagine the journey of the crumbs. They start at my children's laps and then burrow down to cracks in their car seats and eventually are devoured by microscopic life-forms with fangs and antlers who make my minivan their home.

I can't worry about that now.

2007

The salesman in the home department of Belk had hooded eyes and wore a shiny lavender button-down with a white collar and cuffs. Most of the time, he explained, he worked in men's shoes. They were short on staff over Memorial Day weekend.

Just in time for the sale.

After three failed login attempts on a Dell computer the salesman pulled up our registry: Desmond Arnold and Ramona Burkhalter. He presented a light gray scanner with a yellow button, first to Desmond, and then me, trying to determine who would get to hold the scanner.

Which was fair, I thought. This guy shouldn't have to guess who makes decisions in the relationship.

This isn't even his department.

Desmond reached for it.

Ooooh, he said, tilting the scanner sideways. He pressed a button and it beeped.

Let me try, I said.

I pointed the scanner at a crystal wineglass and pulled the trigger. It produced a satisfying tone.

I like that, I said.

That's not the sound you want, the man said.

Oh, it's not?

He spun the goblet. Tiny diamond shapes of glass caught the light.

You gotta aim it at the bar code, he said. The sticker, I mean.

I did as I was told. The beep changed. This tone was higher, almost a chime. Maybe it was supposed to make engaged couples think of wedding bells.

The registry department was aggressively air-conditioned. I had goosebumps on my arm, linked with Desmond's, who smelled like sweat and sausage biscuits from breakfast. Me, I smelled like seven different scents I had sprayed on myself in the cosmetics department on the way to the home section.

The salesman seemed content we were on our way. Now he could ignore us. He flipped his tie over his shoulder and stuck out his bottom lip at the computer.

Desmond asked, can I have it back?

Yes, I said, pulling out folded papers from my frayed canvas messenger bag. I had a checklist of wedding registry essentials from the Knot and a burgundy fine tip gel pen. We gotta start with every day, I told Desmond.

Every day what?

Plates we use every day, I think. And like, forks.

Oh, okay.

It was fun at first. We picked out a stoneware set in creamsicle, mostly because we thought the bowls looked like they wanted chili and Honey Nut Cheerios. There were more decisions. The two of us shuffled around displays of floral platters and All-Clad pots, pointing the registry gun at dishes anticipating a life we couldn't imagine yet. Future meals. Brunches. Dinner parties. Thanksgiving feasts. Christmas Eve. Vessels for things we'd know how to make when we were married grown-ups.

I don't know how to make a meat besides chicken, I said.

Like, meat from scratch?

Meat from raw.

I can grill a burger, Desmond said. I can scale a speckled trout but then I don't know what to do with it after that.

I consulted my list: Okay, we need a gravy boat.

And tiny life jackets for the passengers?

Ha. Sure. There's one.

I pointed to an ivory ceramic pitcher with a spout and a bronze stripe around the rim. The stack of silver bangles around my wrist slid down to my elbow. I wondered if it had to coordinate with the other china. Matching freaked me out.

Should I beep it, Desmond asked me.

Well, I said, shrugging. Do you like it?

Do I like this gravy boat?

Yeah, I said.

Can you put other stuff in it?

Like, what?

Barbecue sauce? Salsa?

I don't see why not.

Who, Desmond wondered, is going to arrest us for not using the gravy boat correctly?

Your mom.

That's right.

She doesn't have to know if we put barbecue sauce in there, I said.

She doesn't. We can do whatever we want.

We don't have to be grown-ups.

My fiancé pointed the registry scanner at my chest.

I just want you, he said.

He pressed the button and it made the alternate beep.

The man at the desk in the wedding registry was exasperated on the store phone. He informed whoever was on the other line that he didn't know when Chantelle was coming back from her break—he's supposed to be in shoes right now. When we looked over, he rolled his eyes and pointed at the receiver like, are you kidding me with this.

Desmond had longer hair then, burnt red waves that twisted in different directions around his ears and chin. He was chewing gum, Hubba Bubba Max Strawberry. He'd gotten slightly addicted to gum after he quit smoking. I used to smoke, too, but I never had a habit, I was a social smoker.

Just me?

Well, Desmond said. He busted out his wicked smile. And our three kids.

Three?

Samoa, Tagalong, and Trefoil.

THOR

KRI

xxxxxx2422

Exp: 1/3/2023

Item: 0010091563410
YA FOREST

Again, not naming kids after Girl Scout cookies. Two, maybe. Depending on what kind of breeder I turn out to be.

I don't care how many, Desmond said.

I love you.

I love you, too. I don't care about gravy boats.

Me, neither.

I kinda, he said, just want to be married to you.

We leaned into each other. My forehead came up to his chin. I wrapped my arms around his waist, which was squishy, and the back of his T-shirt was damp with sweat. My right hand still holding the registry list, which I printed out on the computer at work because I was too lazy to buy new ink for mine at home.

Someone bought us the gravy boat and I can't remember if we ever used it. Now I know how to make a few dishes. Another thing you can put in a gravy boat is gazpacho. I make a peach one with cucumbers.

7

VIVACIOUS SEX CHEETAH

3:13 P.M.

We see a sign for Subway so I steer the minivan toward the exit. I do not put the choice of restaurant to a vote because in my experience that does not end well. *Subway, eat fresh!* Down the street is a miniature golf course—peculiar because a) we're in the middle of nowhere, Georgia, and b) I didn't know Putt-Putt was still around. Of course the kids notice.

"Can we go golfing after lunch?" Alex asks me. "Or dinner? Whatever this is."

"Yeah!" Nanette says.

"Really?" I say. "You want to go? Bailey, do you golf?" At the mention of his name Bailey jumps to attention, and shrugs.

Well. Christopher mentioned that he might not be home from work until six. The desolate golf course might be open. No golfers, but there's a red truck in front of the entrance and a sign with marquee letters encouraging customers to "Putt your Butt off this October with 2 for 1 Tuesdays."

Regular Ramona would have nixed this idea, saying, there's a hurricane chasing us, so we should head to Christopher's house pronto. I wouldn't want to deal with supervising a kid's activity. The truth is, we've got nothing but time. And I'm not myself today.

"Maybe," I tell them. "If you goobers do a good job on your sandwiches. I'm not buying everyone Subway so you can pick at it and be hungry ten minutes later."

My children erupt in joy. You would've thought we just discovered a pirate's treasure chest in the Subway parking lot, with sparkling diamonds and rubies. And puppies and kittens and strawberry Starbursts.

I check on Clarence Thomas. He has kicked a few wood chips outside his cage. I open the door and reach forward to pet him but he scuttles over to the opposite side of the habitat uttering what sounds like panicked pigeon coos so I yank my hand back and pull the clasp shut.

"Clarence Thomas, be cool, okay? We'll be right back."

Inside Subway, Bailey insists *he's fine, he's not hungry, Mrs. Arnold.* When I ask if he has any cash, he doesn't appear to or maybe he's saving it for something more delicious than Subway. I propose he splits a footlong with me because turkey is the Sub of the Day but I can't eat a footlong—it's too much sandwich for me. This is a lie. He goes along with it. You really do get more bang for your buck with the footlongs.

In the booth, Nanette announces, "I wanted Doritos."

"I got you Doritos," I tell her.

Her eyes scan the tray. "You got them for Alex."

"I got one bag of BBQ chips and one bag of Doritos, so we can split them in half and you both get two kinds of chips."

"Oh, okay," says Nanette, now delighted.

"Parented," I say, smugly, to Bailey, which I realize is creepy of me. But he's the closest thing to an adult here, and while ordinarily Desmond and I congratulate each other on avoiding drama with the kids, he's not here, so I substitute Bailey. He offers a polite smile—I'll take it.

Nanette loses interest in lunch before everyone else and she's wiggly so I whip out a green gel pen and start drawing on a napkin. Art project! I start to sketch Hurricane Matthew, or my interpretation of him, which is a cloud with a face, one eyebrow lifted mischievously, the rest of him clad in an Adidas track suit. He's wearing activewear so he can be comfortable as he wreaks havoc on the Southeast. I push the napkin toward Nanner.

"You color him in."

She accepts the challenge. "He needs polka dots."

I have a question for the table: "What is a cloud's favorite kind of shorts?"

"Thunderwear!" Alex says. He has taken too big a bite and I watch the remnants of his sandwich slosh around in his half-open mouth.

"Mrs. Arnold," Bailey says. "That's really good."

"Mommy's good at art," Alex says. He's bragging on me and I'm moved for a moment. "When we get back you should see the painting in Nanner's room."

"It's got a sloth in it," Nannette explains. "In a tutu."

"Can you paint Allen Iverson dunking on the side of a van?" Bailey asks me.

"Probably. Do you have a van?"

"No," he says.

4:07 P.M.

We were starving and the sandwiches are good. I notice that Bailey ate his whole sub and wonder if that was enough for him. Word out on the street is that teenage boys eat half their weight in food every day and I can't imagine what my Kroger bill will be once my son's balls drop. We replenish our cups with Dr Pepper for me and watered down Hi-C fruit punch for the kids. At a desolate BP I top off the tank and then steer us to the parking lot at Putt-N-Stuff.

"You sure it's open?" Bailey asks.

"This is a good question," I say.

"It's gotta be," Alex says.

"I don't see anyone golfing, guys," I tell them. "Then again, I've got a hunch this isn't their rush hour."

We push open the front door, which jingles. Putt-N-Stuff, as it turns out, is open. A peach-fuzzed boy in an Atlanta Falcons jersey grunts at us when we walk in before returning his attention to his phone. Inside the entrance is an arcade, or small conglomeration of ancient video games as well as a sugar candy column and an air hockey table. All of this is thrilling to my kids, who start running around the small room pushing buttons on the games.

"Hey," I say to Peachfuzz. "Is the golf course open?"

"Yes, ma'am. Prices up there," he says, pointing to a sign above his head. "How old is she?" He gestures to Nanette, who's clasping an orange rifle at Big Buck HD, *Pew! Pew!*

"The sniper? She's three."

"Three and under is free."

"Sweet. For once, something's going my way today."

Peachfuzz snorts. I buy tickets for the kids, which may have been unnecessary, since they seem content to watch 1990s graphics on the screen and spaz out. After a gentle reminder—*you said you wanted to golf!*—they remember the course and spend ten minutes deciding which clubs to use before teeing up their balls on the first hole.

I have onion breath from my Subway sandwich. After following the kids outside, I take a seat on a wooden picnic bench under an army green canopy. The wind is starting to pick up. The sky is covered with clouds bearing shades of deep charcoal. The course doesn't appear to have a unified theme—just large, plaster animals and structures. A looming T-Rex. A flock of pink flamingos. A lavender hippo spending time with a UGA bulldog in a sweater that was probably red once but now it's pink. A rainbow striped hot air balloon and a coiled snake.

The kind of place Desmond would love.

I have to know. I fumble in my purse for my phone.

"Ramona?"

"Hey," I say, purposefully monotone. I like to think the effect is not unlike when they change people's voices to protect their identities on *Dateline*.

"I'm so glad you called," Desmond gushes.

"I didn't plan on it," I tell him.

"Where are you?"

Seriously, he's gushing. The overflow of affection in his voice throws me off my game for a minute.

"Halfway to Augusta. We're at a random mini-golf in the middle of nowhere."

"Okay, cool," he says.

"I need to know how long you were with her."

He takes a deep breath. "Not that long."

"How long?"

"A couple months," he says. "It started in the summer."

"Beginning of the summer or end?"

"Beginning," he says.

"Have you been with other women?"

"No! Ramona, no. It was just that. Just the one."

My finger traces a swirled gnarl on the picnic table. "Just one woman, huh."

"It was dumb. Meant nothing."

"Less than five times?"

"Uh," he says. "More than five."

"That's officially more than a couple times. Less than ten?"

He hesitates. "Yes. Less than ten. It didn't mean anything. I swear."

I feel my anger, a slime covered alien of rage, claw its way out of my chest.

"Stop saying that!" I yell and slap the table. "It doesn't make sense!"

"What?"

"If it didn't mean anything," I say, "then why did you do it?"

"I don't—"

"If it was such a non-thing, you could've decided against it. You could have resisted temptation. That thing that didn't mean anything to you? It means everything to me. It feels worse when you say it didn't mean anything. You threw a grenade in our marriage—this special thing I considered beautiful and sacred— for something that didn't mean anything?"

My voice is growing louder. Alex hears me shouting and turns around. I offer the thumbs-up—nothing to see here—and my son, placated, returns to his golf game.

"You're right," he says. "I shouldn't have said that."

"Why didn't you tell me you were unhappy?"

"What?"

"Happy people don't cheat. Why didn't you tell me you were miserable?"

"Well, I wasn't," Desmond says. "Not necessarily. I wasn't un-happy but I wasn't happy. See, I love you. I love everything about our life. Even though it's stressful with little kids. Even though you and me aren't necessarily close right now. But I also love sex. And we didn't have it anymore."

I watch a white-haired woman toss a cigarette out of the win-dow of a burgundy sedan before launching it onto the entrance of US 25 North.

"Fuck you. Just sayin'."

I press end on the call.

Right. It's all my fault. It's on me I wasn't in the mood to give my husband a blowie after dressing and feeding both kids in the morning, driving them to separate schools, shifting content into spreadsheets for Kenneth, picking up the kids, making dinner, cleaning the kitchen, and putting the kids to bed. Listen. All I want to do at eight thirty is pull on jammies, glaze over during an hour of crappy reality TV, and go to sleep. If I'm lucky, nobody will wake up in the middle of the night needing something, so I might—just maybe—catch five and a half hours of shut-eye before I start it all over again the next day.

"Bailey got a hole in one, Mommy!" Alex exclaims over the back of the hippo. Nanette leaps up and down with her blue golf club in the air. It's way too big for her but she dismissed the idea of using the little kid size. Bailey peeks into the ear canal of the hippo before he realizes he's being praised, and he looks up, a big smile spreading across his face.

I call out, "Awesome! You can join the pro tour in no time."

I have to use the bathroom, I shouldn't have gotten that refill, I don't want to go back inside with Peachfuzz and use the tiny powder room where he can probably hear me pee. So I sit there with my bladder bursting and watch the kids navigate their way around eighteen holes. They hop up and down, argue, celebrate, sulk. Nanette rests her hands on her hips as if she's giving the T-Rex a talking to.

Fuck Desmond.

I am drowning in expectations I find impossible to meet. Patient mother. Supportive spouse. Diligent employee. Master chef. Thoughtful daughter. Punctual chauffeur. Scrupulous cleaning lady. Enthusiastic classroom volunteer. Not to leave out the most important job, according to Desmond, vivacious sex cheetah.

2014

When we heard the squeak, we were naked from the waist down. We both paused like we were playing freeze tag. It was the doorknob twisting across the hall from the master bedroom. I was propped up on my left elbow, my tongue was in Desmond's mouth and his hand was between my legs.

Did you lock ours, I whispered.

I think so, Desmond said. His hand kept going.

I giggled: You think or you know?

C'mere.

Okay.

We didn't hear anything else so we kept doing what we were doing. Maybe that sound came from another section of our rickety house. The thing was built in 1934. Just in case I pulled up the sheet so it covered our legs. Then our door burst open, light from the hall flooded the bedroom, and Desmond shot up to a seated position like a player flipped up on a foosball table. Four-year-old Alex hovered in the threshold, his hand still on the knob.

Hey, buddy, Desmond said.

Hi, Daddy.

I rolled over to my side. I said, Alex, honey, you okay?

You both in there?

Uh-huh, I said.

What you doing? Alex asked us.

We're going to sleep, Desmond said. We're really tired.

Yeah, I said. Super-duper tired. Long day.

Aren't you sleepy, buddy, Desmond asked Alex.

No, Alex said. I wanted some water and I couldn't find you guys.

Okay, I said, Daddy will get you some water. Desmond pinched my upper arm—with feeling—and I realized it would be inappropriate for him to get Alex some water because he had an erection. But hello, I didn't have any underwear on.

I will get your sippy cup, Alex, I said. How about I meet you in the kitchen?

Where is Daddy's shirt?

Sometimes he sleeps without a shirt. Daddies do that. It's like daddies and bathing suits.

I have a swim shirt, Alex said. With sharks on it.

My son turned around and trudged to the kitchen. Next to me Desmond threw back his head laughing and bonked it on the headboard. I was giggling, too, and couldn't find my underwear. I patted the fitted sheet in a circle trying to find them with no luck so I rose from the bed, pulled up some new ones, and tiptoed to the kitchen to find Alex cross-legged on the floor in front of the fridge.

Where are your jammie bottoms?

I was hot. It was hot in Mommy and Daddy's room so I took them off. It's okay just to sleep in your unders if you want.

It took Alex what seemed like four hours to gulp down two

sips of water. I walked him back to his room, arranged his stuffed animals around him, pulled his quilt up to his chin, and kissed his head.

Okay, sweetie petie. Let's get some rest now.

Back in our room, on our bed, door closed, door locked.

That was close, Desmond said. It was still humid under the sheet and this time I straddled him and I had forgotten about my fresh underwear so I planted my hands on the pillow on either side of his head like a down-dog and lifted my hips up and he started to pull my panties down. I was still in down-dog when we heard the doorknob move again. I hit the deck and landed on Desmond with a slapping sound.

Did you lock it, he asked me.

I did, babe! I totally locked it.

Again we listened to the squeak of the doorknob.

Maybe he'll give up and go away, Desmond said, both his hands on my butt. At this I pinched him hard, now I'm the crab, and he was the giggling one.

The sound stopped. We listened for Alex's steps down the hall. Instead we heard him knock.

Mommy?

Desmond and I looked at each other. This time my underwear was still wrapped around my left ankle so that was easier. I swung my legs off the bed and opened the door.

Hey, sweetie.

Are you guys still in here?

Yup.

Why is Daddy under the pillow?

131

I could see Desmond hiding his face under the pillow, which was shaking as he laughed. Then one arm emerged to wave at our son.

It's bright when the door is open, Desmond said, his voice muffled.

We're really tired, Alex. It's time for everyone to go to bed now, I said.

Yeah, Alex said.

Yup, Desmond said.

Alex hesitated at the door. But the sweet sweeper came by my room.

The sweet sweeper, Desmond repeated.

Of course. The goddamn street sweeper. That very helpful vehicle which cleans up the shelf of decaying leaves on the side of the road but also has an unpredictable evening schedule and makes a rumbling shushing sound, indicating the End of Days for my anxious preschooler.

Can I come in here with you guys, Alex asked us.

Wait, Desmond said, tucking blankets around him.

What are you doing, I whispered.

I didn't want him to, like, I didn't want him to see. Okay, now it's cool.

Relieved, Alex mounted the bench at the foot of our bed, crawled up between us, and settled down on his back, his small feet flopping away from each other.

Scratch my back?

So Alex turned his body toward Desmond, resting his head on his father's chest, and I twisted to become the big spoon, made my hand into the shape of a claw and started to draw circles on my son's back like my fingernails were an ice dancing couple practicing figure eights. Then Desmond reached across Alex's tiny body and rested his palm on my thigh.

I love you, he said.

I love you, too.

Maybe tomorrow night.

The moment was over. That was okay. I scratched Alex's back until I heard his toddler snores. I burrowed my face into his sticky hair, inhaled the detergent smell of his pajamas, and allowed my body to get heavy.

It was only 9:15. It wasn't hard for me to fall asleep. It may have been tougher for Des. Because his penis was hard. I'm not sure about these things.

5:22 P.M.

I push the scan button on the car stereo to find a song. On 98.7 the River they are playing "When Doves Cry" so I turn it up.

"Yes!"

"Huh?" says Bailey from the back-back.

I lower the volume, just a little. "You like Prince?"

"The old show with Will Smith?"

"No, no, no. That's the Fresh Prince. I'm talking about Prince the musician. Tiny guy? Tight pants. Wore a lot of purple? Recently died."

"Oh, *that* Prince. I don't know many of their songs."

I almost slam on the brake: *"What?"*

"Maybe I do. My teacher is a big fan. Maybe I'd recognize it if I heard it."

"Bailey."

"Sorry. My mom likes country."

"Ew."

"Yeah," he says. "She had a Shania Twain phase that went on way too long."

"This song is almost over but I want you to listen."

"'Kay." Bailey pulls his headphones down.

"This was one of Prince's big hits off his *Purple Rain* record. The video starts with a close-up of him getting out of a bathtub. As a kid I found that really weird."

"How much did they show?"

"Like, mostly his shoulders and chest. And then he reaches out to the camera like, come on in."

"To the bathtub?"

"More like, come into my world and listen to my story."

"Oh, okay."

"Then he starts crawling across the floor in his bathroom, which is purple, with stained glass windows, and there's all these flowers on the ground. Doves flying all around. You're looking for his towel but I really don't think he was wearing one. I think he was just crawling around his bathroom naked."

"Why wouldn't you," Bailey says.

"Anyway, it's a classic Prince song about being in a relationship that's not working and fighting a lot and there was love at one point and good memories but maybe it just wasn't meant to be."

We listen for a second.

"Mrs. Arnold," Bailey says. "It sounds like animals dying, sort of."

"Sure. Part of that is him making his guitar sound like doves. I guess his voice, too."

"I'm still hungry, Mommy," says Alex.

6:04 P.M.

Christopher's boyfriend Frankie is tall and has a drop of ketchup next to one of the buttons on his lavender shirt and for this I like him immediately. Also endearing to me is the way everything about him seems to be spilling over: his belly over his belt, his chest hair from his undershirt, his cuffs over his ankles.

"I quit the Whole 30," he confesses.

I suck down a Diet Coke on a metal barstool in the shiny kitchen of the town house Christopher and Frankie share. Christopher is not home from work yet. This doesn't bother Frankie, who rummages through cabinets on a mission to find something to feed my kids, currently sprinting in circles outside in a courtyard at the complex.

"I tried one week," he continues. "I was shaking from sugar withdrawal and I ate too many nuts, which made me a gassy mess. Also they have delicious food trucks that park outside my work. My favorite has one with fancy grilled cheeses."

"I don't blame you," I tell him.

"Like habanero jack with pears and prosciutto. I'll take you this weekend. We can look on their Facebook page and find them. Where they're going to park or whatever. Anyway, I was like, enough with the Whole 30. The entire day you have to think about what you're going to eat next because you're hungry the whole freaking entire day."

"That sounds exhausting."

As I sip my Diet Coke I learn more about Frankie. He grew up in El Paso. Here in Augusta he's a clerk for a judge, who most people consider a crusty conservative white guy but Frankie has tremendous respect for his boss's steel trap brain and ability to pull cases from his memory. Like keys from his pocket. He's been such a mentor.

Also Frankie can't believe we haven't met before. My painting is the only thing Christopher owns that he doesn't want to take to the dumpster. He's never been to Savannah. A woman from his office went on a trip and had the best time on one of those ten person bicycles where people get drunk. Have I seen those around?

I have.

"My nieces and nephews eat these things—they're like peanut butter and jelly pockets?"

"Oh, yeah?"

"Uncrustables!" Frankie throws both arms wide like a baseball umpire calling, *safe*. "You know what I'm talking about?"

"I do."

"I tried one. Absolutely delicious. I should have got some on the way home from work for you guys. I'm mad at myself about that now."

It is so kind of Frankie to worry about feeding them that I don't have the heart to tell him Uncrustables have so much sugar I might as well give my children crack cocaine.

I hold up my empty can. "Do you guys recycle?"

"Here, I'll take that."

I watch him spin around the kitchen, open the door of the fridge and then close it, wipe his hands on his pants and then the dishtowel. He has a few white streaks at the temples of his almost black wavy hair, thick stubble, and eyeglasses too big for his face.

"Frankie, you're sweet. Please don't worry about us. We're so grateful you two are putting us up. If you don't mind I'm going to duck out for a minute to check on the kids and call my mom."

6:38 P.M.

I wander down a dark hardwood hall to the back of Christopher and Frankie's house. As I pass their living room I spot my painting hung in a prominent spot over a sleek leather sofa. Then I push open the back door to a view of three of Christopher's pieces— massive abstract metal installations—picking up the light in a tiny courtyard.

It makes me smile and choke up at the same time. I didn't expect a visit with the ghosts of art students past.

I haven't checked in with Mom since this morning. That seems like forever ago. By now she's road-tripping with Susan, being annoyed, only barely containing aggressive-aggressive feelings about the radio situation. God bless Susan. I take a seat on a pollen dusted papasan—after three rings my mother answers her phone.

"Well, hello," she says.

"Hey, Mom."

"Y'all make it to Augusta?"

"We just landed," I tell her. "How's Guyton going?"

"Funny thing," she says, and my stomach drops.

"Mom. Where are you?"

"I'm home," she says. "Darlin', I'm still at home."

Jesus, take the wheel: "Mom!"

"I know what you're going to say."

"Where's Susan?"

My mother releases a long sigh. "Probably in Guyton by now. I don't know, I don't care."

"Why didn't you go with her?"

"Because Ramona," Mom says. "She wouldn't take my fur babies."

"What?"

"Sophie and Peyton Manning. She said I couldn't put them in her car. She's such a bitch. Seriously. And I didn't even ask her about the chickens. I was going to leave them here in the shed. With extra meals of course."

I almost drop the phone. My mother is devoted to her rescue creatures. Sophie, the antisocial tabby cat, and Peyton Manning, a senior collie mix, are near to her heart. Sometimes, probably most of the time, preferred to me and my children—her grands. It is a noble quality, however this means now my senior mother is planted in her ranch on the water while Hurricane Matthew is half a day away.

"What are you going to do now?"

"Nothing stupid, honey," she says.

"Mom! You already did something stupid. We're supposed to leave Savannah. You, in particular, can't stay there. Your house is going to be the first one the storm demolishes."

I realize I am shrieking.

"I have survived plenty," Mom says. She's changing her tone now to the steely voice she'd use when my brother and I were wiggly in church. "You need to calm yourself down."

"Can you get a ride with someone else?"

"I am not going to go around calling people like some kind of desperate crazy person. I will go to the Publix and buy water and batteries for my flashlight. I have plenty of peanut butter. Progresso soup. I'll be just fine."

"Okay, why don't you load up the creatures and at least go to our house."

A pause.

"Y'all hide a key under a rock or anything?"

"No but Nicole's got one."

"She still in Savannah?"

"Well, no." I am racking my brain. Why couldn't I have found time during all my child-rearing, Prince-grieving, husband-alienating, and boss-hating to hide a stupid key under our welcome mat?

"Mom," I say. "I don't think this is okay."

"Well, it's gonna have to be, isn't it? Now you give Christopher a big hug for me and tell my grandbabies I love them and I'm sure glad they're safe from the storm."

"Mom."

"Bye, now."

She hangs up. I feel a little dizzy. I lean back against the pillow of the chair and tuck my knees into my chest. They *are* currently safe, Mom, I tell myself. But you're not.

This is not good. Despite my mother's bravado, currently she's a senior on her own in a flimsy ranch on the water, surrounded by ancient trees with thick branches, practically issuing Hurricane Matthew a letter-pressed invitation to roll over her like a monster truck. My eyes brim with tears. I am here—I evacuated. What if something—beyond debris or power surges—really awful happens to my mom?

My phone buzzes.

Thank God, she changed her mind.

Nope. It's a text from Kenneth.

Hey, girl! Sent you an invite, haven't seen your response yet. Google Hangouts tomorrow with Laserlife @ 11:35 AM.

8

THE HOLE SOUNDS NICE

7:03 P.M.

Back inside the town house I'm greeted by a blast of air-conditioning and my friend Christopher. I rush to squeeze his rail-thin body, clad in a serious pinstriped suit and derby shoes in burnished brown leather.

"It's the refugees!" he says. I feel energized by the presence of my friend, someone who remembers the me who wore overalls and shimmering seafoam polish on my toenails and knows nothing of the shitshow that's my personal life. Christopher kisses the top of my head. He smells like ginger and sweat.

"Christopher," I coo.

"I see you met my Franco," he says.

"I did, and he's lovely."

"My Spanish is better than his. Did he tell you that? What kind of Texan is out-Spanished by a white guy from Valdosta?"

"I know *chinga te*," Frankie says. "So, *chinga te* and that's all I need to know."

"Kidding. Well, I'm glad y'all get to meet, finally. Ramona, this is Frankie. Frankie, Ramona. I was her gay best friend before gay best friends were cliché."

"Aw. That's both sweet and reductive."

"Where are the kids?" Christopher asks. He stops at Clarence Thomas's habitat. "Or did you cast a spell on Alex and turn him into this rodent?"

"If I had that power, I'd pick Nanette. They're outside, annoying your neighbors."

Christopher deposits an insulated lunch tote on the counter and peeks through a window over the sink in the kitchen.

"Alex has shot up since I last saw him." He frowns. "Did you have an extra kid when I wasn't looking? With, like a 6'4" Swedish man named Mattias?"

"That's our neighbor. Bailey. I kind of, I don't know, I'm giving him a ride."

"Where the hell are his parents?"

"His dad is deployed and his mom is out of town," I tell him.

"Oh, goodness," Frankie says.

"Where the hell is Des?" Christopher asks me.

"I left work early because of the hurricane and found him right after he finished fucking one of the moms from Alex's school."

Frankie gasps.

"That piece of shit," Christopher says. "Let's unpack that later. In the meantime. Y'all want to get pizza?"

I nod vigorously. "Yes."

NONE OF THIS WOULD HAVE HAPPENED IF PRINCE WERE ALIVE

7:46 P.M.

At the restaurant Christopher picks up his menu and Frankie's and stacks them at the end of our table. He pulls out Whole 30 approved lettuce wraps from a tiny royal blue cooler he's brought and places one in front of Frankie, who rolls his eyes at me before nudging it off his place mat with a dull knife.

Frankie seems bewildered by the way my children squirm in their chairs, inhale slices of cheese pizza, press oily fingerprints into my sleeve, and spend the rest of the meal darting back and forth from our table to a jukebox where they push buttons and jump up and down.

"So much energy!" he says. "Did they see those packs of crayons? We can ask for more. They can color on their place mats."

I nod politely.

Yeah. My kids don't give a rat's ass about that stuff or if they do, it only occupies them for three minutes. I can't remember a time when I ate my meal at the same speed as other adults instead of taking flurried bites between cutting up food for my children or relocating chicken tenders so they don't touch the noodles.

At the end of our table Bailey stares at his phone with his head propped up by his fist. He's got to be exhausted by Alex and Nanette. I know I am.

Still, eating pizza is awesome and I'm happy to see Christopher—there's something calming about him. Christopher has always been a grown-up. The kind of person who takes his car in for an oil change before the mileage sticker says you should. The friend in college who knew the deadline for registering for classes or how late the library was open. Even the way he came out in an email to our freshman dorm: *I want y'all to know after nineteen years of research I have concluded I am in fact gay, and if anyone has questions or would like to discuss this I am happy to set up a time, Thursdays are good for me.*

"Can I interest anyone in dessert tonight?" asks our waitress, a lanky brunette wearing enough foundation to hit the pageant circuit. "Y'all. We've got a peach cobbler that's to die for. The chef picks the peaches himself at a farm not two miles from here."

"We're all set, thanks."

I wasn't planning on telling Christopher about Desmond. If the secret stays a secret, it's not really real yet. Also I should protect Desmond from my friends taking out a hit on him if we stay together. *If we stay together*—a creepy new phrase I've never had to use. I reach for Nanette's abandoned crust and wonder why I care about protecting Desmond, if that's what's really going on here. Maybe I care more about what people think than being honest about the fact that my marriage is a slow-moving raccoon with rabies.

What I *should* tell Christopher but I don't: Mom is still in Savannah and that freaks me out. He'll probably say the same thing Desmond or Nicole, or other grown-ups might.

My mother made a choice. She is fully aware of the danger of the hurricane and she chooses to ignore it. She is an obstinate arse. Still, she's my mom, and considering her all alone on the water is rough. Oh, Adelaide, you and your stubbornness and your rescue pets, you're killing me. When I tried to call her again before we left for pizza, she didn't answer.

I've got sea monkeys jumping around in my stomach, I've chewed the fingernail on my right thumb to a dangerous level, and I find myself twirling a strand of hair around the ring finger on my left hand like I did in elementary school.

I don't share any of this with Christopher and Frankie. Instead I listen to stories about the partner at Christopher's firm, his "inappro-pro" behavior at the company picnic, Frankie's obsession with *The Walking Dead* and their vision for the garden in their tidy backyard. Do I think a lemon tree will flourish in Augusta?

Maybe? In partial shade.

On the ride back to Christopher's town house, the kids are freakishly quiet—they're beat. Frankie marvels at the amount of seating in the Toyota Sienna. It would be perfect for gay softball, he says—they could make a spreadsheet and choose one designated driver for each game. Nanette falls asleep in her car seat. In the guest room I spread out towels on the futon in case she pees, I pour her onto it, I wriggle off her shoes and make a barrier with pillows so she doesn't fall out. Bailey and Alex brush their teeth and not-so-quietly collapse on air mattresses. When I flip the light switch, Bailey's face is blue with the light of his phone and Alex cranes his neck to peek at the older boy's screen. Please baby Jesus, don't let it be porn.

10:11 P.M.

"I liked him," Christopher says.

"You tolerated him."

"Why are you using past tense?" I ask my friend."

"Should I not?" Christopher asks me.

I shift on their giant, plush sofa.

"I don't know," I say.

"Me, either. Well. In the beginning he was good for you."

"How?"

"He took you out of your loco brain and forced you to have fun."

"Hey," I say. "I was already fun."

"Sometimes you're fun and sometimes you're broody."

"I guess."

I sip from a stemless glass of rosé, which tastes fine to me yet Frankie and Christopher worry it's shitty, and interrupt each other with apologies that their booze supply is lackluster because they started the Whole 30 and they only have this half-filled bottle leftover from a super awkward BBQ they went to where you couldn't even drink yourself into having fun.

"But sometimes I feel like Desmond eclipsed you. He's a big personality and when you're together I don't know that people realize how funny and strange you are."

"I'm not funny anymore. Just strange."

Christopher continues, "I don't know when hetero people are going to accept the idea that traditional marriage is dying."

"It's not dying. And that's an insult to gay people who couldn't legally marry for the longest time and now they can and do it way better than assholes like me and Des."

"That's fair. I like the idea of finding a soul mate, I do."

"But."

"Eventually you want to have sex with other people."

"Not everyone."

"A lot of people."

"Well."

Christopher releases a long sigh. "You can accept that uncomfortable fact and talk to Desmond about it, even forgive him. Or come to an arrangement."

"What kind of an arrangement?"

"Like me and Frankie."

"You and Frankie do what?"

"We sleep with other people. We don't tell each other about it but it's understood."

"Does he know?"

"Of course. He has his things, and I have my things. Just nothing serious."

"I don't think he knows."

I am looking toward the master bedroom like Frankie might hear this conversation from the shower.

"He knows. And I love him and he loves me and right now things are great."

"I'm happy for you."

"All right. Are we finished pretending like you could forgive Desmond for his lying cheating cold dead beatin' two-time double-dealing mean mistreating loving heart—"

"Patty Loveless? Respect."

Christopher shrugs. "Earned all this money but they'll never take the country out me."

That one is harder: "Rihanna?"

"Beyoncé. Sweet Jesus, what has happened to you?"

"I know. I know!"

"Ramona?"

"Huh."

"If we're done pretending you could handle an open relationship let's consider a different scenario."

"Wait, don't I have other options?"

"I've got a friend I want you to call. When you're ready. She's a Law Dawg in Savannah and she gets women what they need."

"For what?"

"Divorce, sweetie."

Frankie emerges in striped pajamas with a beige towel wrapped around his head.

"Much better," he says. "What'd I miss?"

The word *divorce* hangs in the air like a zeppelin blocking the sun. I make room for Frankie on the sofa and the three of us watch the Weather Channel. Dan is back, no sign of Daphne, a new guy is hanging out in Jacksonville. The update on the impending disaster reminds me that my mother is alone on Wilmington Island and I wonder if you can give yourself an ulcer combining terror and rosé.

At eleven I creep back into the guest room, gently shift Nanette's body from the center of the futon to the side, and lay under the covers, listening to Christopher's toilet gurgle on and off, my muscles tense, my eyes wide open, and I think about Mother's Day.

2013

I had a third glass of pinot grigio on Mother's Day eve because I knew I got to sleep late the next morning. *Late*, a relative term. More like I wasn't in charge of all the morning business. That felt like luxury, the Mom version of Egyptian cotton or aged Asiago.

At four a.m. Nanette woke me with low moans. I nursed her, set her down in her crib, and then tiptoed back to our bedroom, where I slid under the duvet next to Desmond, dead to the world with his left arm thrown over his head. His body was a nucleus of heat in the sagging center of our queen-size bed.

In the dark I listened to Nanette's sounds and prayed they would grow quieter and farther apart as she fell back to sleep instead of building into full alert mode. I got lucky that morning. She must have nodded off again, so I fell back asleep. Around seven she began to chatter, so I pushed Desmond to tend to her.

I heard whispers and giggles in the hall, and I smelled bacon. I shrugged a nubby hoodie over my pajamas and padded into the kitchen.

Des opened up his palms like he was about to catch a bounce pass. Happy Mother's Day, he said. Alex was watching *Curious George* and Nanette was chewing on a crinkly Rainbow Fish. Des smiled, sheepish, in our tiny kitchen. In his old T-shirt I detected the beginning of man boobs. He cleared his throat, tried again: Happy Mother's Day!

This time toddler Alex picked up the cue.

Mommy, he said, and darted toward me in his distinct running style involving more elbows and shoulders than necessary. When I scooped him up, Alex wrapped his arms around my neck and squeezed me tightly. I breathed in his smell: Tide, Cheerios, slightly wet diaper.

A bright orange envelope rested on the kitchen table. On it: "Ramona" in Desmond's small, slanted letters and "Mom," in Alex's writing. It appeared Alex had more confidence with the second "m" than the first one. Pressed in one corner of the envelope were Lightning McQueen and Mater stickers.

Okay, the bacon's almost ready, Des said. You can choose the toppings for your omelet. And we got you pineapple.

Pineapple!

Gurt, Nanette called out from her saucer. Gar.

It was BOGO at Publix, Desmond said. So Alex and I bought an island's worth.

I love pineapple, thank you! I set down Alex, who scurried back to the sofa.

And there's your Prince mug next to the coffee, Des said, moving the frying pan from one burner to the other. You can serve yourself or if you want to lounge, I will pour you a cup.

Look at you, I said to Desmond. I chose a spot on the sofa, folded my slippers under my butt. Look at me!

Nanette started squawking. The novelty of my boobs being in the same room and unavailable to her had worn off. When she held out her arms, I picked her up and started feeding her, propping her head in my elbow nook on a throw pillow. Desmond delivered my coffee and slid a catalog below it for a coaster.

Thanks, baby, I said. I kissed his stubbly cheek.

After breakfast Des declared, that's not all, and disappeared through the screen door. The tailgate on his truck slammed shut. He reemerged, heaving a huge box with more *Cars 2* stickers decorating it. American Standard, the box said.

Happy Mother's Day! Des said.

A toilet? I asked.

Yes, Des said, his face lit up. To replace the one in the hall bathroom.

A toilet, I repeated.

On cue Nanette bit my nipple—hard. Holy Mary, Mother of God. I jerked her from my breast.

No, honey. Not okay. No biting, I said.

Nanette did not appear remorseful. Still I reattached her to nurse. Desmond was standing in front of the microwave next to the American Standard box, his arms extended, like *ta-da!*

You hate the one in there, he said, with glee.

It was true. I hated our toilet. We have two bathrooms. The toilet in question was the one the kids shared—it's also the one people used when they visit. Installed in nineteen seventy something, we'd replaced the lid three times, the bolts were eroding, and we'd swapped out the flush lever twice. At Christmas it broke again so Des MacGyvered a solution using a chopstick. And it backed up all the time. Not sure if that was related to the tree roots under our house, the size of our poop, our overaggressive use of toilet paper, or all of the above.

Damn straight I hated that toilet. But Mother's Day? I pasted a smile across my face. It was starting to hurt.

Monie? Desmond said. Did I mess up?

No, I said. No. It will be awesome to have a new toilet.

He studied my face and said, you look like you're going to cry.

Nope, I said.

You told me not to get you anything. So, this was a surprise.

Because I didn't think you were expecting a present. I got paid for the Tybee contract.

I know, I said.

Then I did start to tear up. Nanette wriggled free of me. She crawled across the carpet in order to pull up to the sofa, where she grabbed Alex's stuffed puppy.

No, Alex said, jerking the toy to him with such force that Nanette spilled backward, bonking her head against our coffee table. We waited in the silence before the big cry. I reached for her, pressed her to my shoulder, and started swaying, shushing her, in between the wails.

I could take it back, Desmond said. You could use the money for something else. Like new shoes? Or a pedicure? I don't know how much those cost, he said.

I don't know why I'm crying, I said.

You don't know?

It's practical and thoughtful. It just makes me sad. I don't know why but it does.

Nanette continued to howl in my ear. I could see Desmond frantically scanning his choices trying to figure out where he went wrong.

Well, okay, he said. Okay.

Let me just sit with this and then I'll get excited for the toilet.

All right.

When I said I didn't need anything for Mother's Day, that was true. We didn't have extra money for anything—at that point our budget was so tight that I'd try to add up everything in my cart at Target using the calculator in my head, then I'd circle back to aisles I'd just visited to return items to the shelf.

If anyone asked me what I wanted for Mother's Day, my greatest wish would be to sleep and be alone and read a book or watch a movie Des would never pick. That would be the best day ever. But I was too new at the Mom game to actually say that.

I didn't want to be one of those people who said one thing but meant another or expected my husband to read my mind. But the gift of a toilet made me more sad than no gift at all.

I snapped the dangling flap of my nursing bra back in place. For the first time I heard a voice inside my head: I'm not happy.

I'm sorry, I said. Something in me is just—

Bummed? Des said. Thinking your husband should disappear in a freak boating incident?

No, I said, pulling the soft lobe of his ear, slightly spiky at the back where he trims his ear hair. Something in me is still adjusting.

Oh, he said.

I can't explain it.

Do you want to keep it? I was going to install it today.

Of course. And I want to be the first one to pee in it.

You will be, Des said. Because it's your special day.

I found my fake smile again and I put it on.

FRIDAY
6:54 A.M.

My phone is buzzing. I'm half-awake, twisting under periwinkle sheets. I struggle to remember where I am, why my back is so stiff, why my stomach is gurgling, why my neighbor's teenager is tiptoeing across the room.

Oh, right. I have a fuzzy memory of all three kids waking up and bad-breathed Alex informing me that Christopher has Netflix and Amazon Prime TV, the holy grail of series that will continuously play. *Next episode begins in 5, 4, 3, 2, 1.* I worry about the kids bouncing unsupervised on his fancy furniture before I fall back asleep.

The buzz is persistent. Who is texting me at the butt crack of dawn? I fumble for my phone, expecting messages from Mom or Desmond. It's Nicole. There are actually six text messages from Nicole.

Please tell me you got out of Savannah.
Where are you?
GIRL. Is your phone dead?
Just text me back and tell me where you are, pls?
I'm a worrier, so what, deal with it.
And I'm worried.

Minneapolis looks over at me from the mountain of towels Nanette kicked to the side. Did I eat anything yesterday? Am I still married? My fingers look for letters to respond to Nicole and can't find them so I press call instead.

"Thank God," Nicole says. "You're alive."

"Barely. How are you?"

"I was worried," she says.

"I'm sorry to call so early. Did I wake you up?"

"That is one thing you can count on with moms. We are always awake."

"Always," I repeat. "We are always."

"Well, I'm glad I caught you."

Nicole sounds like she's about to hang up. I don't want to.

"Hey," I tell her. "Desmond has been cheating on me."

She gasps. "What?"

"I needed to tell someone. Sorry."

"You're the one who told me to stop saying, 'I'm sorry,'" Nicole says. "Hold on."

I feel satisfied with Nicole's reaction after Christopher's suggestion I should consider an open marriage or lawyer up. I hear a rustle on the other end of the line and Nicole's plea to one of her kids—"Give Mommy a sec!"—and another, less subtle, command to her husband, "Jonathan, get in here, I need to talk to Ramona. Yes, right now." Next, the sound of a door closing, now less background noise.

"Start from the start," she says.

"After I got Nanner from your house," I tell her. "He was there. With a woman. One of the mothers from Alex's school."

"Nope. You're kidding me."

"I'm not." My voice sounds a pitch higher than usual. "It really happened. I am a Lifetime special."

"Or. An episode of *Snapped*."

"Right," I say. "Same channel. I think."

"Were they in the process?"

"They had just finished."

"Maybe that's better," she says. "You don't have images stuck in your head for eternity."

"Maybe," I say. "Glass half full."

"Oh, man," she says. "What the H-E-double-bendy-straws."

"I know."

"Goddamn it. Oh, Ramona."

I sniff. "Thanks."

"What are you going to do?"

"What should I do?"

"You're asking me?" she says.

"Your guess is as good as mine."

"This happened on Wednesday? Is he there with you?"

"He's not. I can't imagine being in the same room with him. Or house. Or city. I want to smash his head in. Like in *Game of Thrones*."

"See, that's why I don't watch that show. Where is he?"

"Atlanta," I say. "I think. I'm not sure. Who knows what else he's lied about."

"Is he apologetic? Wait. That's not the word I wanted. Conciliatory. Is he conciliatory?"

"Yeah."

"Well, that's good, right? At least he's not like, I deserve multiple partners, and this is not how I planned for you to meet your sister wife but here she is."

"I guess. I'm not ready."

"Of course," she says.

"I need to keep it together for the kids. And my mom. I've got to get through this hurricane and make sure they're okay and then once it's gone I can find a little hole and lie in it."

"Of course. That sounds nice. The hole sounds nice."

"Yeah."

"I mean it," she says. "I wish I could be there for you."

"Thank you," I tell her. "You are. You're here right now."

"Come to Macon. Jonathan can take care of all the kids and you and I can go somewhere and get shitfaced."

"You're sweet. We're okay here. We're going to stalk a grilled cheese truck at some point."

"Goddamn," she says.

"I know."

"I'm shaking, I'm so pissed. I don't know what I'm going to do if I see him in the wild. I might ram my car into him. Or grocery cart. Or bike, whatever."

"Also adorable but might add more trauma to my situation. Like, for the kids."

"I don't actually have a bike. What about her? Are you friends with her on Facebook? I'm going to look her up and learn her whole sordid story. I've got time, you know."

"Apparently you do. How's Macon?"

"Who cares?" she says. "You're the one hurting. The least I can do is listen and plan murders with my imaginary bike."

"I know. I don't want to think about me."

"Well. Since you insist. It's amazing," she says. "Last night Robert got terrors and woke everyone up yelling and then stepped on Eva's head so she started screaming. And I'm trying to keep everyone quiet so they don't wake up my in-laws. Oh, and everyone thinks Trump is going to Make America Great Again. And my mother-in-law has tried to give Eva peanut butter—no shit— on three separate occasions despite the fact I have repeated no less than nine times my daughter will go into anaphylactic shock if she eats a peanut. She's like, she'll grow out of it. She thinks I'm making it up. And if I have to read *If You Give a Mouse a Cookie* one more time I'm putting my head in the oven."

"Is that book," I say, "about gateway drugs? Like the cookie is one."

"Now that I think about it, maybe the cookie is a metaphor for cocaine."

It feels good to think about somebody else, even laugh. Even if the distraction only lasts the length of an ad before a YouTube video. Also flaring up: a craving for those normal shenanigans you experience with a young family. I'd give anything to swap them with my current situation.

I am awake, alert, and now I have to pee super bad. I feel another flare of panic remembering Mom's situation.

"Where are you, again?" Nicole asks me.

"Augusta."

"Thank God," she says. "For a while there I thought you were going to be one of those crazy people who stayed."

9

TOO BLESSED TO BE STRESSED

7:28 A.M.

"We have to go back," I announce.

Clustered at Christopher's modern farmhouse table, Alex and Nanette push eggs around their plates while Bailey spoons himself a second helping.

I don't feel connected to the earth this morning. I can't make pleasant conversation or get pumped up about plans to visit the Augusta science center or check out a movie at the new theater with stadium seating. Frankie: *You could take a nap in those chairs.* My coffee, which I needed so desperately, is now lukewarm.

Alex's eyebrows float higher than their usual spot over his blue eyes.

"Back to the golf place?" he asks.

My sweet firstborn. You wish.

"Back to Savannah?" Bailey guesses.

"Yes," I tell them. "Back to Savannah."

Christopher freezes with the pepper mid-shake over his eggs. "Say what?"

"But I wanna watch *Dragons Race to the Edge*," Nanette says.

"I know," I tell her. "Mr. Christopher has a nice TV and there are all kinds of cool shows. But Grandma is still in Savannah and she needs us."

"I wanna stay here," Nanette announces, to which Christopher offers an appreciative pat on the head while Frankie, wearing a different robe—chenille oatmeal—looks alarmed. Nanette reaches a dimpled hand to the middle of the table for a pear that's actually part of the centerpiece.

"Not for breakfast," I tell her and replace the fruit in the bowl. Outside Christopher's window it's drizzling and I also hear the dripping sound of the coffee machine as it brews a second pot. I find the off-tempo rhythm comforting.

"You said we can get ice cream in Augusta," Alex says.

"I did," I tell him. "You're right. Maybe we can find some on the way back to Savannah."

"I want lunch banilla," Nanette insists.

Alex and I exchange looks—we are too worn out to translate for outsiders that Nanette is referring to French Vanilla. Bailey continues to methodically lift eggs to his mouth. That kid can eat.

"Sweetie," Christopher says to me, "I love your mom as much as the next guy. However. This storm is no joke. That's why you're here in the first place. Isn't there somebody in town who can scoop her up? Desmond could go back for her."

"She had a ride," I tell Christopher.

"And?" Christopher says.

"She bailed. She won't go anywhere without her animals."

"Maybe she'll be okay. I mean. You're here now," Christopher says.

"Maybe," I say. "Except, Christopher, she's in that rickety house by herself on the water. Which could possibly make it but then what next? She's trapped on the island without power for a week?"

"Right," Frankie says.

"She's a tough broad," Christopher says. "She reminds me of the judge who presided over my parents' divorce."

I flinch at the sound of that word. Why do people keep saying it? I take a sip of my coffee and sit up straight.

"I gotta go back. I'll just pick her up and find a hotel that takes pets, or force her to come to midtown, and we'll figure it out. We need to go."

Whether I like it or not, the idea of my mother by herself pulls me back to Savannah like a crab scuttling after a raw chicken neck on a string. I didn't feel this way when Dad was alive. I felt sure they took care of each other. Now I have to look out for Mom.

Christopher, rational being: "How are you going to get back in if they've closed off the roads?"

"I'll come up with a plan," I tell him.

"Sounds foolproof," Christopher says. "What can go wrong?"

"Just—Christopher," I say. "Please. I'll figure it out."

My friend shrugs his shoulders. "If that's how you feel."

"Sweeties. Finish your eggs, let's toss your stuff back in the Spider-Man suitcase."

"I didn't unpack. I didn't even change my underwear," Alex says.

He's right. The kids slept in their clothes from yesterday, I only brought my duffel inside, which has their toothbrushes and luvvies. Also still in the car: my laptop and Kenneth's notes, unread. I've got a motherfucking call with Laser Life in a few hours.

"That's kind of gross but okay," I tell Alex. "At least let's brush our teeth."

Before I had kids I had all these dreams that I would raise well-educated and nice-mannered humans. Now my main goal is that they avoid getting face tattoos.

"Whatever is best, Mrs. Arnold," Bailey says. He has long, piano-playing fingers. He rests his fork on the side of his plate.

"I'm sorry, Bailey. I know you didn't mean to sign up for the circus that's my life."

"I'm having a good time. Christopher is really good at bacon and eggs."

"Why, thank you," Christopher says. "I concur. I am indeed good at bacon and eggs. I also have a lot of other great qualities."

Frankie says, "Mmmmmmm."

I am in charge here: "Text your mom, Bailey, and tell her we're going back now. You are still safe on my watch."

"'Kay," he says.

The kids push away from their plates. Nanette ducks under the table and crawls over everyone's feet. She's pushing up one of the legs of my pajama pants and rolling down my sock.

"Hey!" I squawk. "Bring your plates to the counter." They obey and thunder upstairs. Once they are out of sight, Christopher looks at me.

"You sure? Y'all are a pain but you can stay for however long you need to."

"I appreciate it." I pull on his sleeve. "If I stay I'll be freaking out. The whole time I'll be imagining Adelaide on her roof. The water rising around her. Whipping out her flip phone to call for help and then accidentally dropping it in the river."

The coffee machine beeps.

"Okay," Christopher says. "You didn't ask. But. For the record, two things: I think you need to get in touch with Bailey's mom. And I don't know what's going to happen with you and Des, and I have opinions about what should happen, even if you're not ready to hear them, so I need you to call me after the hurricane."

"I will."

My friend lifts his napkin from his lap and places it on the table.

"Ramona. It's not that I don't want to snatch up a crossbow and hunt him down like a turkey. Or fast forward to a time when you aren't feeling so much pain. It's just—I see this stuff in court every day. My love language is logic."

"I know." I'm feeling tears brimming—strange that they surface in Augusta. I seal them off like the top on Christopher's jar of peach preserves. Which no one touched because you can't eat them on Whole 30 and my children only eat Strawberry Smucker's.

8:17 A.M.

I pack my toiletries in a toothpaste encrusted plastic makeup case, stuff it in my duffel bag, and kneel on the inflatable mattress to force the air out more quickly. In the doorway Christopher watches in his undershirt and work pants, a shallow canyon between his eyebrows. *Don't do that*, he mutters, *dork*. When I ignore his suggestion, he unplugs the second mattress, starts to do the same thing.

The air hisses. I make the guest bed and scan the floor for objects we tend to forget: matchbox cars, slinkies from the dentist office, USB cords, rogue socks turned inside out.

As I hug Christopher and Frankie goodbye, I wonder if I chatted at the posh pizza place about what was going on with them or was I self-involved, barking orders to the kids, blabbing on about the hurricane. I remember explaining Kenneth's unrealistic expectations in detail. Did I ask enough questions about Christopher, how his family is doing, if he's happy? Maybe I did, I just forgot the answers.

Thank you so much, you two. You have no idea.

Christopher and Frankie wave at the door, now in work uniform, their faces, half-politely-smiling, half-concerned.

9:04 A.M.

Behind the wheel I can't breathe.

He threw me over. He balled me up and tossed me in the wastebasket like bits in the kitchen: broken eggshells, the slimy skin from frozen salmon, a spot of fuzzy mold near the stem of a green bell pepper.

After I gave him so much—parts of myself I didn't even know were there. After I snuffed out my wildness. After I glued myself with rubber cement to this life because of my love for him and the people we made.

There are moments when I want to hurt him and other ones when I want to reach for him, squeeze him, wrap my arms and legs around him and hold on. Choose me, pick me, I can do better, I will pay attention to you, I will be a present partner, you love me and I love you. We should be together. We promised each other that.

Then I'm mad at myself for feeling that way. Do I have no dignity whatsoever? I am a whole heck of a lot of things but I never considered myself a doormat. Waves of embarrassment and anger swim under my skin and I grip the steering wheel.

A scream rises in my chest. I hold it there. I don't let it escape.

9:06 A.M.

I steer the minivan toward 25 South. Smell you later, Augusta, we're headed back to Savannah. I feel a nugget of relief that we're on the way to rescue my mother. But what happens when I try to get back into the city? Is there a fleet of police enforcing the evacuation border? Lined up side-by-side with riot shields and pepper spray.

Before, the idea of Hurricane Matthew was a graphic swirl on the Weather Channel; now, it looks like a real storm is coming. As we press closer to Savannah, the sky changes from light gray to the lead in a number two pencil. The trees, gently swaying at the beginning of my trip, rustle with more urgency. I can hear the wind from inside the car and every now and then a strong gust pushes us farther to the right.

I take deep breaths. I have a video call at 11:35. I'm driving my children and a stranger's kid right back into the hurricane because my mother can't leave behind her cat—the same animal who once pooped inside my purse.

The kids are plugged in because by the grace of God I remembered to charge the tablets last night. Though somehow the technology is not having the magic effect it did yesterday. Nanette wants to switch tablets because one has a game the other one doesn't, and Alex isn't into it, so they fuss at each other until I use Serious Mommy voice. I decree they play for thirty minutes and then swap.

I'm watching the road, checking my phone every now and then. I get a text from Kenneth reminding me about the call, asking if I have the edits yet. I don't respond. The idea of him panicking for at least half a morning that I'm not going to make the call fills me with euphoria. I have another text from Desmond, wanting to make sure we made it to Christopher's house, and could I call him please so he can talk to the kids. And he's so sorry.

Fuck him. I need to get gas.

"Anyone have to pee?" I ask my gaggle of kids.

"I'm good, Mrs. Arnold," says Bailey.

"Don't need to," says Alex.

"Nope," says Nanette.

"Really, Nanette? Because you didn't go this morning at Mr. Christopher's and I know you must have a bunch of pee stored up in there."

"I went in my pull-up," she says.

"That was apparent," I tell her. "It weighed twenty pounds. Want to try potty here?"

"No," she says. Her eyes are fixed on the screen. "It's too loud."

"What is?"

"The flusher," she says.

"Okay, well, you can go in the car, in the fire engine potty and then I can dump it out and clean it and that won't be as yucky as doing it in the middle of nowhere."

"No," she says.

Fine. I swipe my credit card at the pump. I used to do Kegel exercises while waiting for the tank to fill up based on a tip I read in *Shape* magazine and I decide to skip them today because what's the point? After I replace the nozzle I consider we might need supplies at home—I didn't do any hurricane preparedness shopping—so I press the automatic lock to secure the kids in the van and stroll around the aisles of the convenience store under the watchful gaze of a woman with a camo scrunchie elevating her crispy blond hair in a high pile on her head.

All the generic brand water bottles on the shelf. That's nine, total. Peanut butter—it's Peter Pan and not the "natural" brand we get where you stir it up and get oil oozing over the sides—but what the hell. Granola bars. Chex Mix. Nutri-grain bars. Ooooh, powdered sugar donuts, why not? Next to the breath mints at the counter is a slim paperback entitled *Too Blessed to Be Stressed.*

The cashier is talking to the man in front of me about her dog.

"He's straight up petrified when it storms," she says. "He hides under the bed and shakes and shakes and shakes. I got him a thunder shirt and it was expensive but tell you what, it really works."

I push open the door of the convenience store and I spot a tall man in a leather jacket dialing a flip phone in front of the Sienna.

"These your kids?" he says.

"They are." The plastic bags rustle against the back of my knees.

"I was dialing the police," he says. *The po-leece.* His fingers hover over the numbers. "You can't be leaving kids in the car by 'emselves like that."

A wave of mama bear rage rises up and crests in my throat. Who is this stranger wearing leather in 80 degrees with a flip phone judging my parenting? I'm going to spin the handle of my sack with the peanut butter and throttle this punk until his brain matter spills out of his nostrils and ear canals.

"Well, I'm here, now," I tell him. "So, you can press end on your call."

It takes me thirty minutes to calm down. We drive an hour in semi-peace. My phone vibrates, and I try to resist glancing to see who texted me and fail, instead reaching for it and attempting to type in my code with one hand while keeping the other one on the wheel. I've got a missed call from Sarah Ellen, no thank you. Nanette sings the Batman version of "Jingle Bells"—*Batman smells, Robin laid an egg*—in an earnest soprano. Bailey asks if we have satellite radio or any CDs. Alex farts a lot—gurgly ones— and shoots Nanette looks from hell when she changes the lyrics of Batman "Jingle Bells" to include her brother's smells.

"All right, Nanner. The first version was bad enough. Let's stick to that one."

10:22 A.M.

Signs of the storm intensify the closer we get to Savannah. The grass by the side of the road waves at us. Tall pines sway and bend in creepy choreography. In better news we temporarily have a radio signal and they're playing "Little Red Corvette."

"It's starting to look like a hurricane," Bailey observes from the back-back.

"You're right, Bailey," I tell him. I increase my volume: "Look, I'm sorry this has been chaotic. I thought I was helping you and now I'm taking you right back into the fray. I just can't leave my mother by herself. I need to make sure she's okay."

"Don't worry, Mrs. Arnold. This is the best trip I've ever been on."

That breaks my heart.

"Really?" I ask him.

"Y'all are so nice. And your friend. He made a really good breakfast. Were they roommates? Or more like boyfriends?"

"More like boyfriends."

"I thought so," Bailey says. "That's the first time I ever met anyone who is gay."

"Really?"

"Yeah."

"That's the first time I ever met anyone from El Paso."

"Huh. You like this song?"

"I love this song."

"After Prince died my algebra trig teacher wore purple for a week and played us a song each morning before we started our practice set."

"That teacher sounds awesome."

"He's all right."

In the rearview mirror I see Bailey shrug. "I have a theory. I'm still working on it, but I think Prince's death was a lesson to all of us. Like we can't be complacent that Prince is always going to be around. So we have to get our joy when we can."

"Live your life."

Live your life. Change it if you want to. Bailey's nodding and looking out the window and I sense he is taking stock of things in his sixteen-year-old world and this idea produces a tsunami of affection inside me.

"Look. I'm going to grab my mother and we'll bring her back to our neighborhood because we'll all be safer in my house, okay? There's big trees and we might lose power but it's better than her being near the water. And our plumbing usually works when we lose power. We can flush and stuff."

"Wow, Mrs. Arnold, great pep talk."

"And you made a joke," I say. I look over my shoulder to see he's smiling. Cute kid, one dimple in his right cheek.

"It happens," Bailey says. "Every now and then."

"If we're both joking we're probably going to be all right. Text your mom and tell her the neighbor is still wacko but I'm going to take care of you. Okay?"

"Okay," he says.

We lose the signal. I scan through the stations—there's not a lot out here. Country music and one with Spanish lyrics. I press down on the gas pedal and the van groans, launching us ahead onto the empty highway.

2013

It's the catalytic converter, the man at Savannah Tire told me.

His name was Wayne and I nodded like I knew exactly what he was talking about. He looked down at his clipboard, which meant he could avoid watching me leaking breast milk from my left boob and trying to unwrap ToastChee crackers with one hand. He said, you don't have to deal with it right away. But it'll get worse until eventually the car can't go.

Every crappy expense was stressful. This was before I started working again, and Desmond and I were building a tinker toy column of debt. It wasn't like we bought dumb stuff. We weren't signing leases for Land Rovers or ordering lobster at restaurants. It was just that every time we solved a problem, something else came up.

The catalytic converter. The converter of catalysts. On my way home from the mechanic I wondered how long we could ignore this before we had to deal. I willed the check engine light to dim. The kids gazed out the window. In the rearview mirror I envied their unlined faces, ignorant of the fact that one day they'll be grown-ups who have to pay for shitty things they don't care about.

At home that day I'd be humming along, and then remember, something's not right—what is it? Did I leave Alex's favorite sippy cup at the playground? Did I forget Nanette's nine-month appointment at the pediatrician? Then I'd remember the catalytic converter. It was like a bulging blister on the back of my heel.

Christmas was coming up. Some nuts on my street had already hung wreaths on their front doors. I dreaded telling Desmond.

It's nine hundred dollars, I said, while we cleaned up dinner. He froze, a skillet in one hand, a faded yellow dish towel in the other one.

Fuck me, he said.

Little pitchers, I hissed, but I didn't have to worry because Nanette was in her Gymini in the TV room while Alex was oblivious to the two of us, happily scribbling on a Lightning McQueen coloring book with licorice scented marker. I said, what are we going to do?

What choice do we have?

I don't know, I said.

We gotta put it on the charge.

The Visa? It's got HVAC from August and your new tires. We're not making headway on that.

I know, babe, he said. It sucks. Look. Unless we reduce our weekly budget on everyday things we're never going to get those balances down.

I was scraping Annie's white cheddar shells into the trash can. No, *you* look.

Everyday things? I asked him.

Yeah, he said.

Like, what?

He poured lemon dishwasher detergent into the dispenser. He said, groceries, Target. Starbucks. That kind of crap. Everything else is fixed.

Things I was in charge of shopping for—my debit card purchases.

Before my trip to Savannah Tire that day, I made a special excursion to Publix with both kids, Nanette an infant, Alex a wiggly toddler who needed to move all the time, because chicken breasts were BOGO and I needed Desitin for Alex's diaper rash, which sprung up even though I changed his diaper it seemed like every five minutes. I hovered in the cosmetics section because I was low on Herbal Essences before deciding that could wait because I couldn't spend that much on this trip. Nanette started to scream and a woman wearing a pineapple print scarf walked by and said, your baby isn't happy.

Des, I said. That sounds frickin' impossible. If we spent less on groceries, we would starve. If we spent less at Target, we wouldn't have diapers and your children would crap on the floor.

I know, he said. But maybe we could try.

We?

He had no idea how hard I was trying. At everything! Taking my kids to a public place on a single errand felt like walking around with a bomb. My body existed in two modes: super tense and drooling sleep in odd locations. I was lonely and days stretched on forever. I was trying so hard and nobody gave a shit.

My ugliest feelings, the ones I worked hard to keep a lid on, rose to the surface. Why the hell did I fall in love with someone with no money who doesn't care about making more? Now I was getting lectured about spending too much on diapers at Target and I was stuck.

I used to be cute. I had a thigh gap. I had a lot going for me. I could've picked another guy. Someone with ambition. We would support each other, me and this phantom man. We'd encourage each other and create the life we dreamed of together. Or I could've been by myself. No husband, no kids, nobody telling me

CAROLYN PRUSA

I shouldn't buy an iced coffee. Whoever said love is all you need never needed a catalytic converter.

I felt an atomic fireball in my belly.

Maybe you could try to, I don't know, make more money? I said.

Desmond said, sorry?

I don't know, I mutter. Like make something out of yourself, or in your career instead of talking about the Georgia game on the roof with your buddies and eating wings at Coach's.

Oh, shit, Desmond said.

Like I'm the one causing a financial disaster. I just consigned Nanny's stupid swing so I could buy socks and a jacket for Alex. If anything, I am the fucking hero here.

My face was hot. I felt light-headed.

That's what you think, Desmond said. He is already a red and pink person and in the kitchen he became redder and pinker.

I never thought I'd be standing here losing my mind about a catalytic converter. I hate this.

And it's my fault. Because I don't make enough money.

I hurt him. I felt a tiny bit bad because yes, my situation was not ideal, but at least I didn't have the pressure of supporting all four of us. Hold the phone, though. Fuck him! He has no idea how hard it is to raise humans.

Well, I said. It's not *my* fault.

I waited for him to explode. All right, let's do this. Let's both admit we're frustrated and trapped and we're exhausted and figuring out this stuff fucking sucks. Let's release that energy across the kitchen island instead of storing it underneath our skin.

He didn't. Whatever flare of rage I saw earlier somehow dissipated. It would have felt better if he had exploded.

Ramona, Desmond carefully lined up the towel over the handle of the dishwasher. What you just said? That's the meanest thing anyone's ever said to me. And it came from you.

10

HELL OR HIGH WATER

11:29 A.M.

When I pull over to an Enmarket gas station somewhere between Augusta and Savannah, the Sienna shudders as it comes to a stop. My parking spot is neither near the convenience store nor the gas pump so we probably look suspicious. Like I am stopping to breastfeed or heat up a crack pipe. I flip open my laptop. I've got two bars—this should be awesome.

"What are we doing, Mommy?" asks Alex.

I unbuckle my seat belt so I can fully spin myself around, 180 degrees like an owl.

"Okay, superstars. Here's the thing: I need to make a call for work. A video call. I bet it takes twenty minutes. The thing is I can't have crazy noises in the background."

Nanette: "You have wook?"

"During the hurricane?" Alex says.

"I do, sweethearts. It's dumb but I want to keep my job." I fumble for the package of powdered donuts I bought at the first gas station stashed in the valley of the passenger's seat. "I need you guys to shift over to one side of the van. The right side."

Alex frowns. "Your right or our right?"

My son's concern with logistics is adorable because I'm pretty sure he doesn't know his right from his left.

I point: "Over there."

"Okay," Alex says.

Bailey lowers his Beats from his ears to around his neck, looks at me, then at the seat next to him, slides from left to right, returns headphones to their original spot.

"I'm already over here," Alex points out. "Mommy I think I have a wiggly tooth."

"Where do I go?" Nanette asks me. "I want a donut."

I reach across to unclick her seat belt.

"Maybe," I suggest, "in the back-back near Bailey? Alex, that's so exciting."

Nanette clutches Minneapolis, grabs her sippy cup, piles them next to Bailey. She returns to her car seat for the iPad, her sticker book, a sparkly wand she finds in the pocket behind the driver's seat. I glance at the clock: 11:33. Every snail in the history of mollusks can move faster than Nanette in this moment.

I've got to keep my breath steady and my voice neutral. If I reveal one ounce of the panic I feel under the surface my children will catch on to it the way sharks detect a drop of blood miles away and zoom in for the kill.

"I wonder if the Tooth Fairy comes during hurricanes," says Alex. "She might get sucked up in the crazy wind."

I open the package of donuts, hand it to Bailey: "It's a risk that comes with the job. She probably has sophisticated storm tracker technology. Toothnology? All right. Twenty minutes. Please, help Mommy out, munchkins."

By some miracle I'm dialed into the call—there's a connection. In the window on the screen I'm speaking with Abigail and Jason, two turtleneck sweatered figures in a teal room. The image is mostly clear, though I can't tell if Abigail has a nose ring or if that's a big mole. And of course, there's me in the upper right corner. I never noticed how rippled my forehead looks when I speak. The veins rise up below the skin like ropes under sand.

Abigail and Jason do most of the talking, which is good. Even if it's complaining. That's fine. SEO, Call-to-Action, Meta Descriptions. Sure.

"That's in the proposal," I assure them. "It's definitely in there. I just need to double-check with Xavier on the timeline."

I divert my eyes from Ramona in the Corner to make eye contact with Abigail and Jason. The screen freezes for a second—my heart soars, technical difficulties could truncate the call—and I just hear audio, a squeak from somebody's chair while Abigail prattles on about SEO.

Jason calls out, "Ramona?"

The image on my monitor moves again. It's jerky, like poses captured in a strobe at a club except it's a fluorescent light in a teal conference room in Columbus.

"Still here!" I reassure them.

Dang. Behind me I hear someone's sticker book fall to the floor and a grunt when Alex picks it up.

"Okay," Abigail says. "That was odd."

You have no idea, lady. Right now there's minimal noise behind me and the call keeps going. I'm not sure what we talk about. I feel a natural high at the idea that things are wrapping up—that I'm headed to the finish line and almost achieved my goal of not dropping the ball professionally.

Hold up.

The scent of rotten eggs creeps forward from the rear of the van. A chortle escapes from my son. Oh, no. My heart sinks. Ramona in the corner of my screen looks panicked. I hear an indignant squawk from my daughter; next, the attempted shushing from Bailey, the crackling of the bag of donuts.

On the screen Jason tips his head to the side. "Everything cool?"

"It's fine!" I say. "I'm here, Jason. You were saying."

Behind me the kids explode in laughter. They jostle each other, the boys giggle, Nanette moans in her defense before giving in.

Nothing can compete with a fart. You can't contain the ripples it creates. A fart is its own force of nature, not quite Category 4 but up there. Abigail and Jason freeze in a pose looking at each other before they move again.

"I'm so sorry, you guys. I've got my kids with me in the car," I tell them, shifting my laptop so the camera reveals the group of three behind me, now convulsing. "There's a hurricane. Also a fart. We were evacuating. Well, we were, and now we're going back."

"Nanner did it!" Alex says, before erupting in squeals.

"Oh my God," Abigail says.

"To Savannah," I explain.

"I farted," Nannette admits. "I'm the one."

"Yeah," I say.

Pixelated Abigail and Jason are frozen again in a pose where they are looking at each other and laughing on my laptop, Jason appears to be wiping a tear from one eye.

"Ramona," Abigail says. "We can reschedule."

A moment of mercy. "Really?"

"For sure," says Jason, who squints to examine the action behind me, then backs up when I shift the camera to my face. "You don't have to take a call during a hurricane. That's ridiculous."

1:17 P.M.

"Ma'am, we're not letting anyone through here," says the freshly shaved highway patrolman.

We're stopped on I-16, right around the intersection with 17 before Little Neck Road. I slowed down when the officer ambled out from his police sedan and held up one hand, a bulky class ring on his middle finger.

The minivan hums in park and the check engine light taunts me. For once the kids are quiet, their attention fixed on the officer, who wears aviator sunglasses like Tom Cruise in *Top Gun*. The skin from his neck bulges over his collar. His name tag says Odom. There were some Odoms who went to Benedictine with Des and one who worked with me before I had kids.

I roll down the window. "Oh. You're not?"

"We're evacuating the city on account of Hurricane Matthew, ma'am," he says. "So we're not letting anyone drive through this way."

I nod like this is news to me.

"We know," pipes up Alex from the backseat. "We're going back to get Gigi."

"Sorry?" the man asks. As he leans forward to examine the middle row of my van, his aftershave drifts downwind.

"It's not a big deal," I tell the officer. "We forgot something in Savannah."

"A person," Alex volunteers.

"Gigi!" Nanette says, giggling.

"Gigi is what we call Grandma," Alex explains. Normally my kids hide behind me or transform into mutes when strangers ask polite, not difficult questions, like, how old are you? Of all the times for these two to shrug off their shyness.

"You wouldn't be related to Maggie, would you?" I ask Officer Odom.

"My cousin," he says. "Now she's Maggie Shaw. Just had her fourth."

"Baby? That's a lot of kids."

"Sure is," he says. "Too many for me. Listen. Sorry to do this, but I need to ask you to turn around."

Officer Odom has a gummy grin. He's probably been out here all day by himself. He probably counted the number of anthills by the side of the road while he was waiting or scored his personal best at Candy Crush Saga. I feel confident Officer Odom would never stray from his wife.

"We forgot something," I continue. I can't turn the car around. At this point I don't know where to go. I picture my mother alone in her house. "And we were hoping to pick it up, and then we'll scoot out again. We'll be on our way."

"That's unfortunate," the man says. "Again, I'm really sorry. I can't let you through."

I assess the empty highway stretched out before me.

"Officer Odom? This wasn't my plan. I evacuated. According to the governor's recommendation. I follow rules. I've only had one speeding ticket in my life. And it was in a school zone so I wasn't actually driving crazy fast, I was just going faster than the fifteen miles per hour or whatever they say you should drive in a school zone even when kids are already in their classrooms. And I was a mess that day because my dad had recently died. And then Prince passed. I respect the law, I really do. But I've got to get back into Savannah. I need to get my mother."

"I believe you, ma'am," he says. "I'm sorry about your father. And, I mean, we were all shocked about Prince. Still. I can't let anyone through."

I take note of his firearm, securely fastened to his hip in a holster. I look at his patrol car, the only vehicle for miles. I examine his shoes—shiny Oxfords, laces tied in a neat horizontal bow. I wonder how fast he can run.

"I get it. No worries. We'll turn around," I assure him.

I push the gear into drive and shift my foot to the pedal. He starts to back away. His expression is one of compassion. Or maybe just the practiced politeness that he uses all too often when dealing with an unstable citizen.

I push down harder on the accelerator.

"Hold on, gang," I say.

"Mommy!" Alex exclaims. "We're supposed to turn around!"

"I know!"

I am light-headed and it feels like my heart's beating in my throat.

"We gotta get Gigi," Nanette insists. I am pleased at least one of my children recognizes that every now and then you need to break the rules, although in Nanette's case it's possible this impulse might not lead to a trailblazing career, more likely—prison.

Alex can't believe it: "Still!"

"Well, I'll tell the police I'm sorry," I say, watching Officer Odom in the mirror writing—I assume—my license plate down on a pad. I zoom ahead and the odometer rises from 45 to 60 miles per hour, then 75, while the policeman starts to shrink in the distance. Is he going to chase me? Now he's talking on a device, I think it's a walkie-talkie. "Kids, I don't recommend doing what I just did and for the most part I think you should respect the law. In this case, Mommy made a decision to put Gigi ahead of the evacuation order and if I get in trouble for that, I will apologize."

"We're going really fast," Alex says.

"Weeeeee!" says Nanette.

"Hold on, Adelaide," I say, under my breath. "We're coming, hell or high water."

"I think we lost him," Bailey says.

1:55 P.M.

"Have you ever been arrested?" Bailey asks me. Now he's in the front seat after we visited El Cheapo, a stop intended for my kids yet Bailey was the only one who took advantage of the restroom.

The fact that my daughter has been holding her urine for the better part of three days is a thing. It's just—I've got so many concerns right now. Potty training isn't in the top three.

Here are things I could have been arrested for but wasn't: tagging graffiti in Pike Creek, sneaking into multiple movie theaters when I only paid for one ticket, underage drinking, underage marijuana-ing, copying a video of *Dazed and Confused* using two VCRs, accidentally shoplifting eye makeup remover in Publix, stealing a robe from a hotel in Sedona, driving with outdated registration, installing Microsoft Office 2007 with my roommate's disc to my laptop, leaving my children in the car while I go into a convenience store to buy donuts and bottled water.

"Not yet," I tell Bailey. "Have you?"

"No," he says. "One of my friends from ninth grade, though."

"Who's your friend?"

"Wes Gregory. You know him?"

"I don't," I tell Bailey. "Maybe I'll meet him when I go to jail."

"He's out now," Bailey says. "He went to juvie. He was supposed to go back to school but he only went like two weeks, then he started staying home."

"Why did he go to juvie?"

"The first time was assault. He didn't have a gun, though. So that was good. For him, anyway. The second time was selling oxy. Which wasn't good, either, but if he was selling something stronger it would've been worse. I know he'll go back."

"I hope not. I hope he changes his ways."

"Well. That was ninth grade."

I nod. "Forever ago."

"Now I'm a junior."

"How's that going?"

"All right. It's not like, free to be you and me."

"What do you mean?"

"Like, if you're a guy and you don't play sports, or you're not good at them, or you're not in the crazy smart classes, or in a group, you're kind of by yourself."

"Do you ever hang out with ladies?"

"I mean, yeah. Well. I talk to the girls at work probably more than the girls at school."

"Oh."

"They talk to me, I guess."

"So you don't see the kids from ninth grade much anymore?"

"Like, not really."

"Huh."

"Which is hard because now I have to get to school by myself. I ride my bike now. It's faster, anyway."

I remember watching Bailey loping along 52nd Street in his blinding white sneakers when his hair was short instead of the shag he sports now. Didn't he used to walk with a gaggle of kids before he transformed into this gazelle? I never thought to wonder what happened to those kids or why Bailey rides his bike now.

"Oh," I manage. Swirling in my head is curiosity about this side of Savannah, a world with teenagers, many of whom don't have much supervision or enough to eat. A part that I know is there, that hurts my heart, and yet I don't want to insult Bailey by asking naive questions. Next to me he places his left ankle on top of his right knee.

"Mrs. Arnold," he says. "You don't have to worry. I've got a 4.2. I'm way more together than most of the kids there."

"I'm sure," I tell him.

"I am the only one who got over a ninety-five on our trig test. I'm the best at math. When Alex gets bigger, if he needs help with math, you can send him over."

2:14 P.M.

She's calling again. A sane person would hit ignore. Curiosity inspires me to press accept on my phone—it's like I can't stop my finger. You're supposed to be hands-free in Georgia but this conversation is not appropriate for speaker.

"Ramona," she says, her voice still small. "It's me, Sarah Ellen."

"Duh. Why are you calling?"

"I wanted to make sure you got out of Savannah. Last time we talked you were prepping. It's looking real bad. The storm."

Again I am struck by her breezy Southern tone. It's like she's calling me from a salon to confirm a cut and color appointment with Tristan.

"Well, I was," I say. "And we did. And now we're back in Savannah. And I don't know where Desmond is, if that's why you're calling."

"I was thinking of leaving him, you know," Sarah Ellen says.

"Your husband?"

"Before all this. We're not . . . close. We're not like you and Des."

"Not a high bar right now."

"I think we drifted," she says. "We hadn't had sex in six months before this thing started. He probably doesn't even care what happened with Desmond."

"Of course he does," I tell her. "I can't believe I'm reassuring you after the shit that went down."

"I appreciate it. I don't have a lot of people to talk to."

"You don't?"

"No. That's why I like hanging out with Des."

I grit my teeth: "Sure."

"Sorry. Obviously you know he's a great person to talk to."

"Aware of that."

"Sometimes," she says, "the loneliness is overwhelming."

"You should discuss this with your husband."

"I will," she says.

"That's somebody."

"And Ramona. You should try to forgive Desmond."

"Are you kidding me with this? You can kiss my ass."

Next to me Bailey's skinny body jerks to attention like he just spotted a tarantula on the dashboard.

"That's fair. I probably deserve that. Listen, though. I've been thinking about it. I'm trying to forgive myself. And I hope my husband forgives me. Maybe Jesus wants us to, like, pass it on. You know? Forgiveness."

"Oh my God."

"Forgiveness," she repeats.

"This is bananas. I don't want to talk to you anymore."

"Well," she says. "All right. I'll hang up. I just wanted to check in about me telling my husband. And that I hope y'all do okay with the hurricane and everything."

I press end. That time my finger was not involved in the decision. It came from me.

2:19 P.M.

I wonder what eighteen-year-old Ramona would say to Current Me if we were sitting next to each other at the nail salon. Side-by-side with our feet in giant tubs with salt tinting the water blue.

"I like that color," I'd tell her.

She would have picked out a color—canary yellow—without any concern that once her toenails had been painted, the overall effect was rigor mortis. The shade would have called to her as she stood in front of the rainbow display of bottles lined up on glass shelves.

"Thanks," she'd say.

Me, I'd be holding three different hues in the burgundy family. I'd spend some time analyzing whether or not the metallic polish chips more easily. Because who the hell knows when I'll have time to get my nails done again.

College freshman Ramona wouldn't compliment my color because she'd think it was boring. Kinda corporate. At that point in our lives we were honest about things. Still had nice manners, though.

She'd be bare-faced, in paint-splattered overalls with her long brown hair piled high in a messy bun, her hands on her lap, apologizing to the nail technician about her spiky legs and her tiny pinky toenails.

"It's hard to paint them," she'd say. "I'm so sorry. They're like Chiclets."

My legs would be spiky, too, but for other reasons. We'd both find the smell of formaldehyde gnarly and comforting.

She would fidget with the settings on the massage chair and giggle when they were too strong, propelling her forward.

"Whoa, Nelly," she'd say.

She'd give up on the massage chair and look around the salon, her eyes taking in the colors, the people, the drama on the Telemundo on the television. Eighteen-year-old Me didn't have a phone. She'd notice the rotting panel on the ceiling grid. She'd wonder what the gypsum squares would look like if you painted over them.

I'd lean back into the massage chair, which I don't try to master anymore because I never figured it out. I'd roll up the cuffs of my work pants and judge the way they pinch my calves. I'd pull up my calendar on my phone. I'd run through what I should be getting done during this time and feel guilty I wasn't achieving anything. There's always someone to text. Something to buy. Someone to respond to. Something to double-check.

In the massage chair to my left, eighteen-year-old Ramona would think, that lady needs to relax. Slow down. Live in the moment. Stop letting that wee mobile computer control her mind.

And I'd feel jealous of her thick hair and accidentally toned arms. Not her eyebrows—mine are better now. I'd remember how at that age everything seemed possible and at the same time overwhelming. Sometimes a little lonely.

Telepathically, I'd explain, everything seems so simple to you, younger me. You think you know everything. Just wait. We fall in love. And it gets complicated.

That sounds awesome, she'd say, I've been hoping that would happen.

It is, and it isn't. It's hard to remember who you are when you love other people so fiercely. I miss you.

We would both worry that we tipped too little or too much. We'd hobble out of the salon in the free paper-thin flip-flops with the cotton swabs still separating our toes. We'd smudge the polish on the middle toe on the right foot, creating ripples along the top corner of the toenail. Which freeze when they dry like a tiny curtain moved to the side.

2:24 P.M.

"Ooooh!" I squeal and twist the volume button to the right. The faint sounds of finger symbols, now turned up, usher in the opening groove of "Raspberry Beret."

Bailey humors me. "What?"

"This is one of Prince's best songs."

"Cool," he says.

"Come on. I *know* you've heard this one."

"I can't say I have."

"You're messing with me!"

"Mrs. Arnold, I'm sixteen. How in the world would I know the songs on your lite rock station?"

"It's not lite rock," I sniff. "It's eighties music. There's a difference."

"If you say so."

"Just listen."

"Listening," he says and dutifully lowers his headphones.

"So, in the video—"

"Mrs. Arnold, how am I supposed to hear the song if you're talking over it?"

"Okay, you're right."

I am quiet for the first verse. *That's when I saw her, oooh! I saw her. She walked in through the out door.* Then the chorus, which still makes me want to break out in dance incorporating exaggerated shoulder movements.

"In the video," I continue, "Prince is wearing a sky blue suit with clouds on it and he's at this big party where the musicians are standing on circle stages. Everyone else is wearing rainbow colors and pirate shirts and dancing below them in this awesome choreography."

"You're really selling it."

"Shut up, it was cool," I tell him, but I'm laughing, now. "Cheesy things were okay then."

"If you say so."

"So Prince climbs up on his stage and a girl hands him the guitar. Then there's a moment with her when he gives her a look like, well, thank you, and we think she's the one he's singing about. The one with the raspberry beret."

"The kind you find in a secondhand store."

I thump my palms on the steering wheel. "Exactly!"

"Is he saying the hat or the girl," Bailey says, "is the kind you find in the secondhand store?"

"Maybe both."

"All right," Bailey says. "Okay."

"Now Prince has his guitar on the circle stage, he starts to play and then he coughs."

"Because he was sparking up before the show?"

"Possibly. Well, actually I don't think Prince did a lot of drugs. Before the fentanyl. Maybe he has a bug. Like a sore throat. I don't actually know why he coughs."

"Maybe he's allergic to the raspberry beret."

"He's not the one wearing it. Are you listening? Anyway, he coughs and we're like, is he okay? Is he going to perform?"

"I bet he does."

I nod. "He does. The background blends with the musicians. We see that effect all the time now on TV but when that video came out, it was really crazy. It's like the band's performance fuses together with a cartoon version telling the story about meeting the girl and going to the farm and the barn and the magic that happens after that."

"The magic?"

"You know. It's all this symbiotic joy and there's colors and sky. I remember when I saw that video, I knew—I just knew what I wanted to be."

"A singer?"

"No."

"A guitarist?"

"No. I wanted to be at Prince's party."

11

YOU ARE WEARING
DOWN MY BATTERY

3:02 P.M.

I steer the minivan down the gravel road to the modest yellow ranch on the water where my mother lives.

This is not the house where I was raised. My little brother and I grew up in a different ranch on a cul-de-sac in Pike Creek, Delaware, a midcentury three bedroom with a Jack and Jill bathroom he made disgusting and a detached garage with my dad's tools hung up on pegs in neat rows.

This one—this is the dream house Mom and Dad bought after my father retired so they could enjoy their twilight years closer to their grands. It was a good idea, a dump they were going to fix up, a smart investment. No more shoveling snow. Time to sit on the dock in Adirondack chairs, drink Tom Collinses, and wave to dolphins. Then Dad died—a stroke, and then cancer— and nobody touched the house. It's still a dump.

As we rumble up the lane, Alex wonders if Gigi has popsicles.

"Son. I don't know if Grandma has power."

I squint through the live oaks and I see she appears to. One lamp shines through thick blinds in the living room and it looks like one of her bathroom lights is on. As we get closer to the house, the wind grows stronger and the branches shake the leaves like pom-poms. Hurricane Matthew doesn't seem like an obtuse idea anymore. He's real and he's coming.

We spill out of the car and my kids run up an overgrown tabby path to my mother's door. Bailey trails behind them, probably bracing himself for whatever bizarre situation I'm going to subject him to. I need to visit the facilities. My phone tells me I have three missed calls from Desmond, two texts from Christopher, and one from Nicole.

At Mom's front step, we stand in a cluster temporarily shielded from the wind. Three brisk knocks, seven attempts from Nanette to ring the doorbell—the tip of her little index finger white from pressing down extra hard—despite the fact it doesn't work. Behind the door we hear Peyton Manning growl and his nails on the parquet floor. What's taking so long? I have to pee like a racehorse.

Now we hear the dead bolt turning and my mother's voice: "I've got a loaded rifle so just back away."

"Mom!"

Instinctively I plant my body between the door and the children. We freeze like a group of mannequins in the storeroom of Belk. I open my mouth to yelp something—nothing comes. Now my mother cracks open the door, leaving the brass chain in place, her eyes above it, accusatory.

She's surprised. "Monie?"

The kids jump up and down. "Gigi!"

"You almost gave me a heart attack," she says. "I could've sworn you were looters." She ushers us into the small foyer and presses the door closed behind us. "What are you doing here? There's a hurricane coming."

Peyton Manning utters a feeble bark and Mom's cat weaves in and out of her legs. The kids offer Mom limp hugs and push past her, heading, I assume, to the kitchen for unlimited sugar-laced snacks or the guest room to play with my brother's ancient Legos and Matchbox cars.

"We gave *you* a heart attack," I repeat, my own pulse still speeding from the threat on my life. "Didn't you see my car?"

"I didn't check out the vehicle. I just thought, looters."

"Mom. That was bananas. And to answer your question, we came back to save you."

We stand across from each other in a face-off, my heart still racing from seeing the gun and my mother noticeably flustered by the surprise visitors. I don't need an extra person to parent but if the woman who gave birth to me continues to make stupid decisions, I will throw her on the pile. At least she's potty-trained, or used to be.

"Huh," she says. "And who the hell is this?"

"This is Bailey. He's our neighbor. We kidnapped him."

"She's joking, Mrs. Arnold's mom," Bailey says. "They gave me a ride."

"Into the eye of a storm? With friends like these, who needs friends?" Mom says. "And call me Gigi."

I scurry past her into the green-and-pink tiled powder room, where I drain a morning's worth of Venti medium light blend and a 20 oz. Diet Dr Pepper. I emerge to find Alex and Nanette screeching in the guest room while Mom and Bailey square off in the kitchen.

"So, you're in eleventh grade?" she says. "At Jenkins?"

"Yup," Bailey says.

"What's your favorite subject?"

"Math."

"What kind of sport do you play?"

"Track and field."

"Got any other hobbies?"

"Coding."

"What in the world is coding?"

"Like, designing websites?"

"Oh," she says. "That's pretty smart stuff."

"I'm not that good yet. I took an intro class. I get to take another one next year."

"Huh," Mom says.

"I like your house."

"We'll see if it's still here tomorrow."

"I think it will be," Bailey says.

"Yeah?"

"I like how"—Bailey gestures to the window—"you can see the waves."

Usually there are no waves. Today the water is slate gray with whitecaps. When I drop my purse on the green linoleum counter, Mom and Bailey look up like I'm interrupting.

"Does your crew want hot dogs?" Mom asks me.

"No, thanks," I tell her, but then I see how Bailey's face lights up, so I edit: "Maybe. Maybe the kids want one, thanks."

"I'll put a bunch in the toaster oven," Mom says. "I can't remember if I have ketchup."

"I didn't know," I say. "That you had a gun."

"Oh, well, yeah."

"Oh, well, yeah? I thought you gave away that stuff after Daddy died."

"I hung on to the one pistol," Mom says. "I gave the rest to a bunch of my Alzheimer's buddies from the club."

"Not funny."

"Oh, come on. Ramona. You gotta loosen up."

"About you having a loaded gun in a house where I have dropped my children a minimum of eighty-seven times, without me being here? Are you kidding me?"

"Ramona," she says. "I keep it in a safe. I'm a Southerner, I'm not an asshole."

I'm still pissed. Even though my parents owned firearms when I was growing up in Delaware. Even though I'm used to the gun culture in South Georgia now, revolvers in the glove compartment, pink pistols on your fifth birthday, Fourth of July celebrations where you guess Is-That-a-Bottle-Rocket-or-Someone-Firing-Bullets-in-The-Sky. Children shooting themselves and each other in the news.

"After lunch," I tell my mother, as if I can reclaim power somehow, "we're taking you back to my house."

My mother, Adelaide, is a force, all one hundred and fifteen pounds of her. She won't leave the house without eyelashes coated with mascara and Estée Lauder White Linen dabbed at the back of her neck and inside of her wrists. Now she plants her manicured hands, fingernails painted bright coral, on her hips, cloaked in her navy track pants, in a defiant stance.

"Says who?" she says.

"Come on. I will indulge you being a stubborn fool about certain issues but not this one."

"I will accompany you to the mainland," she says, pursing her lips. "If and only if we can take my fur babies."

"We'll take your damn fur babies. If they don't eat our guinea pig. But we better head out soon because Matthew is going to huff and puff and blow your house down."

"All right," she says, then, in a softer tone, "You're sweet to come back, cookie."

"I'm an idiot to."

"Where the hell is Desmond?" Mom asks me. I feel a drop of sweat roll from my bra hook down to my belly button.

"He's with a friend," Bailey explains, "in Atlanta."

"Instead of with his family?" Mom asks, eyebrow raised. "During a natural disaster."

"It's a long story, Mom." I move my eyes to the water.

"I've got time," she says.

Again, I feel tempted to tell her about Desmond and Sarah Ellen. I could use someone on my side. Someone to tell me what to do. What is the grown-up version of my mother marching over to Shoshanna's house and demanding the return of Carmen, my stuffed elephant? I feel a sinking feeling upon the realization there's no way my mother can get me out of this one.

"We don't, though. We should get off this island. Alex, Nanette. Gigi's making hot dogs. Nanny, let's try to go potty here while we can still flush. Then we'll head out."

"No!" Nanette yells.

"Fuck me," I mutter under my breath. I walk down the shag-carpeted hall past framed photos of me and my brother, me in fourth grade with shiny neat braids, me at my high school graduation, me and Desmond at our wedding, lifting champagne glasses. Also on the wall: an abstract portrait I painted of my father the summer before I graduated from college. I've never been good at faces but I got something right about his eyes. When he laughed he would tip his head back and they disappeared into half-moons.

Before I was a project manager I was a graphic designer. Before I was a graphic designer I was a painter. Before that, Mom and Dad took my brother and me to the Ground Round for dinner sometimes. On the drive home I sat in the backseat with my brother, pressed my cheek against the window and followed the electrical lines as they swooped from one to the other.

I tried to draw them when we got home. In a conference my second grade teacher asked Adelaide why I drew transmission towers and dumpsters instead of houses and rainbows. And why they were upside down. I held my mother's hand in my mittened one as we walked from the school to our station wagon in the parking lot. I told her, it wasn't upside down! It was reflected in a puddle.

I know, cookie, she said.

In high school I pedaled on my longboard to school or to my friend Brenna's house under the power lines and I'd imagine I was skiing along them. I started to put them on paper playing with different tools: pencil, chalk, paint, clay.

There was something beautiful to me about ugly modern things juxtaposed with nature. I liked to play with angles and colors, to layer textures on top of each other, to use a vibrant pink for a building which in real life was drab and brown. I loved to turn an industrial landscape upside down, add imaginary strings overlapping or intersecting power lines.

My college professor told me if you feel inspired by an idea try to make four or six pieces from that feeling. Produce a litter, she said. Also, not everything has to be important, not all your work will be good, there is value in making mistakes. She used to bring undercooked zucchini bread she made to the studio and asked me if I could tell she had drawn on her eyebrows. I lied and said they looked natural. When I read in an alumni newsletter that she passed away I felt a door slam shut somewhere inside me.

I don't miss painting. I'm not resisting a desire burning under my skin to create; sitting at a computer doesn't feel like wearing a straitjacket. When I watch *Wonder Pets!* with my chin resting on the crown of Nanette's head I don't feel like leaping from the couch and making a mural on the wall with whatever materials I can find: crayons, apple juice, avocados.

What I do miss, maybe: the way making art made me feel—capable, resourceful, peaceful.

Without art, I feel like I can't make anything happen. Like I can't make something beautiful.

3:30 P.M.

On the phone Desmond is incredulous.

"You went back?" he says.

"I came back."

"Monie, what the hell?"

"Guess what?" I tell him. "I don't have to consider your opinion anymore. That ended when you broke a vow in our marriage. The only person you have to thank is yourself. I don't have to call you. I did because I'm a nice person and I thought if I call you back maybe you will quit bugging me because it stresses me out and I have no idea how long I'm going to have battery or service."

As I walk toward the water, the wind tosses a plastic Gatorade bottle across my mother's gravel driveway. The smell of the marsh is powerful today. It's like Matthew is pulling up all the salt from the water and hurling it at my face.

"Ramona," he says.

"You are wearing down my battery."

"You were safe and sound in Augusta and you drove back for Gigi."

"I did," I tell him. I sit down crisscross applesauce on my

mother's dock. "She wouldn't go because of the animals and I couldn't leave her here by herself."

"Gigi made a terrible decision," Desmond says. "That house is made of popsicle sticks. Still, I can't believe you evacuated and then came back."

"It's called love. Something I thought you understood but apparently you do not. By the way, tell your sidepiece to stop calling me."

"What?"

"Sarah Ellen. She called me. Twice."

"She called you?" Desmond repeats.

"Don't worry," I snap. "She didn't tell me anything juicy or more devastating than the crap I already know."

"This sucks," Des says. "This sucks so much."

"It does."

"I hate that I hurt you so bad."

"Badly. You really, really, really did. I can't imagine not feeling like this. Listen, I gotta go. I need to get everyone back to midtown."

"Wait." It's hard to hear him over the wind. "Don't hang up."

"Des. We're fine. Not you and me. The kids and I will be fine."

"All right," he says.

I hang up on him. I think he was starting to say he loves me but it got cut off. A gust of wind blows my clothing sideways, the laces on my sneakers reach toward the neighbor's dock. Sharp ripples dance in the creek and the floating dock bobs up and down. On the swell of my right ankle there are imprints of the grains of the wood.

I stand up and my legs feel sore. I have to be strong enough for everyone else. I tell myself I am and squash any tiny voices of doubt.

2012

Desmond's cousin Bridget invited us to a Halloween party. I like Bridget although her husband, Sammy, has the personality of cardboard. She has a snort I find endearing—it escapes when she lets her guard down—and they live on Coffee Bluff in a crowded split-level where they consistently deliver Bloody Marys to friends around a firepit. Bridget's toddler, Lucas, is six months older than Alex, and his birthday was near Halloween, so it was a combo party.

The kids looked adorable. I saw two toddlers dressed as crayons—one I'd classify as red-orange and the other one more of a violet—Thomas the Tank Engine, a bat, an octopus, and two Disney Princesses. They darted around Bridget's yard against a backdrop of jack-o'-lanterns and skeletons, skin flushed under polyester layers on a hotter than usual October day.

We, the Arnolds, had a family costume. Pre-Nanette, Desmond, Alex, and I were attending the party as the family from the film *Raising Arizona*. For this look Des had been growing a mustache—with patchy results—and wore a Hawaiian shirt I recognized from the spring luau party in 1999, slightly snug these days. As Edwina I sported a black hat and plastic badge from a sexy policewoman costume I snatched up from Walmart with a black button-down and pants. And Alex? For

Nathan Junior he wore a diaper, sneakers, and three gallons of bug spray.

We were proud of our costumes. We took a thousand pics of ourselves before we left the house. The reason for that number is because toddlers don't like to stop moving or look at the camera. They, do, however, enjoy both partial and full nudity.

It was divine out. On the bluff the water stretched out gold and when the breeze hit the green grass, it swayed. When we pulled up we set Alex loose with his plastic jack-o'-lantern in his hand. I speed-walked after him with a stuffed gift bag for Lucas. Hugs for everyone.

Hey, y'all. Oh, you dressed up, too? How's your Dad? What are you—oh, there's Des, I get it, I love that movie. You look great. Thanks for having us. You want a beer? We're going to do cake in about a half an hour. What has Nic Cage done recently? Well, there was much debate between whether to go as Jasmine or Belle, so I threw up my hands, to hell with it, just get in the car, kid. Y'all are too funny.

Desmond's mom was there—Cindy. I knew she was coming and that she had a full dance card with the friends she missed since she'd moved to Florida. Unlikely we'd earn a time slot. She greeted us with dainty hugs and delivered the predictable response to our costume, *that's ridiculous*, and *someone put some clothes on my grandson for the love of God*. Half-joking, half-not. I expected nothing less of my mother-in-law. My parents were there, too—sweet of Bridget to include them. Adelaide wore a tiny violet witch hat clipped into her hair and Dad held her hand. He got so thin at the end. They didn't stay long.

Sweaty in my police uniform, I was having fun, working my

way through a Coors Light wrapped in a Publix koozie, sucking a Tootsie Roll Pop my son discarded after two licks. I was sitting on a canvas lawn chair with Alex on my lap, the two of us trying to transfer confetti cake from the fork into his mouth. His curls tickled my chin. My right foot fell asleep so I wiggled it in circles to bring it back to life.

Mom, can I get you something, Desmond asked Cindy.

I'd love a chardonnay, honey, Cindy said, and she turned back to the couple she was talking to, which included a jolly man in suspenders who didn't realize Desmond was her kid but apparently knew him from one of Des's projects.

He said, that's your son? Hell of a roofer.

Desmond had returned to the fire and he was about to tap Cindy on the shoulder, probably to point out, *no chardonnay, Mom, how about pinot grigio or a beer?*

Oh, my son's not a roofer, Cindy told the man. He's in grad school for historic preservation.

Um.

Did anyone hear that? Yes, Desmond took three semesters of classes at SCAD for his master's degree in Historic Preservation. But he stopped. Because of money, because of time, because he had a family. Cindy's lie was awkward because it suggested both that Des was on a career path he'd most likely abandoned and being a roofer wasn't good enough.

My mistake, the man said.

There was Desmond, standing behind his mother, about to tap her on the shoulder. If you blinked you would've missed it: Desmond's face fell in a moment of grief. The next second it was gone.

And Desmond, the happy-go-lucky man I married, who always has a grin and a goofy comment for every occasion, was back.

Mom, got a second choice?

I'm not sure if Cindy realized Desmond heard her. I don't know her well enough to detect the difference between her tones. I do know she's a seasoned professional at changing the subject when things get sticky.

Yes, this is my boy, Desmond, and that's his boy, if you can believe it, the one that's practically nude over there.

The couple turned to us and I waved with Alex's fork.

Trick or treat, Alex said. *Twick o' tweet.*

Ramona, Cindy said. He's starting to get bit, did you see those gashes near his ankle? If y'all didn't bring any extra clothes, I'm sure Bridget will loan you some.

Desmond found my eyes. Now his expression was one I knew— that, *isn't she a piece of work but what are you going to do* look.

Alex did have a bug bite on his ankle and I felt defensive. I was new to feeling like my parenting choices were constantly being judged by other women. It hit harder coming from my own mother than Desmond's, because despite her bullishness, I consider Adelaide a great mom. So I care—probably too much— about my mother's opinion. Desmond's mother excels at pairing the perfect earrings with her Lilly Pulitzer shift dress yet never learned how to hug with her whole body.

I sucked down the rest of my Coors Light. Alex started to glaze over. He let his head fall to my chest, his bottom in the nook of my elbow, and I leaned back in the chair and tried to squeeze five more minutes of peace from the afternoon.

As the light retreated from Coffee Bluff the expressions on the melting jack-o'-lanterns glowed brighter: mischievous, surprised, menacing, disappointed. That one stood out. The most powerful evil that Halloween: unmet expectations.

On the ride home we caught the tail end of "I Wanna Be Your Lover" and Alex didn't fight sleep in the car seat—he let himself fade. My husband and I didn't mention his mother's comment. Des was quiet, though. He'd unbuttoned his Hawaiian shirt, now he looked even more H. I. McDunnough with a faded Hanes undershirt peeking out. I tried to cheer him up by hinting we should get naked when we got back home. That seemed to help, or I could see the beginning of a grin below his Halloween mustache. I told him if he wanted I could wear my Walmart police hat and nothing else.

I need a baby, Hi, I said.

There it was. I saw his smile coming back. He reached for my knee and it was a thank you.

We say we conceived Nanette on that night. If I were an organized person who kept track of her period and grocery apps on her phone and Band-Aids in her purse for emergencies, I might know the exact day we made Nanette.

For now we'll say it was that night and leave it at that.

4:37 P.M.

"My teachers probably miss me," Nanette announces. My kids race Hot Wheels cars around the dusty braided wool rug in my mother's living room and Bailey hovers over his charging phone while Mom and I half-ass hurricane proof her house.

We duct tape rotting plywood from Mom's shed over the windows facing the water. We stack lime-green plastic ottoman chairs on top of each other and carry them to the storage shed. We dump Mom's produce, if you can call it that, into a lavender scented Febreze garbage bag and place salvageable snacks—cold cuts, pickles, bacon, string cheese, boxed wine—into a cooler.

"This feels familiar," I tell her. "Like déjà vu. Oh, wait, because I did all of it at my house."

"Nobody asked you to come back," Mom says. As the wind blows her hair across her face, I notice how thin it is, and I see the skin hanging off the back of her arms as she clutches a garbage bag in each hand.

"You're right," I say, because she is.

"If you ask me," she starts, and in my head I retort, *I didn't,* "we should all be more worried about the election than this storm. Did you watch that circus that was the debate last Tuesday?"

Truth. I had the channel on though I was trying to pay bills online at the same time and I vaguely remember Donald Trump gripping the podium and repeating the word, "wrong," while Hillary bristled in a red suit.

"Some of it."

My mother reaches into a coop with both hands, clutches a reddish chicken with a black face, coos *there, there, Matilda,* and plunges the bird into a separate cage. She repeats this process with the other two until three of them are crammed in a smaller enclosure and not happy about it. Their clucks are screechy and panicked.

"The man knows who he appeals to," she says.

"Mom. He's not going to win."

"Who is going to vote for him."

"You don't need to get worked up for no reason—he won't win! He's a reality show star. And orange."

"You don't know conservative voters like I do! Or old people. Usually the same thing," she says, picking up the crate of chickens. "Believe me. It's a clear and present danger. I went to lunch with Susan at the Yacht Club last week? Had a niçoise salad that was to die for, by the way. Anyway, you're not going to believe this but people have Trump signs on their boats."

It's not that I'm *not* concerned. Or repulsed. It's just—I've got other fish to fry. Not bigger ones, just fish right in front of me, or currently, chickens.

In the storage shed I stack plastic boxes on top of each other and then we place the wire crate on top of those. I'm not sure if that's sturdy or high enough so I push the cage against the wall of the shed. One of the chickens pecks at me and I yelp and pull my hand back. I wedge my mother's artificial Christmas tree against the crate as an additional buttress.

We dump Mom's cooler into the back of my van, where she meets Clarence Thomas, and devise a strategy to transfer him to the way-back so he'll enjoy a separate address from Mom's fur babies and hopefully avoid murder. He does look like a delicious snack for an anxious cat or dog.

Lightbulb: If I bring back the corpse of the class pet, saying, *I'm so sorry about that,* will it change the conversation from, that's the woman whose husband slept with Sarah Ellen to that's the lady who killed Clarence Thomas? Don Draper said, if you don't like what people are saying, change the conversation.

We're almost ready, or ready as we'll ever be. I need to clean up the hot dogs and gather my troops together. My mother holds open the screen door for me.

"Seriously," she says. "Where's your brawny husband when we need him?"

"Not here, obviously."

"What's going on with you two?"

"Nothing."

"Ramona."

"Okay, not nothing. Something. Don't worry about it."

"Mommy," Nanette calls from down the hall, and my heart sinks because I know what she's about to tell me. "I had an accident."

"All right. Is it number one or two?"

A pause. Through the walls I sense her evaluating the situation.

"Just pee pee," she says. "But it's on my unders. They're all wet." She lets out a cry of anguish.

"It's okay, sweetie," I call out, and follow her voice to the bathroom, where she stands in the middle, the sides of her mouth turning down, a dark stain covering the front of her Little Pony leggings.

She starts to sniffle. "My pants are wet, too."

"It's okay," I tell Nanette. "We'll get to the potty next time. I know you can do it, I just know it."

"I don't get an Oreo when I have accidents."

"Well? No, but that gives you something to work on." I shimmy her pants down her legs and her wet underwear, she leans on me to step out of them. "It's good to have goals."

I have clean pants for Nanette in the van. That seems too far right now. Instead I recall a pair of Alex's jammies we used to keep at Mom's house. I stomp into the guest room and slide open a drawer in my brother's old dresser where I find a basket of Zaxby's salad dressing. Nope. The next one—score—I pull out a pair of red briefs and Carter's pajama pants.

"Here we go," I say, bustling back into the room, wrangling the underwear and then pants up and over Nanette's bottom. "These are so cool!"

She looks down. "They have soccer on them."

"You bet!"

"But they're too long," she says, and from her voice I sense she's on the edge of another tantrum if I don't think fast.

"We can fix that," I tell her, and I tuck the hem of one leg of the pants to make an eighties tapered cuff. "Now they are even cooler! And you know, girls play soccer. Actually the US women's team is way better than the dudes'."

Despite her dubious expression—pursed lips, furrowed brow—the sniffling slows down.

"Okay," she says.

"Feel better?" I ask her. She nods, and I say, "Give Mommy a hug." Her body is warm and she smells like my kid. And still a little bit like urine.

Alex is ready for the next adventure: "You guys, can we go?"

"As soon as you two pick up all the cars from the racetrack and put them back into the box," I say.

The kids scramble to action, including Bailey—bless you, child—and I realize the futility of sticking to my rules So My Kids

Don't Grow Up To Be Entitled Pricks in the face of a natural disaster. As if it makes a difference if the cars are scattered on the ground or placed in a box when Hurricane Matthew hurls himself at this dilapidated ranch.

Still: "There's some under the sofa. See them? I spy a purple Camaro with a thunderbolt on the side."

You've got to stand for something.

Mom chases the cat into the crate, and he yowls as if this is the least dignified part of the day, when I'm sure it will get much worse for all of us. I click the cooler shut and nudge my trio of children out the front door onto the gravel sidewalk, while Mom coaxes Peyton Manning outside, encouraging him to "do his business," before locking the dead bolt behind her. The dog ambles across uneven grass.

The kids squeal and shout as they charge through gusts of wind to the car. Nanette bows her head of red curls forging forward in saggy pajama pants. Miraculously, all five of us are in the car, buckled in. The cat is still mewing, though less urgently, in her kennel in the far back with Bailey, and Peyton Manning pants between Alex and Nanette's car seat, thwacking his tail against the second row.

"Okay!" I say.

"We're off!" Mom says, tugging the seat belt across her chest and securing it with a click. "Like a dirty shirt!"

"Like Nanette's pee pee pants," Alex says, giggling.

"Alex," I scold, quickly, an effort to squash the sentiment before Nanette realizes she's been insulted. Then, cheerful Mom voice: "See you, Wilmington Island, we're headed to higher ground!"

"Take it sleazy!" says Alex.

I turn the ignition. The car starts, then every single warning light comes on—oil change, check engine, scary other ones I don't even know what they mean, before the van makes a groan and everything goes dark.

A chunky branch crackles and falls in front of us, landing on my mother's hedges.

Holy Mary, Mother of God.

My car is dead.

12

OFF THE CHAIN

5:40 P.M.

Breathing in, breathing out.

"It's fine," I say.

"The car?" Mom asks. "Or the situation?"

"Both. No, the situation. The car is a piece of shit. But I can't worry about that right now."

"Mommy," says Alex, "not a nice word!"

"I know, honey. I'm sorry. That's what happens when I hang out with your grandmother."

"Hey, now," Mom says.

"Okay." My mind is racing, Usain Bolt in yellow Pumas. "All we have to do is get our crew home. This is like a word problem on a math test. We've got five people and three animals. The house is eight miles away. We're not talking a different state, here."

"But Mrs. Arnold, we don't have a car," says Bailey.

"We'll call an Uber," I tell him.

"We can't all fit in a regular-size car," Mom says.

"We'll get an Uber XL," I explain. As the words emerge from my mouth, I realize there are maybe seven Uber cars in Savannah, and the chances of finding an Uber XL driver hanging around during a hurricane are probably slim.

"Okay," Mom says, and after a pause: "What are you waiting for, call him!"

"It's not a person, it's an app."

"Oh, an app," she says.

I release a big sigh. "There's not going to be an Uber. Maybe we could call a taxi company? Take two cabs? Do you have any cash?"

"I have, like, seven dollars," Bailey says.

"Hell, we just need a car, Ramona," Mom says. "Take the kids in my Civic and then come back for me and the animals."

"Two trips? Mom. I can't leave them at our house without an adult. Look around you! The storm is here!"

In the passenger's seat my mother raises her eyebrows and I realize my voice is getting shrill. That whole protect the kids by remaining calm thing—I'm not a natural.

"Is the car broken, Mommy?" Alex asks.

"Looks like it," Bailey says. "The check engine light has been on all the way going to Augusta and back."

It's irritating having an older kid catch on to things when I'm used to issuing sweeping generalizations and lies to smaller people who believe them.

"Let's go next door and borrow Jerry's," Mom says.

"Your neighbor?"

"Yeah," Mom says. "He has two trucks and a van. I have no idea why an old man needs three semi-functioning cars but he's got 'em."

"He's probably not there," I tell her. "Mandatory evacuation and everything."

"He's there. He's having a party."

"How do you know?"

"Because we have relations, honey," she says.

"Mom!"

"Or, did. It's been a while because he's mad at me for throwing his Trump/Pence sign into his pool."

Oh, hell to the no. I do not have experience with my mother dating people, let alone sleeping with them. And Jerry? A bachelor pushing eighty who talks to shrimp more than people and as it turns out, supports Donald Trump?

"That's so gnarly," I say.

"You're gnarly," she snaps. "I deserve a life."

"You do, Mom, absolutely. Also, ew."

"What's gnarly?" Alex asks from the backseat. "Jerry's party?"

"Yes. Jerry has some gnarly friends," Mom says.

"Do they eat their boogers?" Alex asks.

"Hold up," I turn around. "*You* eat your boogers."

"Not anymore," Alex says.

"Well," I say. "I guess it's as good a plan as any." I let go of the keys, which I didn't realize I've been gripping fiercely, as if I could spark the engine from the strength of my fingers. "Come on, team. Let's visit Gigi's neighbor and see if we can get a lift."

"Just warning you," Mom says, "things might be weird."

I open my door. "As opposed to anything else that happened today?"

"Okay, weirder."

6:17 P.M.

In order to get to Jerry's house, we have to trudge down the gravel drive to Wilmington Island Road because Jerry has a long, wooden fence, most likely to be blown over in an hour, separating his property from my mother's. Which makes me wonder how their trysts occurred, mainly if my mother made this Coastal Walk of Shame or if she scrambled over the rocks that buffer the water along the coast. It's awkward to dwell upon and you're sure as shit I'm doing it.

Mom and Jerry. It makes sense now. How she brought him up in every other phone conversation. That phase this summer where she started wearing a bright red lipstick that I'm certain if I wore she'd say I look like a streetwalker. That time she declined dinner with us at Sandfly Bar-B-Q because she said she was waiting on Comcast.

We bring Peyton Manning on our quest because the cat and the guinea pig are safely separate in my Toyota. My kids sprint down the path, shouting into the wind, while Bailey trails along with Mom and me. I can see Nanette's right pajama cuff is starting to unroll and I worry she might trip over it.

At Jerry's mailbox, Mom says, "Let's grab this." She snatches a stack of envelopes and a circular for Kroger, and slams the mailbox shut with a bang.

"Picking up his mail, huh?" I say.

"Oh, shut up," Mom says.

"Shut up isn't nice, Gigi," says Alex.

"You're right, Alex," I say.

"Well, I'm sorry. Don't make it into something bigger than it is, Ramona."

"I'm just saying"—I shrug my shoulders, I can't help it, I feel a grin—"picking up mail is a little more than an arrangement."

I am just as annoying as Desmond. My mother rolls her eyes. The wind snatches the newsprint ad from her hand and wraps it around the trunk of a palm tree. As we close in on Jerry's house we see no less than fifteen cars parked on the grass.

"Who are these people?"

"Neighbors," Mom says.

"Like, the whole island?"

"Most people stay, cookie," Mom says.

"They shouldn't! We were evacuated for a reason!"

"Oh, Ramona," Mom says. "You didn't used to have so many rules. That was your brother. You were my free spirit."

"Silly me. I'm just trying to keep my kids alive during a raging tempest."

"And so sensitive," Mom says.

6:38 P.M.

I deposit Nanette's car seat on a step next to a coiled green garden hose. We don't ring Jerry's doorbell—we just walk in through the side entrance. Don't think I didn't make a note of that.

Inside, we pass a galley kitchen with laminate counters piled with Coors Light boxes, a cutting board with frayed limes, Bud Light cans lining the windowsill above the sink. Down a dark hall we find Jerry's living room, where we're greeted with the smell of weed and the sounds of Bob Seger.

Mom strolls into the thick of it, a sunken den with faux wood panel walls and eggplant shag carpet. If there's a theme to Jerry's decor it's fish—he's got fish lamps and fish art and fish freaking everywhere. People mill about, women and men of all ages, crusty bearded guys, drinking and smoking and talking and cutting up.

Now my kids cling to me. Bailey scrutinizes the situation and I wonder if he's more or less aware of substances than I was at his age. Does he recognize the smell of marijuana? There are also intriguing scents for Peyton Manning, who sniffs an abandoned plate of celery sticks next to a puddle of ranch dressing.

I'm sensing this gathering isn't age appropriate for my posse.

"Mom," I hiss, "can we find Jerry?"

"I'm on it," she says.

"Hey, Adelaide," says a tanned man I recognize as the Captain, who used to come to Mom and Dad's oyster roasts before Dad got sick. I'm not sure if he actually has any naval experience. He's always been the Captain with crinkly blue eyes and a thick head of white hair supporting that moniker.

"Hey, Cap." Mom gives him a peck on the cheek. "How are you?"

"Can't complain," says the Captain. "Might be a hell of a

storm, though. This thing's gonna blow harder than a hooker at a truck stop."

That's just great.

"It might," says Mom.

"I see you got your crew today," says the Captain.

Cap smells like he uses Jack Daniel's for cologne. I offer a feeble smile. Nanette digs her head into the outside of my left thigh, she's exhausted, and Alex opens his mouth for a giant yawn, exposing his indigo-tinged tongue from the blue raspberry Jolly Rancher he nabbed from my mother's candy bowl.

"It takes a village," Mom says. "Where the hell is Jerry?"

"Ventured out for reinforcements," says the Captain.

"Huh?" says Mom.

"Tequila."

"Oh," Mom says. "Shoot. We were hoping to borrow his van."

"Won't be long," Cap says. "Y'all stick around and have a drink. Someone brought fried chicken, not sure if there's any left."

Mom looks back at me and I shrug. At this point, what else could I do in front of my innocent children and the neighbor kid? Let's see, besides driving them away from a hurricane and then right back into it, I've already lied to them about their father, multiple times. I encouraged them to decimate the snack room at my office. I cleared out all the breakfast meats of my thoughtful gay friends. I disregarded a policeman's orders and sped. I exposed them to the vocabulary and antics of my mother at gun point.

"Fine, whatever," I say, "but as soon as Jerry gets back, I'd really feel better getting the kids home."

"Hey, guys," Cap says to Nanette and Alex. "Y'all want to check out Jerry's aquarium? You can toss in Cheetos for his fish."

Bailey looks at the Captain like a bottle rocket just shot out of the man's butt. My kids appear mildly intrigued, could be about Cheetos or marine life, possibly both. Their faces tilt to me for permission.

"Sure. We'll just be here a minute, guys. Nanette, tell Mommy if you need to go potty."

They follow the Captain to a sunroom adjacent to the den. When Mom reappears at my side, I jump and pretend I wasn't biting my nails.

"Here," she says, handing me a Miller Lite. "Or would you prefer a white wine spritzer."

"At this point," I tell her, "I'd huff rubber cement if it would transport me from the crazy of this day."

"You made a joke. Now tell me what's going on with Desmond."

I take a huge breath in and sigh it out. My mother waits for me. Her eyes bore into mine and I blink. It's possible my brain is too fried to concoct even a crappy lie about my husband's whereabouts.

"He cheated. On me. Okay? He cheated. I don't know what's going to happen with us."

Now her expression is one I don't recognize: "Oh."

"So I could use a skosh of kindness about now."

I brace myself for a smart-ass remark. Like, *surprise surprise, I*

always thought he was a snake, or *that's what you get for marrying
a boy from South Georgia,* or *your daddy always thought there was
something off about that kid.*

It doesn't come. Some lady from Tennis League glides over
and pulls on my mother's elbow. *Wasn't it a riot that Coach paired
Suzie and Charlie Pierce in mixed doubles? That match was the
highlight of the season.* The lights flicker off. The crowd buzzes in
minor tones and then cheers when it comes on again and Jerry's
microwave beeps for someone to set the time.

"I went to the Depot to buy a generator," says a tiny white-
haired woman in a green polka dot rain slicker to her friend,
"and the only ones left cost three thousand dollars. I was like,
are you kidding me? Forget it! That's a down payment on a
boat!"

I wasn't planning on telling Mom about Desmond just yet.
Now she knows and for some reason this feels like the point of
no return for my marriage. I look down at the Miller Lite. Hello,
gorgeous.

From this angle I spot the kids' feet. I see Nanette mounting
an espresso La-Z-Boy, the hem of Bailey's track pants, and Alex
standing on his tippy toes. Wandering around, I find one section
of the house that doesn't feature fish décor. To the right of Jerry's
television is a cluster of pictures, the kind with paper cutouts in
circles and rectangles so you can fit a lot of photographs in one
frame.

His kids. His wife. A life on the water. Looks like Jerry is a wid-
ower, too. Inside guilt churns like those oil-based stickers I used
to love, the ones where you press one side and another color

would swirl and darken the other end. Maybe Jerry even has a jerk daughter who judges the choices he makes in his social life.

The Miller Lite is cold and I sink into Jerry's faded chocolate couch for a second. My body is heavy. My phone buzzes.

7:08 P.M.

"I haven't told my husband yet," says Sarah Ellen.

"I don't care."

Her voice is always soft and far away.

"I think I should," she says. "Tell him."

Me: "Fine."

"Soon," she says. "Maybe tonight."

"It's a plan."

I take a swig of my beer.

"I think I've got problems," she says.

I cross my right thigh over my left. "Again. Don't care."

"Since you saw us," she says, "I haven't slept at all. Dave has OxyContin from when he slipped his disk and I took it with us to our friend's house in Alpharetta."

"Well."

I kind of care. Even though I consider myself a woman of many talents, it's becoming difficult to find joy imagining a humiliating demise for this woman, who as it turns out, has as much backbone as one of those neon yellow wind dancers in front of car dealerships.

"I took, like, three," she says, "to help me sleep and then I drank a bottle of Malbec."

"That's probably not your best idea."

"And I was kind of hoping when I woke up that Dave would know—that you would have told him—and he would kick me out or I could go somewhere else for a while."

"I'm not going to tell him, Sarah Ellen," I say.

"I slept for nine hours and when I woke up it was eleven o'clock and Dave had taken the kids to the Legoland at Phipps Plaza."

"Yeah?"

"And I was sad."

"That you missed Legoland."

"That I woke up."

"Sarah Ellen. You're right, you've got problems. You messed up. So did my husband. People are hurt. But you have to woman up to what you did and the consequences. You're a mother. We have to be tougher than everybody."

"You're right," she says. "You're right, you're right."

It's hard to hear her once Cap starts blending what appears to be a daquiri in a blender from the McCarthy era so I increase my volume.

"Sarah Ellen."

"What?"

"Do you love him? My husband?"

"I don't think so," she says. "Do you?"

After a pause the blender resumes a churning and grinding sound and I watch my mother's doubles partner bestow Cap with a plastic yellow lei.

"I think so," I tell Sarah Ellen. "I don't know anymore."

"Oh."

"I'm hanging up now."

"Okay. I just want to say you're a really nice person, Ramona," Sarah Ellen says. "I can see why Des loves you so much."

"That's enough."

"In another situation," she says, "we might be friends."

"Goodbye, Sarah Ellen."

7:14 P.M.

"Ramona?"

"Uh-huh?"

Standing over me is a young man in trim dark jeans and a weathered Pink Floyd T-shirt who knows me. He must be from my office, and I've forgotten his name, dang it, I'm not trying hard enough to be social there. Maybe if I did, I wouldn't resent the millennials and I'd be less disposable.

Those revisions. I've got to send Kenneth something. I can't remember if I texted him about the botched Google Hangouts which will forever linger in my mind as the fart smelled around the world.

The stranger hovers. It would be nice manners to stand up from Jerry's couch, only the cushions suck me down, invisible tentacles wrapping around my thighs.

"Ramona Burkhalter?" he says. "Didn't you go to Cab Calloway?"

I blink at him. "First graduating class."

"Thought so! Josh Tillerson. We were on the paper together."

Josh. Now I remember him. His face is fuller now, he's got a five o'clock shadow, he's grown-up.

"From the paper!"

"That's right, wasn't sure if you'd remember me. You were a senior."

"You were," I start, "like a BMX guy. Josh Tillerson!"

"I wish you didn't remember that."

"And a photographer. They were great," I tell him. "Your photos. What the hell are you doing at Jerry's hurricane party?"

"I live here," he says. "In Savannah, well, for now. I'm teaching for SCAD. It was a summer thing, it was supposed to be just summer, they asked me to stay."

"You live with Jerry?"

"No, I live downtown. He's a friend of the family. Sometimes I help him out with stuff."

"Oh, random," I tell him, nodding my head. "I mean, cool. I don't know."

"That your mom?" I follow his gaze to Adelaide, currently cracking the top off her second Heineken with somebody's sunglasses. I imagine Josh Tillerson has been a witness to the comings and goings of my mother.

"That's my mom, yes."

"You live here, wow. Who would've thought I'd bump into someone I knew from Delaware? I'm the only person here who knows what scrapple is."

"Oh," I tell him. "I'm cool with scrapple staying there. I do, though, live here. In midtown."

"Smart. Your house might be standing tomorrow."

"We'll see."

Josh Tillerson has tattoos winding up his forearms and defined biceps. I believe the kids call those sleeves. I bet he buys Mexican street corn at music festivals and does drugs I've never even heard of.

"It's so great to see you," he says. "We should hang out."

"Yeah," I tell him, in the way people say we should grab coffee and you never do.

"We should."

"You look pretty great."

"You look great also," I echo, "and well rested."

I lift my Miller Lite to my lips again. I try to straighten up on the couch so the overall impression is less Jabba the Hutt. If I remember Josh Tillerson played Dungeons & Dragons and wore a boot after breaking his ankle on a BMX racetrack. The grown-up version seems to be flirting with me. Tired, married, panties from Target me.

I feel a second wind in Jerry's sunken living room. With another gulp of Miller Lite I enter a wormhole in my imagination where I am no longer married. In this fantasy it's not the most horrible thing that could ever, ever happen to me. Rather, it's made me resilient, more compassionate and oddly, more attractive.

I live in a charming rented bungalow, I have most of the custody of my kids, I never worry about the bulge over my waistband, I stay awake reading nonfiction everyone says is great, I start sketching again, I play Prince whenever I want without anybody asking if we can change it to Widespread Panic, I have beachy hair that happens naturally without a curling iron, every now and then I grab dinner with friends during the week. I get to try new restaurants when they open, instead of hearing about the next big thing and one month later that they closed. I sometimes indulge in an extra glass of wine, and I don't worry about being hungover or confusing which kid eats ham instead of turkey on sandwiches or forgetting to sign the permission slip for a field trip to the strawberry farm. I just don't worry about that stuff. On the weekends Des has the children, I sleep late, and then I have wild sex with my lover(s) and I watch whatever I want on TV.

"You ever go paddleboarding?" Josh asks me.

"No," I say, taking another sip of my beer. "I should start."

Totally I should start. What if I'm amazing at paddleboarding? I probably am. There are so many gifts I would never have discovered if this awful thing hadn't happened. I should really thank Sarah Ellen. I have her number in Recent Calls, maybe I will.

"I thought you were a great artist, you know."

I shrug my shoulders. "You're sweet."

"Those cartoons—off the chain."

It's a good thing if something is off the chain, right? Maybe not because it would be terrible if an aggressive dog were off the chain or someone's boat in a hurricane. I bet the weed I'm smelling belongs to Cap and he'll give me some. I visualize Josh Tillerson's tattooed arms around me and I feel a heat wave cross my undercarriage. You know. I've been looking at this all wrong. It's a new beginning. It's the reinvention of Ramona. Is that a hip-hop record? It should be. I'm probably also a fantastic rapper—off the chain.

"I thought you'd be, like, famous in New York," Josh says.

"No, not quite. I painted my kids' room, though. And I work with graphic designers."

"Digital art?"

"More like, branding for clients?"

"Oh, that's cool."

I spill a little beer on my jeans and dab it with the bottom of my shirt. It's not, really, and growing less cool by the second. He's being kind. And why do I give a Funyun about looking cool in front of a stranger at this geriatric hurricane party? Am I embarrassed in front of teenage Ramona, art editor of the school newspaper, for not living up to her potential? Am I embarrassed in front of Prince, for never becoming the person I wanted to be? While he was here.

It's not that simple. This is a sentiment I want to explain to sexy Josh but I don't know how to verbalize it myself. He's losing interest. Maybe he can't reconcile whatever image he had of me twenty years ago with the person currently slumping on the sinkhole sofa. I get it—it's a challenge I struggle with on a daily basis.

"Mommy."

That word breaks the spell. It's like in the movie *Labyrinth* when Jennifer Connelly's character shatters the bubble she's dancing in with David Bowie because she has to find her brother. Alex appears at my side. "Mommy."

"Yes, my love."

"Nanette ate all the Cheetos so there's no more for the fish. And Bailey is outside, he could fall off the dock."

Josh Tillerson lifts his eyebrows, too nice to show his disappointment. I don't bother with introductions because the moment is gone, blown away, just like Jerry's tiki torches smacking against my mother's fence.

"All right, honey, let's go find him. We're going to leave soon."

Inside the aquarium room I locate Nanette on the floor licking her fingers. She's sitting on her heels with Minneapolis's head lolling out of her pocket. I pick her up, and she doesn't resist, she rests her head on my shoulder.

"You need to go potty?" I ask her.

"Nope."

"You tired?"

"Yeah."

13

THAT, AND OTHER TRANSGRESSIONS

7:34 P.M.

We push through the side door. Behind Jerry's house is a tidy yard about the size of Mom's, only it has a pool, with contents rippling the same direction as the water in the river, stone paths, and a catawampus birdbath that has seen better days. I spot Bailey halfway down Jerry's dock hunched over his phone.

"There's Bailey," I tell Alex and Nanette. "He's probably calling his mom."

As we approach Bailey, the wind rushes around us and Nanette burrows her head into my sleeve. I reach for Alex's hand—now I only have one arm to support Nanette, and girlfriend is getting bigger, so that limb starts to feel like Jell-O real quick.

"You okay?" I call out to Bailey. He spins around and hides something, but not before I recognize it—it's not his phone, silly Ramona, it's a can of Budweiser. "Aw, dude. Is that a beer? That's a beer. You're drinking." Nanette's interest piqued, she picks up her head, then lets it drop back to my shoulder. Her sigh is a warm puff next to my ear.

"Just one," Bailey says.

"Listen." I shift Nanette to my opposite hip. "You're not in trouble with me. It's just, we don't have time for teenage rebellion or pushing boundaries or whatever today."

"I'm sorry, Mrs. Arnold."

Bailey looks like he might cry. I am frustrated with him and at the same time I want him to feel better immediately. In an odd way Bailey seems like the only friend I have right now. Impatient, Alex wrenches free of my hand, darts down the dock, and leans over the railing.

"Bailey, it's perfectly normal to try that stuff. I don't want your mom to be upset that it's happening on my watch, though, and we need to get moving."

"It's not my first drink," he says.

"Oh."

"I had vodka at a wedding once. That was nasty."

"Yeah. Vodka is pretty gross at first."

Just have two kids, grow a gulf the size of Oklahoma between you and your husband, and get back to me on vodka. The wood around us creaks as the wind weakens the hardware attaching the decking. A Sea Ray hitched to a dock two houses away bobs up and down in a violent nod.

My mother is now aware of my husband's affair, Hurricane Matthew has laced up his gloves and stepped into the ring, and I'm not sure which of those things is worse. Regardless, we've got to get a move on. Nanette is a bowling ball in my arms. If she falls asleep now and wakes up when I transfer her to the car seat, she'll lose it—overtired for a toddler is worse than no sleep at all. Bailey waits for a mandate from me.

"Just. Maybe leave it there."

"Here?" Bailey says, looking around him.

"On the dock. In the pool. I don't know. My friend, we've got to go. Alex, come on. Bailey. Did you tell your mother our new plan? Got any power left in your phone?"

"Yep," he says, no eye contact.

"Bailey. You didn't, did you? Alex, *now*, buddy." Bailey doesn't answer me. It's starting to rain and the wind is whipping my face. Alex pulls out pebbles from his pocket and hurls them into the water before climbing down from the railing. "Bailey, you're not in trouble. Why didn't you text her?"

He shrugs. "I'm cool. She won't be worried."

"You're sixteen. Even when my kids are forty-five, I'll worry. Why don't you give me her number, I'll call her before my battery runs out."

I reach out my hand, palm open, but Bailey is a statue.

"It's okay," he says. "Mrs. Arnold, seriously. When we get back to your house, I'll just go next door. Thank you for everything, though. Subway and stuff. The party with all the old people."

"Dude. What's going on?"

We hear cracking branches behind us. Headlights shine on Jerry's rotting shed as more partygoers show up. Alex manually wiggles his tooth with his right hand and Nanette starts to whimper.

"She's not here," he says. "My mom. I'm thinking she's not coming back."

"What?"

"She left some money. And I have some from my job. You know I work at Party City. I'm going to graduate and then I'll figure it out."

"She, just, disappeared?"

"Please don't tell anyone," he says. "I want to stay in the house. My dad pays the rent—like, automatic withdrawal—from over there. I'm almost grown-up, anyway. I pay my phone bill and the power. I've been doing my own dinners since I was like, twelve, and I ride my bike to school."

I'm starting to feel dizzy: this news, Mom's face when I told her about Des, the Miller Lite, Nanette's curls rustling against my cheek, my stomach rumbling, my arms burning, the raw wind.

"I am sure you can take care of yourself, Bailey, you seem wise beyond your years. In fact you're more of a grown-up than me. But you're too young to be on your own. Someone should know what's going on."

"They'll put me in foster care. There was a kid in my bio class in foster and he said the family only wanted money from the government and they sold his Game Boy on eBay."

"Honey, no, don't—don't jump to conclusions here. Nobody is putting you in foster care if you have parents."

"Okay."

"What about your dad?"

"My dad's deployment started in February. But I don't think things were good the last time he was home anyway. My mom, she started traveling for work and then the trips were longer, and then the last time, I called her office and they said she doesn't work there anymore."

"Oh, no."

"Yeah."

"Okay," I say, and to myself, "okay."

"Please don't call the police, Mrs. Arnold."

"The police? No, don't—we gotta think about this. It's not safe for you to be by yourself."

"You're not going to call the police?"

"No," I tell him firmly. "I'm not. But I need to do a little research. Please trust me, okay?"

He looks down at his shoes.

"Okay."

This beautiful boy. This sweet kid. What kind of person up and vanishes on him? His mother always seemed nervous. How could Desmond and I fail to observe the absence of an adult coming and going next door for weeks? Or not notice that a teenager was living on his own? My heart hurts and my arms ache.

"We will figure this out. All right, Bailey? Look at me. We will. But we're not going to solve any problems getting swept away by an eight-foot storm surge on a rickety dock on Wilmington Island. We need to survive the hurricane and then we'll make a plan."

We leave the half-drunk can of beer by the pool. That's littering but I imagine it won't be the first time something gross ended up in Jerry's pool. I drag my cluster of kids back into the house, where we find Mom, who's exasperated because she just saw Jerry's truck pull up and she's been looking for us everywhere. This is about as believable as when Alex says he can't find *Diary of a Wimpy Kid* and it's on the top of his bookshelf, right next to *The Giving Tree*, which he won't let me read to him anymore, because it makes me cry. *And the tree was happy.*

I scoop up Nanette's car seat—semi-soaked—from the side steps. I have to get everybody to my laundry room and then I'll figure out the rest after that.

"All right," I say. "Anybody need to use the restroom?"

2013

At Monkey Joe's, Alex's preschool buddies threw themselves into the inflatable party zone like they were tripping on Molly. They hurled their tiny bodies at the bright yellow and purple bounce houses, ricochet-ed off netting, scrambled up slick ladders, and tumbled down slides without looking back to their parents, who traipsed after them with diaper bags and water bottles.

Except my kid.

Alex clung to my leg, gripping my light maternity jeans with dirt encrusted fingernails and burying his dark curls into my thigh. I let him for a couple minutes while I narrated the fun the other kids were having, broadcaster-style. Look at Lucas over there. He sure is bouncing high. Boo-yah! Isn't that your friend, Sally? She looks like she's having fun on that slide. Desmond took off his baseball cap and stuffed it in his back pocket.

I was seven months along with Nanette. During my first pregnancy, I couldn't wait to show—I wanted to wear a cute polka dot maternity dress Adelaide had bought me. It seemed like with the second one, my belly and boobs exploded right after the plus sign showed up on the test. They were like, this isn't our first rodeo.

Alex admitted it looked like his friends were having a good time. He'd be up for trying the slide. If we did it together.

I'll go with you, buddy, said Desmond.

No, Mommy goes.

Desmond raised his eyebrows.

Cool, cool, okay, I said.

During the last few weeks of my pregnancy, my son seemed to realize that his time as an only child, or the center of the universe, was coming to a close. So he stuck to me like butter on a popcorn kernel.

I slipped off my flip-flops. We mounted the bouncy slide together, me following Alex's diapered butt at a snail's pace. Clinging to the plastic handles, I felt an urge to bite the waistband of his pants and hurl him up to the platform like a lioness tossing her cub by the scruff of the neck. The baby pressed down on my pelvic floor and my belly dragged against the yellow fabric.

Once we made it to the top, however, Alex lost all apprehension, scrambled ahead of me, and launched himself down the slide. On all fours at the top, I panicked—we were supposed to go together—I called out his name. Then I felt warm liquid escape from downstairs.

I had peed my pants.

A lot.

Alex? I called.

The last sign of my kid was a flash of red sock as he picked himself up from the base of the slide, and with newfound confidence, scurried after a friend to explore the pirate ship.

Meanwhile, kid traffic had not slowed down. A scrawny girl with freckles and sunflower leggings crouched next to me.

Your turn, she said.

Not now.

Why not?

I'm scared, I said. I tried to back myself to the far corner of the landing at the top of the slide but it was tough with my belly.

Oh, the girl said, before throwing herself down the slide.

Alex! I called again. I peeked around the top. Desmond! Nobody could hear me over the white noise of the fans and piped-in soundtrack encouraging Monkey Joe visitors to *left foot, let's stomp, now cha-cha real smooth.*

I considered sliding down and pretending I sat in something. It's a kid party venue—there could be rogue liquids anywhere. Who cares what other parents think? I don't know these people. And why would they be looking at the crotch of my maternity jeans in the first place? Weirdos.

But I didn't budge. Inside me, the baby stretched, an elbow or knee pressing against the uterine wall, making my shape morph in front of my eyes.

Sunflower Leggings was back, this time with a smirk.

You can't stay up here forever, she said.

I'm not!

That punk should mind her own business.

I still had to pee more. Who knew how long I would be up there? It could be a while, I figured. Maybe I should release the remaining pee. Surely Alex would cycle through again and he could retrieve Desmond for me.

As I lurked at the top of the slide, enormous in my drenched maternity jeans, I considered that perhaps I was wholly unprepared to have a second child. Was the universe kidding with this? How was I supposed to keep two people alive when I was barely crushing things with the first one? What was I supposed to do when the new kid was suckling my boob and the other running around, unsupervised? Alex could pull out knives in the kitchen or climb on top of the dryer, reach the container of bleach, and chug it. Let's face it, I was never, ever going to sleep again. And with a second human emerging from my vagina, there was definitely going to be lasting effects down there.

Damn these extra hormones.

I really didn't want to cry in front of Sunflower Leggings.

A pair of twins in coordinated dino shirts inched their butts toward the sharp decline holding hands. When I shifted to make room for them, my phone pressed into my butt.

Wait—I had my phone.

I typed out a message to Desmond: *Help, please.* After that I added seven blushing emojis. *Help me.*

I waited. Sally from Alex's class flipped by me without acknowledging my presence. Sally! Whatever. Three dots under my message.

Hey. Where r u?

Thank you, Jesus, Mary, and Joseph Gordon-Levitt.

I've got, I typed, *a situation. Come to slide near Dasani machine. Look up.*

I waited. Then I saw the toes of my husband's work boots come around the corner. Des squinting up at me.

I peed my pants. Help?

As he read my text, his expression went from concern to amusement to sympathy. He looked up at me again and down at his phone.

Take my keys, he typed. *You go home.*

Change and come back?

Now he was calling up to me: Ramona, no, just, it's fine.

I had to come back. We were only fifteen minutes into the party, for Christ's sake. Plus however long I'd been stranded up there in my soggy knickers. We were celebrating the end of the year for Alex's three-year-old class. I had a note and a Fresh Market gift card for the teachers in the pocket of my diaper bag. I hadn't even said hello to them yet. And I needed to ask them about summer camp.

Desmond texted me, *I can watch Alex.*

I guess he could. Sometimes I forgot I wasn't the only one raising my children. I mean, I could go home. Switch my pants. Maybe take a nap.

I scooted myself forward and slid down, fast, because I was pushing 180 pounds. Desmond was at the bottom, waiting. I rolled over to the side and tried to press myself up. My husband reached out his hand. He pulled me up.

Well, hello, there, he said.

I hoisted up the maternity band of my pants and tried to yank my T-shirt down over it. Desmond pressed his truck keys into my hand.

I'm so embarrassed, I said. Tell Alex Mommy wasn't feeling good. No, don't say that. He'll worry. Tell Alex—

Ramona, Desmond said. I can take care of this one. Go on home.

I realized he was right.

So I did. I waddled so quickly to the exit you wouldn't even have known I was there. Except for the part about being massively pregnant in stained jeans. I turned the ignition in Desmond's truck, and thought, well, that was a humiliating experience no one needs to know about.

Except later when I told my mother about it. And Nicole. And a random mom at the playground. And the delivery nurse at Candler Hospital. And a recap with Desmond on New Year's Eve when we laughed so hard about it I probably peed a little that time, too.

7:52 P.M.

My phone buzzes with a text from a 912 number I don't know.

Ramona, it's MacKenzie. Kenneth asked me to get in touch with you. He doesn't know where you are or if you have service. You need to update us on the Laser Life call. Thnx

I experience the knee-jerk reaction of fear in the pit of my stomach that always follows a kerfuffle at work. At the same time, Hurricane Matthew just plucked Jerry's mailbox off the wooden post and heaved it into a hedge, so my job seems like a distant memory. I can't worry about it. Kenneth, I will get back to you, I promise. And sorry, not sorry, MacKenzie.

One time in the break room we were talking about our first concerts. I didn't reveal mine—New Kids on the Block—because I already feel like a fossil around people at work. MacKenzie's first concert was Taylor Swift, a fact she seemed embarrassed about.

"My dad brought me and my friend Haley," she said. "He found our seats for us and then he bailed to read *Sports Illustrated* on a bench outside the colosseum."

For once I recognized a subject my coworkers were discussing.

"I like some of Taylor Swift's jams," I said. "I think she's a better role model for girls than other singers. Because she's not naked. But there's something about her dancing that reminds me of a baby giraffe. There's this book I read my kids called *Giraffes Can't Dance*. It's about this giraffe named Gerald who can't really dance at the jungle party and all the other animals are dicks to him, especially the lions, and then he figures out that he needs to find the right song and dance if he's feeling it and the other animals can just fuck off. Anyway. That's what Taylor Swift makes me think of. Gerald. So good for her. Dance your heart out, Taylor Swift."

Everybody stared at me. MacKenzie looked annoyed, like I stole her spotlight, when I was just trying to jump in to share my thoughts on T-Swizzle. Maybe they think Taylor Swift is an amazing dancer and she doesn't resemble a giraffe, not even a little bit.

MacKenzie. I'm not calling you back. Or Kenneth. You should listen to Prince. He's really good at guitar.

7:54 P.M.

The rain comes down harder in thicker, heavier drops.

"I'm hungry," Nanette says. We pass Jerry's kitchen, where the party is picking up steam, Steely Dan floating out an open window, a woman's laugh like a horse braying.

"We've got peanut butter and jelly at home," I reassure her.

"You ate two hot dogs. And all those Cheetos," Alex accuses his little sister. "You had more than the fish."

"Not the buns," Nanette says. "I didn't eat the buns. It's really dark."

It's we-wee dock.

"Take heart, maties," Mom says. She's leading the way, Peyton Manning trotting by her side, as we stomp across Jerry's yard to his truck, where he appears to be still sitting in the front seat. "What is that jackass doing in there?"

I shudder to think of my children's new vocabulary when they get back to school. If they ever return, if their schools are still standing. Then again, it won't be just my kids, maybe all the first-graders hanging up their bookbags on hooks in cubbies will have new expressions, like, *it's the goddamn roof* or *motherfucking branch* or *holy shit my dock blew away.*

A searing crack of thunder follows two rapid blinks of lightning—it sounds like it's all around us. Nanette screams, I clutch her to me and out of instinct grab Alex and Bailey, who lets me hug him. For a moment I am confident I can keep everyone safe with this one hug. My mother, nonplussed, charges over to the truck.

"Jerr," she says, yanking open the door on the driver's side. "You got a whole party in there waiting on refills."

It's so Savannah. This storm is going to obliterate the city and they worry about guests being underserved.

"Nice to see you, too, Adelaide," Jerry drawls.

"What in the world are you doing?" my mother says.

"Checking on my league."

"What?"

"My fantasy football league."

This statement propels my mother into a tizzy. She throws up her hands and swings her head from side to side like Jerry just announced the earth is flat, which I found out from my coworkers during an ice cream sundae teambuilder, is actually a thing people believe.

"Ramona's car just died"—at this, I wave from my position lurking behind her—"and she's got a flock of kids and creatures to haul back to her house so we need your van."

Apparently 3 kids + one guinea pig = a flock. Even though Jerry's focus on his phone is steadfast, he releases a long sigh.

"In civilized cultures," he points out, "it's polite to make a request in the form of a question."

"Jesus Christ," Mom says.

"Hypothetically. Say you're asking someone for a favor."

"Jerry?" I pipe in over Mom's shoulder. "If I may, I'd like to apologize for my mother. I mean, *rude*. The truth is, my Toyota died and I'd like to get my kids to a safe spot before the storm really picks up. I'd be so grateful for any help in the vehicle department."

My mother: "Christ on a cracker."

Now Jerry looks up at us.

"You can use the van," he says. "And I'll drive y'all. For the record, ladies, I am doing this for Ramona. You seem like a nice person. Your mother and I are just neighbors, not friends, and I am still waiting on an apology from her."

"For the sign in the pool?" I feel a rush of sympathy for Jerry—we both know what a strong cup of coffee my mother can be.

"Ramona!" Adelaide says.

"That, and other transgressions," Jerry says.

Gross, whatever. Bailey's eyes shift back and forth as the adults talk in a non-adult fashion. He kneels down to scratch Peyton Manning behind the dog's ears while Nanette and Alex spin in circles and make their mouths into O's to catch raindrops.

"Kids," I tell them, "I got an idea. Can you guys be the presidents of the fur babies?"

In the half-dark Alex frowns: "What's that?"

"Can you guys go back to our car at Gigi's house to get Clarence Thomas and Sophie so we can load them into this awesome van we're going to borrow?"

Nanette howls—not about my request, she's dropped Minneapolis, and she's rooting around for him in the leaves at her feet.

"Please, sweeties," I say, and something in my voice must alarm them, because they look at each other. "If you head to Gigi's"—in a calmer tone—"and gather the animals, it would really help. A lot."

"There you are," says Nanette to Minneapolis.

"Okay," Alex says. "But Clarence Thomas's cage is pretty heavy."

"Silly guy," Nanette says.

Bailey appears to understand what the hell is going on and I am pleading with my eyes, *please help me, neighbor kid, oh, please.* I am keeping a secret of yours, can you help me preserve this faux fortress of calm I've created so my children aren't even more traumatized by whatever is going on here. Please.

"Come on, y'all," Bailey says. "Let's race!"

Miraculously it works, the three of them start to gallop down Jerry's lawn. For a moment I panic, watching my children frolic under what feels to me like a canopy of danger, as one of these swaying trees could drop a branch on my babies at any moment, and I'm tempted to chase after them.

"Now. If you'll excuse me," Jerry says, "I am going to drop off my reinforcements and I shall return with the keys to the van." With a grunt he reaches across the passenger seat for a cardboard crate filled with bottles, lowers himself from the driver's seat of his truck, and slams the door.

"Fantastic!" I say.

"Fine," Mom says.

The containers clink as Jerry shifts the box to one arm, extracts a bottle of pinot grigio, and hands it to my mother.

"I know you like that kind. It was three dollars off."

We watch him trudge down the gravel driveway to his house. Next to me Mom clutches the wine and blinks rapidly as the rain speckles her face.

"You okay?"

"Of course, I'm okay," she snaps. "There were no feelings, Ramona, it was just sex."

It didn't mean anything. It meant everything.

"Mom, I'm not—"

"Just shut up."

"Hey!"

"Just shut up and let me think," she says.

I am quiet, and annoyed—it doesn't feel good when anyone tells you to shut up, least of all, your mother. I try to squash that feeling and now I listen to the muffled music and laughter from Jerry's, the leaves on the ground crackling as rain beats down, and a gutter pipe dangling from Mom's banging into the side of her house. I watch the trio of three skipping off toward the road, Nanette trailing behind Bailey and Alex, the lights on her Elsa sneakers blinking.

8:07 P.M.

My mother yanks the hood of her raincoat over her damp hair and nods to Nanette's car seat: "Let's strap that in."

"All right."

We're briefly illuminated by rapid flashes of lightning. When Mom heaves open the rusty handle of Jerry's van, a dull light reveals a small rummage sale worth of boxes and fishing supplies piled high on the middle bench.

"Good Lord," Mom says.

She plunges into Jerry's van, begins grabbing items and tossing them on the wet earth. It's a lot. Cardboard boxes of fishing magazines, empty Sherwin-Williams paint pails, an orange traffic cone, a gunmetal toolbox that appears to weigh as much as a piano.

"Mom." I'm not sure she can hear me. "Let's wait until Jerry comes back. He might have opinions about where this stuff should go."

She pulls out a broken lawn chair, one of those old models with pastel vinyl webbing, which reminds me of the pink glitter jelly shoes I used to wear as a six-year-old. The straps of the chair hang off the aluminum frame like limp fettucine noodles.

"All this shit!" she exclaims, only to disappear again into the van.

"What are you doing?"

She tosses a pair of rubber boots on the ground.

"I'm playing Scrabble, Ramona."

I lift Nanette's seat over my head to use as a temporary umbrella. "Hey. I realize you are missing Dad and suffering and this thing with Jerry is a coping mechanism but I don't think I deserve to be snapped at."

"Ramona."

"What?"

"Did you ever stop to think," Mom says, "that maybe I'm just fine? That I feel lonely and I miss your father but instead of hiding in a mourning shroud I am trying to get an ounce of living in before I kick the bucket? Did you ever think *you* might be struggling and maybe that's why you're so goddamn angry all the time?"

"I'm not angry."

She rolls her eyes. "If you say so."

"I'm not angry!" I repeat, my voice louder.

Mom shakes her head: "Just trying to help."

"I'm. Not. Angry."

She surveys the pile of Jerry's equipment she just pitched from the van.

"You know. Your father and I had a similar situation when you were little."

"What?"

"Whatever you want to call it. An affair."

My head feels fuzzy. "Dad cheated on you?"

"Other way around."

Now my mouth falls open. I feel the familiar flush—purple, orange, red—pulsing at my temples.

"You? Cheated on Dad."

"Not my finest moment."

"Why are you telling me this?"

"I don't really know," she says. "It was a long time ago and I was an unhappy person."

"You cheated. With whom?"

"Does it matter?"

"I thought you and Dad had a great marriage."

"We did."

I wipe the rain from my eyes. My mother did this to my father, my favorite person in the whole world, who is now gone, a loss I feel every day. My mother did this thing that I know feels like being prodded in the gut with a hot poker. I am tired and—fine, she's right, I'm angry—this news is more than I can handle.

"You're awful," I tell her.

"I can see how that would be your reaction."

"Why can't everybody just be nice and stop having sex with people they're not married to? It's not that hard."

"Listen, cookie," Mom says.

"I can't believe I came back for you. I should have let the stupid hurricane wipe you off the map."

My mother freezes and her face crumples.

I have seen this expression three times: when my brother told us on the phone one Thanksgiving that his wife lost her baby, when my father got his diagnosis in a consulting room at Memorial Hospital, and when the soldiers handed Adelaide the perfectly folded flag that covered my father's coffin at the cemetery. I feel wretched I am the reason for her face. And delighted. I want her to hurt. Maybe not in the same way Dad did, or me two days ago. But a hurt made worse by the knowledge it was triggered by her own mistake.

She returns her attention to the contents of Jerry's van. I slide my feelings inside the tiny pocket inside the pocket of my jeans. It is a tradition handed down from her mother, and now to me—there is no time to unpack feelings when you are a woman with a job to do. The rain is now blowing sideways. If any section of me was dry, not so much anymore—my clothes are drenched, my sneakers squish with each step.

And I shake with rage.

Jerry's back, now sporting a yellow raincoat and a bucket hat and holding a navy umbrella that the wind turns inside out. He looks like the little girl in the dress on the cover of a Morton Salt cannister and appears visibly annoyed at the sight of my mother heaving his belongings into the rain.

"Adelaide, dammit. Get out of the way."

14

THE ANGELS PLAY LASER TAG

Peyton Manning starts barking at the return of the kids, who are now moving more slowly, Bailey gripping Clarence Thomas's cage, Alex staggering under what appears to be ten tons of Sophie's travel kennel. I feel a small moment of relief that we are one step closer to transporting the team to a safe zone in midtown. Then I remember Bailey's secret and the fact my mother just turned my memory of a relatively happy childhood upside down.

Jerry begins transplanting the stuff Mom threw on the ground into the trunk of the van and I'm helping him.

"You okay?" Bailey asks my mother. He doesn't know what to call her. "Gigi? Adelaide."

Under a skinny palm tree my mother clutches her right forearm with her left palm. Through the sleeve of her jacket a stain is spreading and blood dribbles from between her fingers.

"I scratched my arm on Jerry's junk," she says.

"It looks like it's really bleeding," Bailey says.

Jerry, holding a rubber boot in each hand, shuffles toward Mom to examine the wound.

"Let me see that," he says. Mom pulls back her sleeve and it's tricky to make out the damage in the dark but it looks like there's a deep gash about four inches long.

Shit.

8:12 P.M.

Bailey's eyes grow as big as Tervis lids.

Jerry says, "That's a bad slice."

"I'll tape it up," Mom says.

Jerry: "Reckon you need a few stitches. Let's wrap it up and get you to Urgent Care."

"That's ridiculous."

"All right," Jerry says, turning around, throwing up his arms, making a bow-legged path back to his van. "Bleed to death. I don't care."

"Gigi, it looks like you got bit by a dinosaur," says Alex, still holding the cat kennel at a precarious angle. "Like a dromaeo-saurid. Or maybe an ornithomimosaur."

I am trying to cultivate empathy in my children but it's hard for me to tell if that statement reflects concern or fascination.

"Are you okay, Gigi?" asks Nanette.

There, that's better.

"Of course I am, sweetheart. Y'all did a great job rounding up the creatures. Want to load them in the back?"

I'm desperate to see my mother's gash and yet I'm furious

with her, so I don't budge. Nanette is currently sucking on Minneapolis, and Jerry swings one of the boots he's holding in the direction of my daughter's blanket.

"Bind it with that rag until we get you some medical attention."

"No!" I yell. It's so loud—I didn't mean it to be that loud. "I mean, we can find something else. I'll look for a towel. Mom, someone needs to stitch that up."

She pulls her sleeve back down to her wrist. "Y'all are the most lily-livered evac crew I've ever encountered. But, fine."

Jerry's found a chamois rag in the glove compartment, which Mom dismisses as disgusting, yet allows Jerry to fashion into a tourniquet. It is both sweet and confusing to watch them huddled together as the storm dumps gallons of liquid on all of us.

I clap my hands.

"Let's load up, people."

I pick up Clarence Thomas's cage, the class pet racing from one side to the other in terror, and wedge it in the storage compartment in the back of the van. I am about to hop into the backseat with my kids when Jerry hands me the keys.

"Darlin', how 'bout you drive? I'm a little woozy. I don't know if it's the whiskey sours or all that blood."

8:14 P.M.

Do you remember when Prince was the halftime act for the Super Bowl? It was the Indianapolis Colts versus the Chicago Bears in 2007. You bet your britches I do. It's possibly the only memory of a professional sport event in my brain. And I don't even know who won.

Desmond and I watched the Super Bowl on a crappy LG flat screen that technically belonged to his last roommate, eating Asian Zing chicken wings from Buffalo Wild Wings. My engagement ring was so new, I'd get distracted by tiny spots of light reflected on the interior of my car when the sun hit the stone.

The Super Bowl was in Miami. Nobody expected a storm in Miami in February. Yet it poured for an entire day. Palm trees swayed against a cloudy sky and raindrops speckled the television camera lens.

The commentators wondered what would happen with the halftime show. Will Prince still go on? Is it safe to perform? When halftime arrived, the whole stadium went dark. In the midst of the downpour, twinkling lights appeared in the crowd, punctuated by bolts of lightning. We weren't sure if it was real lightning or holograms. We heard the opening of Queen's "We Will Rock You," sped up, and the lights rose to illuminate a stage shaped like the Prince symbol.

And there he was! Holding his guitar, Prince appeared in a turquoise suit over an orange button-down with a do-rag on his head and he started "Let's Go Crazy." Twin dancers with long, dark hair, pirate sleeves, and knee-high boots threw themselves around him.

It was still raining—really raining—and Prince was wearing high heels on a slick surface. People rushed the stage, soaking wet, screaming the lyrics, their expressions indicating that their entire lives had been building up to this moment. A marching band joined the fans on the field.

That guy is incredible, Desmond said. He stood up and announced, I'm going to take a shit before the second half.

When it started to rain even harder, Prince asked in song if someone's getting the best of us before playing a sick guitar solo. As he launched "Purple Rain," he pulled off his head scarf and his hair was perfect, a slick pompadour, incapable of being mussed by the storm. A big sheet dropped from the sky and we watched Prince's shadow as all five foot two of him grew into a giant, guitar neck as a phallic extension.

It was like Prince landed on a spaceship in the middle of a new planet while hundreds of thousands of people watched him. He commanded the storm like a god, mesmerizing everyone who watched him in the stadium, and those of us watching on our TVs.

I am so tired. I'm standing in so many storms. I'm soaking wet. I'm heartbroken. I'm scared. And yes, Mom, I'm pissed as hell.

What would Prince want me to do? Squat down and cover my head to shield myself from Hurricane Matthew? Or do I let the storm awaken my dormant powers like Prince at the Super Bowl, so I rise up, tear off this flimsy costume made up of people I think I should be, to become myself?

8:16 P.M.

We are on the road. Two women, two children, one teenager, one cat, one dog, one guinea pig, one Jerry in a vehicle I'm not sure I'm qualified to drive.

I'm used to my Toyota Sienna, and though this van is bigger and crustier, we should be fine. Behind us, we leave the party, still going strong thanks to Jerry's booze run. I navigate the van down the long driveway and take a left on Wilmington Island Road, heading to Johnny Mercer Boulevard.

Next to me my mother grips her bandaged forearm and scowls. Now that I'm closer I see the blood from her wound has soaked most of the bottom half of her sleeve and the top of her right thigh. She doesn't have much skin or fat on her these days. How in the world is she producing that much blood?

"You okay?" I manage.

"I'm just dandy."

"You're not my favorite person right now," I tell her. "But please don't go to the light."

"Today, anyway," pipes in Jerry from the second row.

She snorts. "I am definitely not dying before you, Jerry."

This is bizarre. I didn't even know my mother was dating, let alone getting naked with neighbors, and here we are, in the middle of some kind of sexual tension I don't understand. It's like Mom and Dad are fighting but this guy is not my dad. And it turns out the man who was my dad was a cuckold—an old-timey word that reminds me of my mother's unstable chickens—just like me. I always knew I took after him.

Also, I'm freezing. Jerry's AC blasts across my wet skin and I can't figure out how to turn it off.

We hug the right lane of the street as it parallels the curves of the coast. Thunder. An extended rumble sounds like a dump truck pouring boulders into a pit, followed by flashes of lightning. It feels like Hurricane Matthew is in the car with us.

"I don't like that noise," Nanette says.

"Nanner," I say. "Know what my daddy used to tell me? The angels are bowling."

"That's right. He did, didn't he," Mom says.

I grit my teeth. Like you care or even loved him.

My daughter doesn't buy it. "What's the light thing, then?"

"The angels play laser tag," Bailey offers.

Mom claps and twists around like she wants to give Bailey a high five before she remembers her bloody appendage. We appear to be the only car driving on this godforsaken island. Even though the windshield wipers work their hardest to keep up with the rain, my view is mainly a blur. The traffic lights still have power at the intersection in front of Ace Hardware. They rock up and down like kids pumping their legs on swings.

"Ramona, if you're cold," Jerry says, "you can push that button under the radio."

It works. Now that the jet blast has ceased, inside Jerry's van is silence—a bizarre contrast to the wind howling outside the car, the beating of the windshield wipers.

We see sparks on the power lines above Basil's Pizza and hear the sound—*pop, pop, pop*—as a shower of lights explodes into the air.

"Fireworks?" Nanette suggests. *Figh-wooks?*

"Kinda," I tell her, as I swerve to the left of the telephone pole.

I brake when a stray shopping cart from Publix blows across the road.

"Chill, puppy!" says Alex to Peyton Manning, who is whining and pacing, obsessed with the smells in the far section of Jerry's van, but too weak to jump over the seat, "Take a chill pill, dude!"

"Animals always know about disasters before we do," says Mom. "They're smarter than humans in that respect."

"Like hurricanes?" Alex says.

"And earthquakes," I add.

"And volcanoes?" Alex asks.

"Alex is super into volcanoes this year," I explain. "They talked about Pompeii in STEM."

"They have some in Hawaii. That's where I was born. I don't remember it, though," Bailey says.

"You were born in Hawaii?" I say. "That's a fun fact. Let's look up Hawaii on the map when we get home."

Alex pipes up, "I know where it is. It's really far from us."

"Your grandpa and I were going to go there on a trip once," Mom says, "until I got shingles. And he wasn't a great flier. We went to Key West instead. Lots of cats there. And ex-cons."

How did that vacay go? I want to ask her. Did you meet anyone special while you were touring Ernest Hemingway's house with the six-toed cats?

We've made it to Highway 80. Now we are out in the open, which inspires relief because there aren't as many branches to fall on us, and terror because now we're exposed to a landscape where the wind has free rein.

The rain pummels the windshield. From what I can see the water below the bridge is dark, almost black, with whitecaps. It's pulsing up, reaching for the road. I'm terrified to be on the bridge, and even worse, driving someone else's dilapidated vehicle, so I'm moving, swear to God, fifteen miles an hour.

"You're going so slow, Mommy," Alex says. "We're never going to get Gigi to the doctor."

"Slowly," I correct.

"Better slow than sorry!" Mom says.

Alex is delighted to find an ancient maroon tin of Skoal between the seats in Jerry's van.

"Don't open that," I tell him.

He ignores me.

"Dang," says Bailey. "It smells like rotting butthole."

"Don't knock it 'til you've tried it, son," says Jerry.

In the rearview mirror I see Nanette's eyes getting heavy. She's clutching Minneapolis and Peyton Manning's red leash and is possibly thirty seconds from sleep. I am still navigating the van across the bridge—almost to Victory Drive.

"Okay, sweeties," I tell them. "We're getting there."

Now I'm in Thunderbolt. Which is closer to our destination, only the right side of Victory is flooded—it's a deep lagoon. Jerry's van struggles as I accelerate through the puddle in the left lane, sending up a five-foot high spray on either side of us. The wipers labor under the downpour.

"This is ludicrous," I mutter.

"Ramona!" Mom says. "You're in the middle of the road!"

Her voice next to my right ear is grating and I flinch every time she speaks.

"Mother. I am driving through a lake right now."

"Well, pick a goddamn lane in the lake."

"Stop yelling at me, I am losing my mind, shut up! Shut up. Shut up!"

Maybe I am a little angry.

Next to me my mother stares ahead at the road with pinched lips, strong posture, her hair frizzier than usual, Jerry's wine in her lap, blood oozing through the chamois. The row of palm trees sways and I hear a crack somewhere behind me. In Chick-fil-A the lights shine on an empty dining room with gleaming red tables.

Ramona. Drive. Stay calm. You can do this. You will bring Adelaide to the hospital and then you can head home. You can fit everyone in the laundry room—it has no windows.

"Take a left on Skidaway!" Mom says.

"Skidaway instead of the Truman?" I say.

"We need to get away from these palm trees—they will snap like toothpicks!"

"Shit! I can't see anything!"

"That's why you should take Skidaway! Take it to DeRenne and drop me off at Candler."

I take a left on Skidaway, past the CVS, past the Krispy Kreme, past the movie theater, past the Dairy Queen. The wind is blowing like crazy. I see a couple of cars in the parking lot of the shopping complex of Home Depot and Target. Nanette has reverted to a whimper. In the back-back Alex is quiet, and I wish I could hold his hand.

"What do doctors and nurses do during hurricanes?" Bailey asks.

"Not sure," Mom says. "I hope somebody's there."

I've made it to DeRenne, miraculously, without any trees falling on us, or, I don't know, projectiles smashing the windows of Jerry's van. As we approach the Truman Parkway bridge, a gale force pushes us into the right lane. At the veterinarian clinic the sign has been ripped off—all that remains is a metal frame. The stoplights now are black and still swing with abandon.

At Candler Hospital all the lights are on—that's a positive sign. I swing into the circle drive near the entrance for the ER. When I turn off the ignition the van gives a familiar shudder and I feel a tenderness for this vehicle because it evidently wants me to feel at home.

"Stay cool, everybody," I instruct my passengers.

Then, I hop out of Jerry's van like my pants are on fire.

8:52 P.M.

"Do you need help, ma'am?" I am joined in the pouring rain by a tiny Latino man in hospital scrubs with a bright orange Fitbit circling his wrist. When the attendant sees Mom, he goes, "Whoa," and pulls a small walkie-talkie out of his pocket, pushes a button. "Cecelia. Send a wheelchair, please."

"A wheelchair!" Mom harumphs.

The ER department of Candler seems reasonably staffed at this time. Perhaps locals are getting shot or having heart attacks in the places they evacuated to because here they've got two other orderlies to help us, pretty quickly, and they're pushing a wheelchair out for Mom. She ducks under the ripped ceiling of the van and reaches for my hand so I can pull her out.

"Go on home," Mom says. "I'll get this stitched up."

"Mom."

"They've got electricity here. Think y'all got any?"

"I don't know," I admit. "Let me get you checked in."

"You don't need to. I'm fine."

My house, only ten blocks away, calls to me. In just a few minutes I could be home, my children safe under our roof, peeling off our sopping clothes, hiding under a soft blanket from Hurricane Matthew and the painful revelations of the past three days. From the light at the entrance of the lobby I see Mom's face and it's pale.

I sigh. "How you gonna fill out paperwork when you're bleeding like a stuck pig? Jerry, mind watching my kids for a minute?"

"Sure. They like Altoids?" Jerry ambles over to the driver's side of the van. I'm starting to think he's not drunk, that's just the way he walks. The wind slowly prods a scarlet dumpster across the hospital parking lot. Bailey, hauling open the heavy door of the van, pops out his head.

"Mrs. Arnold," he says. "Is it cool if I come with and plug in my phone for a minute? It's been dead for, like, two hours."

To him: "Sure." To my kids: "I'm gonna get Gigi set up and then we'll go home. Make good choices."

The team steers my mother, who looks tiny and bloody in the wheelchair, through sliding doors. She's too worn out to be a dick to us and for that I am glad. Bailey and I shuffle behind the procession and I toss a look over my shoulder just to make sure Jerry is feeding my kids Altoids instead of chewing tobacco. At this point, whatever.

8:57 P.M.

Inside I collect a clipboard from a weathered redhead in Mickey Mouse scrubs and hunker down on a pleather sofa next to Mom's wheelchair. As Bailey circles the perimeter of the waiting room on the hunt for an outlet, his wet sneakers squeak on the linoleum.

"Mom. Got an insurance card?"

"It might be slimy," Adelaide says. She careens her body my direction so she can dig her less bloody hand into the opposite pocket for her wallet.

"Slimy works."

A towhead in corduroy overalls drifts from his mother's side and starts to follow Bailey's tracks. Bailey notices the kid, pretends to hide from him behind a trash can, and I can't help smiling. Discovering that random people possess freakish abilities to charm or soothe children is one of the pure delights of motherhood.

I try to dry off my right hand on the sofa and start to fill out the form. My wet hair distributes droplets on the paper. The lights blink, people gathered in the waiting room look at each other, and Bailey shoots up from where he's crouching. The receptionist taps on the plastic partition and calls out, "We have a generator, y'all, slow your roll."

On a small flat screen wedged in a corner of the waiting room, Jim Cantore is on the Weather Channel, his teeth are super white, I bet he uses the strips at night.

"As if Mother Nature wasn't playing a cruel joke," he says, "this loops around by Tuesday and is no less than two hundred miles to my east as a tropical storm and potential second landfall."

I wonder if Daphne and Dan got bumped for Jim Cantore, the Big Kahuna, if they suck up to him at the studio or push pins in a voodoo doll of his likeness in their apartments after work. It feels like seventeen years have passed since I scrolled through our channels with my Mountain Dew wine to find the station to check on Hurricane Matthew.

"Ramona," my mother says. "It was a grad student who worked at the library. When you kids were little. I volunteered there."

"We don't have to talk about this, Mom."

"I want to."

My hand trembles as I enter my mother's name in tiny spaces. She has one of the longest names in the history of names. A-D-E-L-A-I-D-E B-U-R-K-H-A-L-T-E-R. I don't need dirty details about something that happened one hundred years ago, not tonight.

"It happened three times and I felt wretched about it. So, I told your dad."

I study the fluorescent tube lighting above me.

"Then what happened?" I ask her.

"He kicked me out."

"What?"

"Remember when I visited your aunt Coco in Birmingham and the babysitter picked y'all up from school that week? That odd girl with the devil symbols on her jacket?"

"They were Mötley Crüe patches."

"I wasn't in Birmingham. I was at a Best Western outside Wilmington."

"You were at Aunt Coco's. You called us from there. You brought me back a Pound Puppy keychain from Alabama."

"It was from the gift shop at the Best Western."

The inside of my mouth tastes like pennies and Miller Lite.

"I can't with this," I say.

"I'm not telling you to stress you out. Or shatter your image of our marriage."

"Too late."

"It was the worst and best thing for us."

I rest the pen on the clipboard. "You're lucky he took you back."

"I know."

On the television monitor, the tie-dye swirl of Hurricane Matthew, orange-red in the center, floats up from Florida like a jellyfish.

"Mom. It seems you genuinely believe you are helping me somehow with this story but it's plunging what's already been a pretty shitty couple days into even more awful territory. It would be so great—just peachy—for one person I love, or used to, to not let me down."

Mom peels back a section of the chamois binding her arm, grimaces, and then puts it back.

"Maybe we could ask, for, like, a Ziploc bag," I suggest.

"Or paper towels."

"Try to squeeze it together. Pinch skin on each side of the slice."

"They used to call it baby blues," Mom says. "When I said my affair was the best thing for us, I also mean me. It forced me to tell Dad I was unhappy and we figured how to make things better."

"Are you proposing Desmond and I should make it work?"

"Hell no. Maybe you try or maybe you don't. It's not my business and these things are complicated. What I'm saying is you're stronger than me. You don't push everything down like we did."

"Who's we?"

"Women. Mothers."

"You don't know."

"I don't?"

"All I do is squash it down."

"It doesn't look that way from here."

I start to cry. "It feels that way. I'm exhausted. And I can't believe Desmond. It's so shitty."

"I know," she says. She reaches for my head with her less bloody arm and kisses the top of it. I breathe in the plastic smell of my mother's GORE-TEX raincoat. "It's probably gonna feel like that for a long time. I'd give anything to take away that pain for you but I can't."

"I know."

"Just like you can't protect your kids from everything awful. You want to. But you can't. It's the worst thing about being a mother."

"I hate it."

"Me too."

We sit there, quiet now. Bailey kneels on the ground, one elbow resting on the seat of a chair, and scrolls through his phone.

"I know you're mad," my mother says, "and I don't expect you to hear me, especially since you and your dad were two peas in a pod. But listen. I love you and my grands and I'd do anything in the whole wide world for you. And I love your brother even though he hasn't shown up for Christmas in five years."

I wipe my runny nose. "But who's counting?"

"You okay?"

"No."

"You are, Ramona. You're the toughest one of all of us."

"Burkhalter?" It's the woman at reception. "Adelaide Burkhalter? We'll get you back there and looked at in two minutes, 'kay, hon?"

Over her shoulder my mother nods and smiles. Her face looks less cadaverous, so that's good. Whether it's related to the promise of medical assistance or the relief of unloading her true crimes confession, I couldn't tell you. Regardless: phew.

Bailey is back. He plops down in the seat across from mine, keeping his eye on his phone charging across the room, possibly sensing he's walked in on a loaded conversation. He clears his throat.

"I got snacks. Gigi, I wasn't sure what you'd want so I got sour cream and onion Ruffles, pretzels, and a granola bar."

"I'll take the Ruffles," she says.

"I was hoping you'd say that because I want the pretzels."

I fill out the last page on the clipboard and flip through it to make sure I didn't forget anything. When I stand up, Bailey does, too. The sofa I've abandoned has a wet print where my butt used to be.

"Want me to stay here?" Bailey asks. "She shouldn't be by herself, should she?"

She shouldn't, I think. Neither should you, Bailey.

"I'm fine," Mom says. "Get gone."

"I mean, Bailey, if you want to? Or we could ask Jerry to stay."

"All right," Bailey says.

Mom: "I can hear you."

"Okay, Mom, want Bailey to stay or I can go get Jerry?"

"I prefer Bailey, thank you very much." She flips open her bloody wallet with one hand. "It's obvious Jerry is crazy in love with me and I don't know where my feelings stand so that's awkward. Now, Bailey, dear, help out a senior, will you, and see if they have a Diet Dr Pepper over there. Second choice is a Diet Coke. None of that caffeine-free garbage."

9:34 P.M.

Outside, the rain has slowed down. When I wring out the front of my T-shirt, water drips down to the pavement. From here I can see Alex and Peyton Manning have now moved up to the front seat in Jerry's van. Of all the unsettling things I have learned today there is only one that still prevents me from putting one foot in front of the other. I turn around.

"Bailey!" I call out. He's at the vending machine and I squish across the floor to him. "Bailey. Give me your dad's phone number. Or email address. Or something."

He frowns. "He doesn't care."

"He doesn't know."

"All right," Bailey says. With a few long strides he crosses the room to the spot where his Galaxy is plugged in to the wall. "I'm going to share a contact. You know how to open it?"

"I'm a mom, I'm not a moron."

He looks up and grins. Bailey has a dimple and eyelashes at least six inches long and when he smiles—the whole enchilada— it gives me the same feeling as holding a golden retriever puppy against my chest.

"Sent," he says.

"Thanks for babysitting Adelaide."

"If you don't have cash," he says, "you can PayPal me."

"I probably can't afford you. What do you make at Party City?"

"Seven fifty an hour."

"Maybe I can."

"I'm just messing with you, Mrs. Arnold. See you on the other side."

9:42 P.M.

I choose a seat next to Nanette in the first row. Jerry fires up the van.

"Next stop, 53rd Street," he says.

"Jerry, I can't thank you enough for the ride. Do you want to bunk with us for the storm? I can't imagine you want to make that drive back to the islands."

"You're a doll," Jerry says. "Not necessary. I'm dead sober and that's a problem."

I can't parent everyone.

"Down came the rain that washed the spider out," sings Nanette.

Alex picks pine needles from Peyton Manning's thick fur in the front seat.

"I'm ready to go home," he announces.

I lean in and sweep his hair from his eyes.

"Me too, love."

Alex should be in his booster, or at least in the backseat and I can't find a seat belt in the dark.

Fuck it.

Jerry takes a right on DeRenne out of the hospital drive and launches the next verse of Nanette's song: "Up came the sun that dried up all the rain."

Another surprise: Jerry has a lovely voice. It's a velvety baritone that warms the damp interior of the car. You really can't do much about the wet dog smell, though.

"Okay, team," I tell them. "Let's go home."

15

IN A DIFFERENT WORLD
WE WOULD'VE HIGH-FIVED

9:48 P.M.

To: Commander Sergeant Anthony Wilkerson

From: Ramona Burkhalter Arnold

Subject: FYI from neighbor

Pls call or email. Your wife has left SAV. Bailey on his own. We care about him. Need to talk.

10:04 P.M.

By some miracle we still have power.

Or at least our neighbors do. As Jerry drives down our street at a snail's pace, I spy lights on in the Mulaney's living room. Also in the brick cottage of that woman who ties the poop bag around her dachshund's leash. Definitely the Glenn family has power—they're lit up like a dang Christmas tree.

The rain is currently a sideways drizzle and the wind is no joke. Jerry pulls his van into the narrow driveway next to our house. Alex spills out of the car, Peyton Manning hobbles after him and relieves himself on our front lawn next to the hostas. I unbuckle Nanette—she's past overtired, now entering zombie mode—and hoist her into my arms.

"I'm hungry, Mommy," she says. "It is late."

"I know, honey bun."

She clutches my neck. "It has been night for a long time."

There's no need to haul suitcases inside because our bags remain in my dead minivan on Wilmington Island, where it may be swept out to sea and live the rest of its days at the bottom of the river with mer-people. I fiddle with the lock to our front door with my right hand while I balance Nanette on my opposite hip. Jerry deposits the cat and guinea pig on my stoop and unceremoniously reverses and points his van back into the hurricane toward his party, which I have no doubt is just beginning to percolate.

Inside it's dark and still and I'm relieved to be home. I know where we keep the garbage bags. I know there's a stale Easter bunny behind the all-purpose flour in the cabinet. In my rumble with Hurricane Matthew, I now feel a home court advantage.

"Can we get pizza?" Alex asks me.

"I wish, love," I tell him. "Didn't we have pizza last night? I think it's PB and J for dinner."

His shoulders droop: "Hurricanes aren't actually that much fun."

"Agreed," I tell him. "They kinda suck." I set Nanette down on the couch, where she pulls her knees into her chest and scratches her elbow feverishly. "Nanner? You want a sandwich? Or are you just ready for sleep."

"Srwich," she mumbles.

"Okay, sweetie. Let's make sandwiches, and then, guess what? We're going to have a slumber party in the laundry room!"

The idea intrigues her.

"With the dirty clothes?"

"We can move those. We'll make the laundry room an awesome fort with our sleeping bags!"

The only room without windows, I think to myself.

Next to the side door I sit on a kitchen chair, wriggle off my wet sneakers, and peel off my socks. I slide my feet into my ragged deerskin slippers waiting beside the mat. This sensation is the closest I have come to orgasm in months.

Under flickering lights I prepare two peanut butter and jelly sandwiches in the kitchen, crusts on. Most of our snacks are still in my Toyota at Mom's house, so I root through the pantry until I find leftover Power Ranger gummies from Alex's Valentines party and fancy cashews one of Desmond's clients gave us for Christmas last year.

"*Bon appétit,* kids."

I'm hoping for an update from Mom or Bailey. Instead, my phone flashes the low power message before it goes dark. My body feels like I've been trying to pull myself out of quicksand for hours. I'm going to find our candles, that's what I'm going to do. And our flashlights, okay, I locate the big one—it's out of batteries.

I scurry through the house, opening drawers and cabinets with Peyton Manning at my heels. I find three decorative fancy candles that normally I would be a troll about lighting and five half-burned votives leftover from hosting a girls' night in 2014. Our plastic fire starter is in the drawer with Desmond's grilling tools. I remember the John Deere flashlights—green trucks with handles that emit a tiny but real glow—and in Alex's room I rifle through the car bin to find them. There they are! Batteries functioning, praise Jesus. Alex pokes his head into his bedroom where I'm sitting on my heels trying to remember what else I'm supposed to do.

"Mommy, can we get on jammies?" he asks me.

"Of course," I tell him. You know your kid is wasted when lights-out is his idea. "You two pretty tired?" Alex nods. "All right, bring your plates to the sink. Let's get jammicized. Then we'll pull the blankets off our beds and bring them to the laundry room."

"My blanket is heavy," Nanette says.

"It's all right, Nan," I tell her. "I'll help you."

I sweep her up—let's pretend like this is any old night. Just doing our evening routine. I pull the T-shirt over her head, yank down her loaner pants and undies, carefully slide a Dory pull-up over her butt, stuff her in purple fleece pajamas. She doesn't fight me—right now she's a ragdoll, floppy limbs, heavy head.

"Isn't it nice to be back with your potty?" I say.

"Yeah," she sniffs. She stares at me before she leans forward, plants a kiss on my lips, and whispers, "You are a smart and strong girl and I am very proud of you."

This is a sentence I tell my daughter every morning before school and it's possible hearing it repeated back to me at this moment in time might transform my body from a solid into tiny droplets of water.

"Mommy," Alex says. "My toothbrush is back at Gigi's house."

"Oh. You're right. Know what? We'll do a swish clean tonight. Let's use my toothpaste"—opening cabinets, rummaging some more—"and put a bit on your tongue and swish it around."

I deliver blobs of toothpaste to two tongues. This seems to delight them. Alex giggles, foam escaping the sides of his mouth, and Nanette doesn't get it. She stares at her brother.

"Now, spit!"

They do.

The laundry room is next to Nanette's room in our miniature hall. In earlier permutations of our house it was also a half bathroom but Desmond and I ripped out the plumbing with big plans to make a Houzz-inspired mudroom with extra storage since apparently people who built houses in Savannah in the thirties did not believe in closets. We never got around to fixing it up. It's a naked sheetrock room with a sad bulb hanging from the ceiling where we throw stuff we don't want to deal with. I step around the crap when it's time to do laundry, which is every five minutes.

Now I take a fluffy duvet and spread it out over the dusty floor. Then an orange and red afghan Desmond's mom left at our house once. A faded quilt on top of that.

"Is that soft enough for the base of the fort?"

Barefoot Alex treads on the surface I've created.

"I think so," he says, smiling a little. Spots of toothpaste speckle his Iron Man pajama shirt.

"Pillow me," I instruct, and the kids scatter, giggling, retrieving pillows. After the pillows come stuffed whales, Curious George, and Alex's nubbly penguin. "Does that work?"

My kids cheer and I shrug. I light two votive candles, place them on the center of the washer, and find a small spot for myself at the corner of the sleeping quarters, in the space left by Nanette's shortness. I switch off the sad bulb light.

"Mommy," Nanette says. "Where's Minneapolis?"

My stomach drops.

This whole time I've been thinking we're doing okay. Of course I forgot Minneapolis. Minneapolis was probably the most important thing not to forget, more important than my purse, phone, or wounded mother. When did we have him last? Was it when Jerry wanted to use him to bind my mother's cut and I growled at him like a badger?

"Sweetie," I tell her. "I have a feeling he's still in Jerry's van."

I brace myself for the tantrum. I make a hasty mental plan, where I will take Nanette to another room while she screams, rock her until she falls asleep, and then gently place her back in the Panic Room next to Alex. But the tantrum doesn't come.

Instead, I hear my daughter's quiet voice: "Okay."

"Here, Nanny," says Alex. "Want to hug Curious George? He is just as soft as Minneapolis." My sweet firstborn—bless his tender heart.

"No," says Nanette. "He's stupid."

Well.

"Okay, my dears," I tell them. "Let's take deep breaths and rest our bodies and when you wake up, the hurricane will be over."

"Are you sure, Mommy?" Alex says.

"Sure, I'm sure."

"And Daddy will come home?" he says.

"Yes," I fight to keep my tone steady. "He will."

Nanette pushes Alex: "Don't put your leg there."

"Everyone has enough space, okay? We're going to have a resplendent slumber party in the laundry room fort and tomorrow Hurricane Matthew will be gone and the sun will come out."

My kids are quiet for a minute. In the laundry room the sound of the storm is slightly muffled. Still, we hear the wind cranking up. It looks like Nanette is on her way to falling asleep.

We are safe here. I did the damn thing.

Except we hear a new sound—the front door opening—and the three of us jump.

"It's another ghost!" Alex says.

"No, pumpkin," I say. "It's probably Gigi. Stay here. I'll check."

"Honey, I'm home," a voice says.

It's not Gigi.

It's Desmond.

2007

When my friend Lindsay asked me to donate a painting to an auction, I thumbed through my canvases and announced to Desmond that none of my work from college was appropriate. I liked the idea of starting something new. I hauled out my supplies from our moldy storage unit and found my best brushes had frozen bristles and most of the paint jars had a crusty layer of paint around the caps so I spent two hundred dollars on new supplies at Blick.

You can do that when you don't have kids.

We didn't have space to work in our basement apartment on Gwinnett so I set up the canvas next to Desmond's grill on our tiny patio. For two weeks it sat outside and accumulated pollen and smoke, which I found dirty and beautiful—it reminded me of a photo I'd snapped of a broad pillar below the Talmadge Bridge. I sketched an abstract version of the pillar and the cables and layered paint over those, creating contrast with gray and deep, almost black, dark greens. It needed texture so I climbed over the rotting fence behind our patio, plucked palm fronds from our neighbor's yard, pulled them apart like I was shucking corn, allowed them to dry, glued them on the canvas, and then painted over them.

A little darker than your usual stuff, Desmond said when I loaded it into the car. Kinda swampy and scary and I dig it, Christopher wrote, when I emailed him a photo of my piece and invited him to the show.

On the night of the auction I clutched the crook of Christopher's arm in a gallery on Whitaker and tried not to stare at people staring at my painting. It had been many moons since I'd made anything new or showed work and I was glad Christopher was in Savannah for it, even though he drove down to see both me and some third-year law student he described as dreamy, like if Kurt Cobain and George Stephanopoulos had a baby.

He snatched the last shrimp from the server's tray before I could grab it. Quit your whining, he said. She'll be back with more. When the lady did come back she had chicken salad in mini pastry shells. Christopher said he was going to pretend like he was headed to the bar and walk by to see if anyone else had bid on my painting.

I held up my clear plastic cup.

You might as well go to the bar, I said. Get you a refill and one for me, too.

My piece was displayed between a black-and-white photograph of the Tybee Lighthouse and a muted orange ceramic pitcher perched on a podium. Fashion-forward couples and students milled about in the warmly lit room with exposed oatmeal-colored brick. I oscillated between deciding my painting sucked and that it had a haunting beauty about it. Christopher and I said hey to some bidders and artists but mostly clung to each other and got tipsier and tipsier until we saw Desmond and both waved at him frantically like we were trying to hail a cab.

Desmond shaved for the occasion and he'd pressed his khakis—poorly, but still—and he hoisted me up, swung me around, calling me his sexy artist almost wife, then released me and gave Christopher a bear hug, which Christopher accepted.

Desmond wondered where they hung my painting. He was the shittiest whisperer. Then he saw it, and scanning the rest of the room, declared the other submissions were junk. Mine was extraordinary. I hushed him but I was also beaming and a little drunk.

My hand in his, the two of us shuffled over to my painting. Now there were three penciled-in numbers on the bidding sheet. Christopher bowed over the clipboard under another mixed media piece. Up close I was pleased how the palm fronds worked out.

Look at those bids, Desmond said.

I'd sell it for a gas station pickle, I said.

He squeezed me tight and I felt a familiar amusement park ride of desire. We could have sex tonight even with Christopher sleeping on the living room couch. Sometimes Trying to be Quiet Sex is the best kind. Or it was possible Christopher would ditch us for the cute Law Dawg and that wouldn't be a problem. At the bar Desmond said he was so proud of me and asked the bartender for a to-go cup.

Y'all have fun, he said to us. I'm going to meet Stu and his buddy at the Bohemian.

What?

This is your night with Christopher, Desmond said. I don't want to harsh your vibe. Seriously, I love your piece. If it sells for less than two thou everyone in here is a goddamn idiot.

Then he gave me a rough kiss on the cheek.

Cool, okay.

Christopher and I watched him sweep out of the gallery, first stopping to give a hug and high five to a couple he knew— Desmond knows everyone in Savannah—then out through the glass door, down the street, phone out of his pocket. Christopher gently tugged on my hair and asked if I knew that was the plan. I was going to pretend like I knew Desmond was bailing. But I can never lie to Christopher.

I made reservations, I said.

For three of us?

I feel stupid. I thought he was coming.

He must have gotten mixed up. Or it might have been me. Maybe he didn't want to go if I was coming.

Christopher. He's known you forever. Are you wearing bronzer?

Does it look dumb?

No, it looks good. I was going to tell you, I forgot.

After three glasses of wine, Christopher's accent got slower and thicker. He said, let's go to Alligator Soul and drink more and stuff our faces. If there isn't some kind of funky butter or new crustacean on the menu I shall be very disappointed.

All right, I said.

Want to get our coats? I gotta piss.

I retrieved our coats from a tiny woman with thick platinum braids coiled on top of her head. I wished I could conjure up my earlier giddiness to replace my disappointment, but it was like pulling a Jenga stick from the bottom and balancing it on the top of the pile—too precarious. I felt so stupid, here in the gallery with my blown-out hair that was starting to frizz and my knee-high boots hurting like all get-out. Maybe I should have told Desmond how excited I was for a night out celebrating my art with my two best boys. My fiancé wasn't very good at reading my mind but he shouldn't have to.

I wondered if we should be getting married. I shrugged my coat over my shoulders and here came Christopher with my painting tucked under his arm.

You didn't, I said.

I did. It's a fucking amazing piece.

I love you.

I love you, too, dork. He lifted up my painting and tipped it from side to side like one of those people holding signs on the side of the road: Store Closing Everything Must Go.

Thanks be to Jesus you made reservations for three, he said, because we need chairs for three masterpieces.

10:44 P.M.

It's only been two days but Desmond looks older, and I hate to admit it, Han Solo–ish: stubbly, threadbare T-shirt, dingy puffy vest, greasy hair, pleading eyes.

I want to throw myself into his arms—my partner is back, the person who helps me handle the wackiness of parenthood—he's here! Then I remember I hate him. These two thoughts produce opposing forces inside me like my organs are trying to escape from their lining.

"What the what?" I hiss.

Desmond slides past me, smelling like the cigarettes he quit before Alex was born. "I never left. I'm not going to bunk on some random couch while my family is stuck in a Cat Four."

"So you're some kind of hero."

"I wouldn't say that." He hovers in our tiny landing with his ancient L.L.Bean bookbag over one shoulder. "How did you get back into Savannah?"

"I kind of," I tell him, "made a break for it past a cop."

He nods. In a different world we would've high-fived and said, *respect*. Or I would have told the extended version of the story and we would laugh about it. I might have included this new juicy tidbit about my mother's sex life, past and present. In the kitchen Clarence Thomas scuttles from one side of the cage to the other and Desmond notices him.

"What in the world?"

"Class pet," I say. "Clarence Thomas. Named after a notable Savannahian."

"They could have named him Big Boi. Kids sleeping?"

"Probably not yet," I say. He dumps his backpack on the coffee table, which irritates me. My husband and I are 180 degrees away from our old lives and he's still depositing belongings around the house like his mother or I will pick them up. He charges toward Alex's bedroom until I redirect him: "Laundry."

"Daddy!" I hear Nanette exclaim. "I just went pee pee in the potty."

It's true, but that was one time out of nineteen million accidents. I trudge into the living room and plop down on a leather chair, cheered by the memory of Tito's in the freezer. Waiting for Desmond to come back, I hear him peeing in the bathroom and it's the longest stream I've heard in the history of urine.

He's back.

"Ramona?" he says. "Will you talk to me?"

"I don't know if I'm ready for all that," I tell him. Then, curious: "What do you have to say?"

"I'm sorry," he says. "I am so sorry."

"That's all?"

"It's not enough."

"No," I tell him, sighing. "It's not."

"I've got to try. I'll do whatever I can."

"You messed up everything."

He sits down on the couch and hangs his head: "I know."

"Stop agreeing with me!"

"But I fucked up. I don't really have a case to defend myself," he says.

"Why didn't you tell me you were unhappy? We could've worked on things before you went and did this."

"I'm not the best communicator."

"No shit, Sherlock."

"Listen. Ramona, please listen. I've been thinking about it. If a marriage is going okay, not great, and not horrible—I think people have the tendency to sort of, just, float by," he says.

"I can't recall any period of you and me I'd describe as *floating*."

"What I mean is that nobody is going to be motivated to change things. Maybe it takes something like this—"

"Inviting a whore into our marital bed . . ."

Desmond's face contorts like he's passing a kidney stone. "Like that. To force things to the light."

"No. I'm not good at talking either but that's not how I operate. We could've gone to counseling."

His eyes light up. "We still can. Let's go to counseling."

"I don't know."

"You don't know what?"

"Anything at all right now."

"Ramona," Desmond says, covering his face with his hands and then letting them drop to his knees. He's still wearing his wedding ring and so am I. "You and me weren't great. So I was worried about us. And clearly out of my mind."

"Why were you worried? I'm the most loyal person, ever. If you hadn't gone and did what you did, you'd never be rid of me, for your whole life. I still have friends from preschool."

"I know," Desmond says.

"And kindergarten. And junior high. Like Vicky."

"I was starting to feel," he says, "like you hated me."

"Huh?"

"You hated me. If I touched you, you pulled away like I was a leper. You acted like I was in the way. You wanted to do everything with the kids your way, you didn't let me help, you were Joan of Arc with your job, my job meant nothing, you didn't want to spend time with me after work, you just wanted to get the kids in bed, and watch your show on the couch."

"Yeah, so. I do everything," I tell him. "And I'm so tired."

"Everything?"

"Yeah."

"Ramona," he says. "I know you want to stab me but you can't claim I'm a deadbeat dad."

"That's not what I'm saying. Still I feel like I'm working harder than you. All the time, at everything. And I don't like that feeling and I don't like myself when most of my day consists of resenting you."

"See?"

"See, what?"

"I wasn't the only one unhappy," he says.

"Every marriage has stuff like that! Everyone goes through phases where they don't like each other. In good marriages you ride it out. You work your shit out! You don't go and fuck the closest Lululemon mom at your kid's school."

Like my parents, I think. In my psychedelic swirl of feelings now I veer toward pride that my mother and father triumphed over infidelity. Unlike my lazy generation of meal delivery kit ordering marriage quitters.

"That's fair," Desmond says. "You didn't want to work on it, though. I didn't think you would even talk about the idea of working on it. Sarah Ellen—it wasn't a plan, it definitely wasn't a plan, but the opportunity presented itself, and I thought, maybe I'll do this thing, and that will give me a little more patience in my marriage. Maybe that thing will tide me over until you come back to me."

"That's the dumbest thing I ever heard."

"Probably is."

"Let me get this straight. You thought if you had an affair, you'd get enough sexy thrills out of your system to tolerate me a couple more years. What happens after that? A new client? Or you call up Sarah Ellen again?"

I don't like my voice like this.

"It was stupid. I don't want to end our marriage. For the last two days I've been trying to figure out why I did it and I'm thinking it was a dumb thing," he says, "to get through the place we were in."

"Well," I say.

"Does that make sense?"

"Not really. People cheat because they're unhappy. That's like Psych 101. It's obvious we were both unhappy but instead of addressing it, which, I'll admit—I sucked at, too—you went and did this. We went from not really connected and going through the motions to one of us feeling angry and distrustful and the other one hopefully feeling like a rotten guilty shithead. If there was any hope of upgrading from the first situation, your thing with Sarah Ellen makes that infinitely harder now. And it hurts like hell. It will always," I tell him, "hurt like hell."

He is crying now.

"You need to know," he says, "how much . . ." He doesn't finish because we hear footsteps in the hall—it's Alex.

"Guys? It's scary back there but we don't want to come out when you're fighting."

"Nice," I tell Desmond. I am shaking. "We're already freaking out our kids and we haven't even split up yet." Alex looks to Desmond and then back to me and bites his lip.

No!

That was too much. What did I say? I don't have control of what's coming out of my mouth. Alex turns around and plods back to the laundry room, I don't think he understood, or hopefully he's too exhausted to hang on to one comment. I wipe my nose with the back of my hand and start to gnaw on my pinky nail.

Desmond stands up. "Yet?"

"What are you doing?"

"They need me," he says. "You're the one who doesn't."

Inside the laundry room the candle on top of the dryer flickers. Peyton Manning paces in the center of the comforter before making a circle and lying down. Nanette is in a half-agitated trance, whimpering and flailing around like she took a bad dose of something. I navigate the pile of blankets trying not to step on anybody. I lower myself into Nanette's corner, and pull her toward me, her head on my chest, hoping my proximity, my smell, and gently rubbing her back will help her calm down.

I shift my position so my neck isn't at an uncomfortable angle against the washer. Desmond chooses the corner opposite from me and extends his arms out to Alex, who stumbles into them. My heart is still beating crazy fast from our talk. What the hell does he mean, *I'm the one who doesn't*? I feel like my insides have been scraped out with an ice-cream scoop. Nanette sucks on the section of my T-shirt she's gripping.

"Daddy," Alex says. "Nanner doesn't have Minneapolis."

I wave my free arm: Stop! Don't you dare bring up Minneapolis when we narrowly escaped a kamikaze tantrum. Oddly enough, Nanette doesn't respond because right now the edge of my shirt is soothing enough. I tuck a stray lock of her hair behind her ear and trace circles on her back.

"It's okay," Desmond tells Alex. "We'll find him tomorrow. Let's get some rest, okay?"

"Okay," Alex says.

"Night, night, buddy," Des says.

Alex pipes up, "I have a wiggly tooth and Gigi cut her arm."

"Cool," says Desmond. "And not cool. You can tell me more tomorrow."

The light from the hallway dims. A moment of quiet before the power surges, and we hear our appliances reboot—a hum, a buzz, a whirr. Then the power goes off again and stays there.

"See you, power," Desmond says.

"Take it sleazy," I say.

I try to deepen my breath so Nanette will match her inhales and exhales with mine. It's working. She twists her body so her head is now on my shoulder. She stretches her arms out and closes her eyes with one elbow over her head. After a minute she launches a toddler snore.

Outside, it doesn't seem as loud anymore. I hear the sound of regular wind, not the wild stuff.

"Maybe it's over," I whisper.

"No," Desmond says. "It's the eye."

Desmond looks uncomfortable. But Alex is on his way to drifting off, too, in which case, nobody moves a muscle or else. *Get some sleep*, Desmond mouths to me, and my instinct is to snap-whisper, *you don't get to tell me what to do, you lying, cheating double-crosser.*

I'm just too tired.

The candles make shadows on the back of the door.

I close my eyes.

16

HOW IT FEELS TO
BE A RODEO QUEEN

SATURDAY
1:05 A.M.

We could work things out.

We could.

We could talk to someone—a professional. He or she—no, it's got to be a she—she might give me space to yell and rant and cry in an office with a tissue box thoughtfully positioned on an espresso end table. She might give me tools. Ideas on how to move forward as a compassionate person in a marriage that has experienced a few hiccups.

I guess my parents did it. Other people, I can't think of examples right now, but I'm sure there are some who worked it out. All right: Bill and Hillary Clinton. There you go—if the future first female president of the United States can forgive, surely I can, too.

It won't hurt this badly forever. I know that.

Even the things that always hurt—rejection, heartbreak, death—eventually they take a backseat to other stuff.

I have the capacity to forgive, or at least I'd like to think I do.

I would not have the same blind trust I used to have. I would be the same me, except with a little edge. That's marriage, right? It's a union between humans—not robots. I would practice becoming a better person. I wouldn't throw Desmond's mistake in his face every time I didn't get my way.

I wonder if my father managed that. When he was dying, did he look back on a full life of friendship, family, travel, grandkids with mismatched socks, sticky hands, and tiny freckles? Or as Mom fussed with his pillows and clipped his toenails, did he look at her and think, I can't believe you went and did that.

I guess I'll never know.

Every relationship is different.

We could work things out.

Or not.

1:40 A.M.

I fall asleep during the eye of Hurricane Matthew and I dream about Jerry. He's still holding his inside-out umbrella and trying to bring Minneapolis to us but the bridge over Wilmington River collapses, leaving him standing on the other side holding my daughter's blanket.

My rest isn't deep and it doesn't last long. I wake up to the sounds of the house creaking, groans, sighs, and pings coming from every corner. We hear cracking and falling limbs of trees. The wind roars through the neighborhood, only it doesn't sound like wind, more like a tidal wave.

Peyton Manning stands up, his ears flatten, he utters a low growl. One of the candles has burned down to the wick, the other one is still going. Desmond is awake now, too—I catch his eyes in the half dark.

It feels like the storm is trying its damnedest to pick up the roof of our house. And when that happens, and it feels likely it will, because the wind is relentless, attacking our house like the Big Bad Wolf, where will our huddled-together group of four go then? This is the panic room—we don't have another one.

An explosion of thunder combined with a crash from what I assume is a major tree down wakes up the kids. Their bodies jolt. Nanette flails her limbs, moans, then she falls back asleep. Alex is awake, alert, and petrified.

"Mommy!" he says.

My sweet seven-year-old, he is still my baby. I stretch out my other arm, the one that isn't holding Nanette and Alex crawls over to me and nestles by my side. His breath is stale and his small body shakes with sobs.

"It's okay," I tell him. "It's all right. The sounds make everything scarier."

"Is it going to pick up our house?"

"No," I say.

"It's throwing trees at us."

"Some branches may come down. But we're safe here. We're inside. Nothing's going to get us."

I squeeze the top of my son's thin arm. I'm telling him that stuff but I don't believe it. Becoming a parent means losing the privilege to freak the fuck out.

Another crash, followed by a ripping sound.

This has got to be the scariest part of this thing.

Right?

Because I am terrified.

I deliver an imaginary slap to my own face. I hear my mother's voice telling me to put on my big girl panties.

There is no time for fear or doubt. I will keep my babies safe. I can get through this.

3:43 A.M.

Thunder like the sound of a cannon firing stirs me from another brief snooze.

It feels so close, like it's right next to us in the hall. Now Nanette sits up, rubs her eyes, starts to cry. On my other side Alex writhes and slings his right arm out from his blankets to thwack me in the jaw.

"It's all right, sweeties," I whisper. "We're safe. Mommy and Daddy are here."

Together, for the time being. Desmond is rooting around the pillows for his phone and when he finds it, it lights up his face.

"It's moving northeast. Hopefully we won't have much more of this," he says.

"It's going away, you guys. We're safe," I repeat.

I like to think this is my finest acting performance of all time. Why, oh, why did we settle in a city with such beautiful and deadly trees and a propensity for flooding? I chew on the nail on my right pinky finger until I draw blood. I never imagined a life in Savannah, Georgia. I thought I'd raise my children some place where I would wear sweaters. A bright yellow wool coat with three tortoiseshell buttons.

It's stuffy in the laundry room and it smells like body odor and kid feet. We all jump again when we hear glass breaking on the other side of the house. Even though it's probably a branch, it sounds like an invasion.

Something has definitely breached the kitchen—now the wind sounds louder and closer. Agitated, Desmond rises, knocking a container of Tide pods off the shelf, looking like a giant in our tiny laundry room. He's Alice in Wonderland after she eats the cake.

"Sit back down," I hiss. "We can't do anything about it now."

He obeys, but not before shooting me a look of irritation. I can tell he wants to be manly and run out and fix something and not doing that drives him crazy. My other hand is pins and needles from its new position under Alex. Peyton Manning curls around in a donut shape to lick his balls.

"Probably the glass in the side door. The screen is two hundred years old," Desmond says.

I know he wants me to reassure him, to tell him it's probably not a big deal, we'll get it fixed, at least we're all right, it could've been worse.

Instead, I tell him, "Yes. It's broken."

4:52 A.M.

I alternate between ankle-deep sleep and delirium. My body gets heavy, my head rolls to the side, then sounds of the storm startle me and I'm jerked back to life. Across from me Desmond uses a rolled up hot pink beach towel as a pillow, one knee is bent, one leg is extended. He's still wearing his sneakers. His T-shirt is drenched with sweat.

Is what we created together a life?

The physical evidence suggests yes. The row of sandy flip-flops deposited inside our side door. Alex's St. Patrick's Day shamrock from preschool secured to the fridge with a stegosaurus magnet. The Savannah United sticker pressed to the side of Desmond's ancient Ford. The red fifteen-pound kettlebells we bought at Dick's Sporting Goods and never used. Nanette's unfinished grape Tootsie Pop we saved in a Ziploc sandwich bag. The Pretend Box, stuffed with polyester Halloween costumes turned inside out. Our toothbrushes, leaning toward each other in a Wet Willie's souvenir cup. The Band-Aid Alex didn't need anymore, curled up next to his Thomas the Tank Engine alarm clock he claims is babyish. The blue goggles hanging on the hook next to the keys. Nanette's bottle of detangling spray pasted to the ledge of the tub with a sliver of an old bar of soap. The plastic Tony the Tiger dish next to the detergent, filled with rocks I take out from Alex's pockets before I put his pants in the washer.

Or if we go our separate ways, does all of this disappear? If we stay together, will I be buried alive underneath it?

I've got to be there somewhere. I will look for me underneath the rubble of the hurricane. When everything is topsy turvy like a giant shook our little snow globe of a house, I will put on gloves. I will drop down to my knees and pull back kettlebells and branches and Halloween costumes and flip-flops and keep digging and digging even if spiky thorns scratch my arms.

I hear my mother say, "You're the toughest one of us all."

1994

In the parking lot of Pike Creek Bible Church, the orange-pink sky was reflected in the windows of a dusty bus, the only other vehicle in the parking lot besides my mother's Nissan. The sun sank slowly. My mother was teaching me how to drive stick shift. A skill, she explained, every woman should master.

I sucked at first. Like, big time.

It's a learning curve, Mom said, sweating by my side in madras shorts and White Linen. You're not going to get it right away.

She was dipping into a bottomless reservoir of patience during this lesson, which should have been reassuring.

Instead, hot lava bubbled up in my belly and reached for my throat.

I need to get things right away— I want to be a natural at everything, I told her.

At that, Mom produced an audible inhale that sounded like the instrument the dentist uses to vacuum out my spit. I squirmed in the driver's seat.

Let's try this again. I placed my hands on the steering wheel, hot from the sun. I pressed the clutch with my left foot, twisted the key in the ignition, and pushed the gear into first. So far, so good. Gently applying pressure on the gas pedal, I propelled the Nissan ten feet forward.

Next I bore down on the clutch again—too hard—and yanked the gear toward my body to second. I slammed my foot down on the gas; the car leaped forward, then started bucking to and fro, sending our heads back and forth, our seat belts searing across our chests, before stalling with an angry hiss.

It's okay, Ramona, Mom said, you'll get it. In the meantime, now I know how it feels to be a rodeo queen.

I was furious—I felt like such a doofus. I moaned and made another effort. That time, it was a little better, I got to second gear. When I tried to shift to third, it didn't take, and once again the car stalled.

You're not giving it enough gas when you lift your foot off the clutch. It's about balance. Imagine a seesaw, Mom said.

Why are we doing this? I whined. I'm going to live in Brooklyn. I won't even need a car.

A white Buick glided by. The driver, an older woman with thick glasses, peered at us before looking away. We sat next to each other in silence. I found a typo in the sign for Summer Bible Camp. It should have said "registration," not "regirstration."

My mother said, let's give it another go, cookie. Remember, you don't have to slam on the gas. Just add pressure and release the clutch.

All right.

It was officially dusk. Now the sky was pink lemonade, a color I had tried to reproduce in my paintings with medium success. I saw a bright yellow light, then another near the entrance of the church, tiny flickers popping up across the parking lot. Lightning bugs.

I took deep breaths and tried again, twice. On the first attempt, I made it to third gear before stalling. I was feeling cocky on my next try so I sent the car jerking forward once again.

I caught my reflection in the mirror—my face was red and blotchy. The corners of my mouth turned down like I was going to cry. I hated everyone, especially my mother, who opened up a channel I did a decent job keeping shut most of the time.

Ramona, Mom said, reaching over to pat my hand, don't be so hard on yourself. I believe in you.

Now I felt bad for hating her because she was so calm.

You shouldn't, I said. I wasn't crying but you could hear a warble in my voice.

That's the thing, she said. Part of the contract. I'll always believe in you even when you don't.

I nodded and tried to psych myself up. *You can do this, Ramona. You are a smart girl. You got an A in pre-calculus even though the teacher seemed roofied for most of the second semester.* The car shuddered as I turned the key once again.

Here we go. Wait a minute, the car was actually moving. I shifted from first to second, second to third, then third to—hold the phone—fourth! I was steering the Nissan around the parking lot; so far the car was in no danger of dying. Exhilarated, I rolled down both our windows with the automatic control.

Wooooooo, I squealed, driving in circles.

Wooooooo, said Mom. By golly she's got it!

The air rushed by us. It tickled my face and sent my hair streaming behind me. I wasn't hot anymore and I didn't feel like crying. It's weird how feelings can change so quickly.

7:16 A.M.

I don't know when I fell asleep. I remember staring at Desmond until the second candle snuffed out and I couldn't see his face anymore. In the dark I listened to the screaming wind, the branches crackling outside, and the soft snoring of my seven-year-old. At some point I must have drifted off.

Because when I wake up the house is quiet. Light peeks from the crack underneath the door of the laundry room. Every neighborhood in my body is sore. My neck, from the angle where I fell asleep against the dryer. My back, from the driving. My shoulders and arms, from carrying Nanette most of the day.

My family, snug in our laundry room fort, is still asleep. Good— they need it. I gently roll Alex to the side and cover him with a blanket. He's not going to wake up, his body is so spent I can drive a backhoe digger through here and he wouldn't flinch. Slowly, quietly, goddamn I'm sore, I rise and tiptoe over sleeping bodies.

In the hall the silence is jarring. I don't even hear the *shhh-shhhing* of the wind in the trees anymore. I turn the corner and there's my living room in the morning light. Yes. The boxy sofa which looked midcentury and sophisticated when we bought it but now it's got pilled fabric and an orange popsicle stain on one arm. The Oriental rug Des's mom gave us that we duct taped to the floor because the kids kept racing by it and slipping.

It's all here. We're okay. Nothing has changed.

Then again, everything has.

17

THE TREES THAT
ARE STILL STANDING

8:39 A.M.

Desmond holds a paper plate of bacon in our neighbor's driveway. Leave it to my husband to transform a disaster into a tailgate. I watch him, chatting and chewing, while I slouch on the
steps in my yoga pants praying for coffee.

The kids make an obstacle course from the damage on our
street. They hurdle over downed trees. They swat branches at
other fallen branches. Every now and then Alex returns to me,
red-faced, and breathless, to make a report. *There's a tree all the
way through that house with the yellow door. I saw a pumpkin in
somebody's pool. The fence next to the baseball field blew over.
Mommy, you gotta see the roots of the tree on the corner of Paulsen,
it's cray-cray.*

And it is, for lack of a better adjective, cray.

It looks like Hurricane Matthew took a green marker and
scribbled all over our neighborhood. Any previous boundaries between natural life and asphalt are gone. The street is

covered in debris: leaves, twigs, branches, pine needles. Two doors down a live oak capsized on a neighbor's garage, its thick branches horizontal now. Its roots have uplifted the earth, exposing a massive underbelly of thick, snakelike cords, and a gash in the ground where the tree used to be. The power lines zigzag across the landscape and I feel an old urge to photograph them. A ripped-off screen door curls around a battered hedge.

Plugging my phone into the charger in Desmond's truck I exchange texts with Bailey, who informs me that my mother has six stitches and attaches a pic of her asleep in the waiting room with mouth and Ruffles bag wide open. I catch up with Nicole, who still considers me an idiot for returning to Savannah though she's relieved I survived. I offer to check out her house but she's already been in touch with her neighbors via an association group on Facebook. I should've known she'd be on it. She suggests we meet for a falafel at Al Salaam Deli when she gets back and I tell her I didn't know we were falafel friends and she says, I think you could use one.

The scary sound we heard during our slumber party? A teenage magnolia crossed the driveway to smash the front corner of our house, severing the roof and puncturing the window over the sink. It's currently chopped up and stacked in a neat pile at the front edge of our yard—Desmond's first priority this morning. I sweep up glass in the kitchen, cover the window with a blurry plastic tarp we use to catch the Christmas tree needles, and secure it with black Gorilla tape.

The sky is a lighter shade of gray today. When I feel a breeze cross my cheeks, I'm grateful it's not moving at 90 miles per hour. I'm semi-social with neighbors assessing the damage, and there are groups of people clustered on the street. Many of them are snapping aftermath pictures for other people—the ones who left. A category formerly known as us.

Desmond keeps looking over at me. He feels familiar, and some of him feels like he's asking if it's okay it's familiar. I want to say, just relax, guy. I'm not going to make decisions about my marriage while I'm picking up Peyton Manning's poop in a plastic Walmart bag and you're standing next to a primitive grill talking to neighbor Brooks about the power grid on the islands. It would be thoughtful of me to convey that idea somehow—I'm not that nice.

I rack my brain thinking of any place in Savannah I could get coffee. It appears a catty-corner neighbor has a generator. I should've been friendlier to that couple. Maybe they'll let me plug in my Mr. Coffee just for a hit. I'm still brainstorming on options when I spot two trim figures at the stop sign making their way toward my house.

Mom. Bailey!

"Guys!" They don't hear me at first. My mother keeps marching down the sidewalk in her tidy clip. "Mom!"

The second time she hears me—her face lights up and she picks up the pace. Bailey offers an exaggerated wave, which shakes his entire body, and soon he's intercepted by Alex and Nanette, who tackle him. I skip down our tiny path to greet them. When I reach my mother, I throw my arms around her.

"What the hell? I was safe at the hospital!"

"I know," I say. "I don't know. I'm all squishy."

My mom is here. My imperfect mother who pisses me off at every turn but will never let me down.

"Well," she says, patting my shoulder. "It's been a time."

"How's your cut?" I ask her.

Beaming, she shows off her bandaged arm: "Stitched up! I guess it was pretty bad."

"Told you."

"Okay, y'all may have been right."

"Once in a while. And Jerry? It was nice of him to help."

"Eh."

"You probably have to marry him now."

"Ramona!"

"Kidding."

"Everyone okay over here?"

"Depends on your definition," I say. Bailey appears at Mom's shoulder with Nanette trailing him. She's stuffing sticks she doesn't want to lose into the pocket of his track pants.

"Mrs. Arnold," he says.

"Bailey!" I reach out to squeeze him. We all smell. I don't care.

"I got an email from my dad."

"Of course you did. I knew he'd write back."

"He's going to call me. Or you," Bailey says.

"Or me," Mom says. "We wrote him back and gave him plenty of numbers."

I kind of want to hug Bailey again or fist bump but that seems dorky.

"Our house is okay," Bailey says. "That stop sign wasn't in our yard before. But nothing big fell on the house."

"Yay," I say.

"We made it, team," Mom says. "We've got cleaning up to do but we made it to the other side."

She looks at me and we're both thinking: well, except for that other thing. My mother's eyes find Desmond. He's talking to a neighbor and when he turns around and sees Adelaide he lifts his beer in a hopeful cheers. He doesn't know she knows but I imagine he suspects now.

"Where did my grands run off to?" she says. "I would kill someone for a Diet Coke."

12:46 P.M.

Mom and I scrounge up lunch for the kids. It's hot. Even though I've got every window open except for the taped-up one, it's still 85 degrees outside. Without air-conditioning or fans, we're unlikely to feel relief until the wee hours of the morning.

Alex and Nanette are filthy from their neighborhood explorations, bright red and sweaty with dirt forming a grimy paste on their faces, necks, arms, and ankles. They're operating on minimal sleep and a natural high following the passing of the storm and the news that school has been canceled indefinitely.

Mom and I serve peanut butter and jelly for lunch with ToastChee crackers and apple slices. Alex and Nanner demolish the crackers and pick at their sandwiches. (What kind of entitled bullshit is this? There's nothing wrong with eating

PB&J for every meal.) They race off to their bedrooms to play with their toys, precious items that weren't precious enough to stuff in the Spider-Man suitcase, leaving apple crescents with one bite missing, crumbs on their place mats.

Bailey's jaw hosts slight fuzz today and it occurs to me he's old enough to shave. My mother eases herself down on a chair next to him and taps her coral painted fingernails on a plastic place mat with a map of the USA on it. Now she's bobbing her knee up and down like she's waiting for the teacher to call on her.

"I got an idea," she says.

I roll my eyes at Bailey. "Pins and needles over here."

"What if," she says, "now, no pressure—but what if Bailey comes to stay with me for a minute?"

Bailey rests his sandwich on his plate.

"Like," she continues, "until the other stuff gets worked out."

I'm looking at Mom to ascertain what kind of crack rock she's smoking. She's no spring chicken. And who wants to raise a teenager after you finished getting two out of the house a long time ago? A really, really long time ago. My instinct to tell her what a ridiculous idea that is rises to the surface, the reasons floating above my head—for one thing, he's got actual legal guardians, hello, and another thing, there's a house—organizing themselves in an invisible bullet pointed list.

"Like, live with you?" he says.

My mother shrugs. "If you want."

"For free?"

"Sure," Mom says. "Why not?"

Bailey looks over at me. I have a lot of experience living in

the same house as Adelaide—it doesn't seem like the appropriate time to share my thoughts on that. When I see her jittering
as she waits for Bailey's response, it occurs to me that the life
Mom has created after Dad's death—Jerry, the tennis league,
Sophie and Peyton Manning, pet-rejecting Susan—might be a
little lonelier than she's letting on. And it's maddeningly difficult to resent my mother for a blunder she made decades ago
when I see the way she's still showing up for all of us: Alex, Nanette, Bailey, me.

"I could do that," Bailey says.

"I have internet," my mother says. "There's also chickens."

"The chickens are assholes," I say.

"Ramona, hush. I could drive you to school if you wanted."

"Ask her," I suggest, "to drop you off two blocks from the entrance."

"Ramona! Who's being an asshole now?"

She's smiling, though. And so is Bailey. Hunched over my tiny
kitchen table, they seem to have established some weird little
friendship. I want good things for Bailey. I feel a flare of joy at the
idea that my mother, and maybe even me, can help with that.

I make myself a sandwich and eat it on the couch in the living room watching through the front window as Desmond and
other men from the neighborhood strut around with power
tools. My children pull out the blankets from the laundry room
and take turns pulling each other down the hall and crashing
into walls. I charge my phone using a neighbor's portable USB
charger. It's the size of a Pez dispenser. I didn't even know those
had been invented.

3:14 P.M.

When I see Kenneth's name on caller ID, I feel a knot in my stomach and the adrenaline of Rocky mounting the stone steps at the Philadelphia Museum of Art. I settle down cross-legged on the kitchen floor between Sophie's empty cat carrier and Clarence Thomas's cage.

"Kenneth."

"Ramona!" Kenneth says. "She lives."

"Kenneth," I repeat, firmly.

"We were worried about you." I can see him striding between the cubicles of our office in his tight pants. "It's great to hear your voice! I didn't want you to get swept out to sea."

"I'm okay."

"Good," Kenneth says. "Kewl. Can we talk Laser Life?"

None of that was kewl. Actually, that was the anti-kewl.

I take a deep breath: "No."

"Not a good time?" he asks me.

I scratch the sand gnat bites on my right ankle. What is Kenneth doing now? Is he pulling on his ear? He's probably lamenting the day he hired this almost-forty-mother-of-two to create diversity (and bless him, he may consider me diverse) in the workplace.

"It's not a good time, Kenneth. We just had a hurricane. I care about my job but right now I have responsibilities as a mother. And a daughter. I can't talk Laser Life right now."

"Okay..."

"So," I continue, "if this means you don't think I can work

there anymore, that's fine. But the stress of trying to pretend like I can do this job and that my family doesn't come first is crazy. It's unnatural to worry about work during a natural disaster. My kids come first."

Clarence Thomas looks up at me.

"Ramona!" Kenneth says. "You know we support families."

"Do you, really?"

"Of course. That being said we expect you to at least communicate when things come up. It's part of being on the team. I'm kind of disappointed."

"When things come up? Like a monster storm? Kenneth, I don't care if you're disappointed. I did on Friday but I don't anymore. I've been through a lot."

"I'm not sure what to say."

"You don't have to say anything."

"All right," Kenneth says.

"I'm really good at my job, Kenneth. Don't you think so?"

"Of course," he says. "You're a valuable component of the team."

"I'm not a component! I'm a human. And I work hard and I'm good at it. Really good. And I actually enjoy my job when I don't feel like you're breathing down my neck. You can plan all the duckpin bowling teambuilding events you want and stock the lounge with organic gummy bears—ultimately you need to respect and trust your employees if you want a business to grow. Also, I don't deserve to feel like my job is on the brink every time my family needs me. That's not fair."

In Kenneth's silence I listen to the buzzing of chain saws and generators outside my kitchen.

"I didn't," Kenneth says, "realize you felt this way."

"Well."

"Like, about me. Not respecting you."

I stand up and sweep wood chips off my butt.

"Now you do. Okay? How about," I say, "you think about whether or not you want to fire me and let me know. I have my laptop. Most likely the kids won't have school next week. So I will be staying home. Or somewhere else. Because a tree crashed through my kitchen. If you don't want to fire me, I can probably check in at the end of next week. Kewl?"

He's quiet, then he murmurs, "That's fine."

He sounds so sad—I feel a rush of compassion after telling him to fuck off.

That only lasts for a minute because then I get the idea to boil water for instant coffee on our grill, which doesn't really work out. My coffee ends up tasting like burgers.

4:22 P.M.

I remember that day in the post office when I learned that Prince died. Squinting to read the words from the glare of the clerk's phone. I love his songs, the way he walked, how he oozed creativity from every pore, like he couldn't stop it. I liked knowing he was in the world. At the time I felt like something irretrievable was gone.

Even though there's a shit-ton of stuff I haven't figured out, I learned one thing—Prince didn't die so that I can live. His passing was a message from the beyond, not unlike the helicopters that buzz back and forth across Tybee Island with advertisements. Only instead of encouraging beachgoers to save more with Geico, Prince's death made me realize the way I was operating was *no bueno*.

I thought becoming a grown-up meant you have to give up things. Some of them you probably should: exotic animals, motorcycles, white furniture, heroin. But you don't have to sacrifice creativity or joy.

See, I wasn't unhappy because Prince died. It was because I completely forgot how to live.

I make a vow to myself things will change. They have to. If I have the Super Ramona strength to survive the last three days, I can learn how to hop off the thankless hamster wheel of Mom life I fashioned with a little help from Des, but mostly on my own. I feel bubbles in my chest—I am my own flavor of seltzer water— lift me up. I can do this. The only person who can infuse the absurdities of parenthood with the humor and sparkle of a Prince song—that's me.

The sun is back. I didn't think it would come but it did. I spot it behind the trees that are still standing.

6:41 P.M.

In the late afternoon we polish off the tin of cashews and continue to work through our supply of booze. We help neighbors Dan and Maddy lift a dense branch from the hood of their Jeep Cherokee. Mom and Bailey shuffle two doors down to stuff a rolling carry-on full of essentials and collect Bailey's school supplies.

Desmond delivers them to the La Quinta Inn on Abercorn in his truck. I brave a lukewarm shower. The kids wriggle out of filthy clothes and pull on their jammies.

"It could have been so much worse," Desmond says, cracking open a beer—his fourth since lunch—on our sofa.

"It could've."

"Tomorrow I'll round up materials. I'll call the guys. The roof patch shouldn't take half a day. Less than that."

As the light fades in the living room, our collection of candles flickers from strategic locations: the mantel, the coffee table, the shelf next to the front door. From my spot on the couch I watch the tarp billow over the sink in the kitchen and I see dark, black rectangles on the microwave and the oven where the time is usually displayed. It would almost be romantic if you subtract the humidity and random potpourri of scents.

"Listen," I tell Desmond. "The other thing. Maybe it can be fixed and maybe not."

My husband rests his beer on the coffee table, reaches for my knee, then decides against it.

"You and me," he says.

"Yup. What you did with Sarah Ellen wasn't okay. And our relationship had gone down the tubes and I'm as guilty as anyone for that. What you did is not right and it's not something I deserve. Even if I were the most rotten wife in the world, which I'm not, most of the time. You can sleep here. But I'd like it to be on the couch."

Desmond blinks several times.

"We don't have to rush to decide on this," he says.

"I don't feel rushed."

His face falls: "Oh, okay."

"I've only decided that thing. About the couch. Well, and one more."

"What's the other thing?"

"Me. I wasn't happy. Even before Sarah Ellen. I want to change that. Now I feel like I know how."

"Ramona," he says. "I love you."

"I know you do. In your weird way."

"You do?"

I examine my husband, red-rimmed eyes and greasy hair, shocked on the sofa, and I don't forgive him. I'm floating around in a pool of pain and anger, which I imagine will morph over time like one of Nanette's Play-Doh creations, into both sweet and scary shapes. I realize I have no idea how to process this and it's okay, which could be a sign of maturity or more likely a sign that I've exceeded the storage in my emotional in-box. The truth is Desmond is a decent man—my word, flawed—but decent.

"Yeah. Right now, though, it's time for me to hit the hay."

I pick up a votive candle and tiptoe down the hall, careful not to wake up Alex and Nanette, who are sleeping with doors wide open to keep the air moving. The light dances in our tiny bathroom as I brush my teeth in the mirror. You know what? A shower, a come to Jesus with your husband, and a little Crest can really lift the spirits.

I shift my weight to one foot, hoist the other up on the commode like Captain Morgan, and scrape my tongue, still sore in parts of my anatomy I forgot existed. And there's another strange and not entirely unwelcome sensation: hope. It's hard to remember the person I was becoming before I met Desmond and had kids—it will be messy and maybe fun to find out. Whoever she was, I liked her.

That night Desmond sleeps on the couch. I don't know if he sleeps well or if he tosses and turns in the heat. If the combination of bacon and alcohol gives him a headache. I don't know these things.

I sweat in a tank top and Target panties sprawled on top of my comforter. I spread out my arms and legs like I'm making a snow angel on the mattress and I sleep so deeply it doesn't feel like anyone is missing. Not even Prince.

ACKNOWLEDGMENTS

My friend pointed out that the process of publishing a book seems like an elephant pregnancy. I feel so lucky to have the most brilliant professionals in my elephant delivery room.

I'm beyond grateful for Trish Todd for riding shotgun next to Ramona on this adventure. Ever since our first chat, which took place in my car because, inside the house, my kids had Zooms cranked up to the highest volume, I felt confident the book was in good hands. Her suggestions were spot-on, her wisdom is infinite, and I'm still thrilled to get an email signed, "TT." Another gracias to the patient and helpful Sean (brilliant in *Succession*) and the vibrant team I'm getting to know and love at Atria. (Y'all, there are many other celebrity deaths I still haven't recovered from.)

None of This Would Have Happened without Maggie Cooper, Super Agent! Possibly the smartest person I know and definitely the pluckiest, her notes on the manuscript were invaluable, as well as her thoughtful navigation was through the process. I will always be grateful for her kindness and emails buffering disappointing news with puppy GIFS. I reckon her stint in NC prepared her well for repping Southern authors who go on long tangents about candles at HomeGoods.

I'm indebted to Amy Condon, who has always had unwavering faith in me and an enormous pig, Gus. Shout-out to early readers Sarah Asquith and Sarah Underwood—y'all were way too nice about my crappy draft, but maybe the margaritas influenced those critiques. I realize how lucky I am to be loved by a flock of hilarious women who support and inspire me. As I type this, one of them is probably lighting up my phone with a delightful anecdote that should be its own book and a killer Southern expression I forgot about.

An enormous, never-enough thank you to Mom and Dad. When I wrote my first story about Julie piling suitcases to the sky, I decided I should be a writer and you guys said, "Absolutely!" I can still see the mug in our kitchen cabinet with everyone's favorite burrowing rodent encouraging us to "Gopher it!" Thank you for giving me the world and encouraging me to be myself. Also, I'm grateful to my sister, Alexa, who has always believed in me way more than I believed in myself, and bubbles over with marketing ideas like champers uncorked. I'm stronger with her standing next to me.

And last but not least, thank you to my roommates. Dale, for being the Emotional Support Napper every writer deserves. Miles and Theo, you are the most fascinating people I've met, and hands down, the funniest. It's my dream that you two find something that brings you as much joy as words and stories do for me. And finally, a super long, no-flinching hug for Kevin. It's tough for a person of logic and spreadsheets to watch someone you love spend years on something and struggle in a tough industry. Thank you for loving me, singing improv jams, and pouring me coffee toppers. And for the weird and wonderful life we have created.

ABOUT THE AUTHOR

Carolyn Prusa studied literature and creative writing at Stanford University and Boston University. She has written for *Savannah Magazine*, the *Charlotte Observer*, and other publications. She lives in Savannah, Georgia, with her husband; two sons; and giant rescue dog, Dale, who looks like a Wookiee and sings like an angel. Find out more @CarolynPrusa on Twitter and Instagram.